THE CALL
of
DISTANT
SHORES

by David Niall Wilson

Hesitantly, Jeremy reached out and rapped on the door. At first he thought no one had heard him, and he was hovering between the desire to knock louder, pounding until they let him in and told him what the hell was going on when the door swung wide. The floor beneath him lurched sickeningly, tumbling him forward, and Jeremy reached out with a cry drowned quickly in the roar of ...

Waves. Crashing, rolling high above and tumbling toward him, foam-tipped and peppering face and eyes with hard, stinging salt-slaps of spray. His stumble brought him up abruptly against a wooden rail, and he clutched the slimy surface tightly as his chest slammed into the solid wood and his knees threatened to buckle from the impact.

The water hit then, and everything else disappeared. Jeremy pressed himself tightly to the wood, clutching with his hands and gripping with his knees, fighting the crushing weight of the cold, relentless pull of the seawater as it pounded, then receded with a sickening, sucking sound over the side and the world tilted backward as quickly as it had leaned forward. Closing his eyes, Jeremy clung more tightly still to the rail, fingers slipping and groping along the wet-slick wood for purchase and feet threatening to slip off behind him and down.

For an eternity of deafening sound and flashing lightning, he hung nearly perpendicular to the sea, then he rushed back the other way, compressed tightly to the wooden rail and his breath left him. Voices cried out, nearly lost in the gale, and Jeremy's mind swam with the words, trying to order them so they made sense, trying to find the courage to release the rail, turn, and step back through the door and into the barber shop – the world.

Contents

Author's Introduction

A lot of authors of dark fantasy and horror will cite H. P. Lovecraft, William Hope Hodgson, Hugh Cave, and Manly Wade Wellman as influences on their writing. Clark Ashton Smith is another name you'll hear, and in this volume, you'll find my tribute to that great talent, as well as a number of others that dip into the wells of darkness and magic – a world I'm familiar with from endless hours of reading, dreaming, and spilling my own words onto the page.

I have never considered myself a huge fan of Lovecraft. Though pulp writing, in general, appealed to me when I was much younger, and in the middle years of my writing career, I pushed it aside. I was, of course, deluding myself. When someone pointed out to me that I actually had a body of work loosely fitting this sub-genre of horror / dark fantasy that was probably enough for a book, I laughed. Then I looked. Then I stopped laughing. What I found was that these writers – these storytellers I grew up with and believed I'd left behind me – were responsible for a huge chunk of my output as a writer. There are elder gods, ancient evils, and everything that attends them walking the corridors of my creative consciousness, and that reader was correct. There was more than enough to make a book.

I also note that, of all my works, most of my favorites, and some that have garnered critical notice, are among the stories you are about to read. "The Call of Distant Shores," the title piece of this collection, is one of my most popular stories to date, and Cockroach Suckers, which is more recent and set near my current home town in the fictional Old Mill, North

Carolina, could not be more Lovecraftian without being set in New England.

Anyway…there are a lot of words ahead – a lot of images – a lot of dark dreams. I hope you'll enjoy them, and I dedicate them to those authors who have gone before, paving the way for an ever-widening realm of new worlds and deep-rooted fears.

Welcome to my nightmares.

-David Niall Wilson
4/9/2011

AUTHOR'S NOTE: Sometimes a story comes from something deep in the shadows of your psyche. Sometimes you are compelled by visions; you hear voices in your head. And then–sometimes–it's a title. I love playing with words, and one day this grouping came to me. I sat with the first paragraph on my hard drive for years...then one day, I figured it out. It isn't the best pun in the world, and it has nothing at all to do with **Zen and the Art of Motorcycle Maintenance** *– but here it is...*

Glen and the Tart of
Mortar Psycho Maine Tenants

One of the only perks of being Building Superintendent is setting my own schedule, so when the doorbell screeched at the ungodly hour of 8:00 AM on Saturday; I rolled straight off the wrong side of the bed. Rubbing sleep from bleary eyes, I staggered to the door of my room, only remembering halfway there that I was naked. I turned back, snagged my jeans off the floor and hopped into them as I made my way down the hall. The doorbell sounded again, and I cursed.

There are only about two things that are worth getting up early for on a Saturday; when I opened the door, one of them smiled at me and held out the round handle of a water valve on the end of her finger. She was tall and freckled with wavy auburn hair and bright eyes that were either sparkling, or just reflecting more sunlight than I was used to seeing on a weekend. I knew her name was Linda, and that it was customary among our people to say "Hi," or "Good morning," but all I could manage was a confused mumble and a lop-sided return grin that probably made me look like the drooling idiot I was.

She laughed and twirled the handle on her fingernail. In the recesses of my depraved mind, I saw the tip of that finger crook and beckon me closer, but I shook my head. Too much time spent in depraved recesses is never good.

"Um," I managed, finally waxing eloquent, "can I help you?"

"I sure hope so," she said. Her voice was as bright as her eyes, and I was so fascinated by it that the words themselves took their sweet time sinking in. Her accent was odd, Boston, I thought, or somewhere in New England. She went on as if I were coherent.

"Daddy was trying to turn on the hose this morning, and this came right off. We're in the middle of some important work and…"

She stared pointedly at the handle on her finger.

That woke me up. This was a real problem, and one that I could handle. At that moment, handling things was foremost on my mind, and I knew that if I bobbled the hand-off of the faucet handle, all other handling was out of the question. I took it gingerly off her finger.

"Let me get my tools," I said. "I'll be right over."

She smiled, and I swear when I said the word tools she glanced about three inches south of my belt. Whether she did or not, my mental image of her did, down in those aforementioned depraved recesses, and I blushed hard. I stumbled in a half circle and staggered back into my apartment. She laughed softly, and called out to me from the doorway.

"I hope you can fix it. There's a lot of work to be done today, and if we don't get some more water out there, everything is going to set wrong and crumble. When things crumble – it can be very bad."

I vaguely recalled that her father made some sort of statues out in back of the building. I never go there except to take out my trash, because I really hate rats and the smell of dumpsters, and because that area is rented, along with suite 1A, to one set of tenants. These tenants.

I found a clean t-shirt and socks, laced on my Doc Martens and grabbed the canvas tool bag I kept just inside the door to my bedroom. I learned early on that if pipes burst, or the roof leaked, or someone's doorknob came off in their hand at three o'clock in the morning it was best to have the tool bag where I was likely to fall over it. It saved me hours of bleary-eyed searching and helped me keep my job. At the moment all I wanted was to get back to the front door before my Miss New England wet dream disappeared back into her apartment and left me outside playing in the water with daddy.

When I reached the back yard, I stopped short of actually entering it to stare. I've seen a lot of very odd things during my tenure in building maintenance. I haven't lived a sheltered or particularly sedate life. In retrospect, I suppose nothing could really have prepared me.

In the center of the lawn, placed in a spiral that ran from what I guessed was dead center in the lot outward toward the fence, statues had been lined up like dominoes. Most of them seemed to be renditions of something that resembled a lobster, though the head and eyes were far too large, and the claws…I think they were claws… had protuberances similar to opposable thumbs jutting out beneath. The very center statue was small, maybe half a foot tall. Each successive creature was a little bit taller. From where I stood at the back door, I could see the center, shrinking in like the guts of a gigantic Nautilus shell. As I stepped closer, staring openly with the tool bag dangling at my side, the center became obscured, and all I saw was the outer ring of taller statues. The last few were darker than the others, and I realized with a start that they were still wet – drying in the sun.

Not far to one side, a large vat of some viscous white paste rested with a hose dangling over the edge. The white paste was slowly setting. Beside it, a sorrowful expression on his face stood the girl's father. He was a small mountain of a man. His shoulders were too broad, and he stood there in a grungy wife-beater t-shirt and jeans – at least I think they were jeans. They were stained dark and puddled over his feet so it seemed they melted into the dark earth. I felt dizzy, and would probably have turned and staggered back into my apartment if Linda hadn't dropped her hand on my shoulder at just that moment.

I turned and cried out, nearly tumbling us both to the ground, but she caught me. She was stronger than she looked, and I found the transition from staring at her father and his lobstrocities (thank you Stephen King) to her smiling face a genuine pleasure.

"What…what are those things?" I managed to ask. "Jesus, they look like some sort of mutant crawdads."

Her smile didn't falter, but I saw from her expression that the reference was lost on her.

"They're Daddy's creations," she said. "They aren't finished."

I glanced at the spiral of statues and shook my head.

"Most of them seem finished," I said.

"They all must be finished," she said. "Every one. They aren't separate works, it's a single creation."

I followed the inward spiral as far as I could. Somehow, as strange as her words seemed, they also rang true. I couldn't imagine one of the creatures standing alone, or a pair of them on the two sides of someone's front walk. They fit together, and there was an eerie symmetry to it - except that something wasn't quite right. I followed the line back to the near end, the unfinished end. The father still stared at me. His expression hadn't changed. He held the limp end of the hose in one hand, and my mind returned to the moment.

"We have to hurry," Linda said. "If the mortar dries, it will be too late. There's no time to mix another batch.

I lifted the faucet handle, flashed on why I was there, and nodded, starting toward the back wall of the building. It didn't matter why they needed to finish the statues. What mattered was they paid for the use of the water, and the hose and it was my job to get it back into commission. Luckily, it was a simple job – a single screw to tighten, and they'd be back in business. If all went well, and Daddy was happy, I thought maybe Linda might take me up on an offer of lunch, or drinks…or more. Except, the closer I got to the faucet, the harder it was not to glance over my shoulder at that growing army of statues. I felt the weight of their cold, collective, lifeless gaze weighing on my shoulders. I told myself if we *did* go to lunch or dinner, Red Lobster was definitely out.

Linda trailed along beside me, not close enough for my taste. If my eyes strayed back toward her father, they met her tanned, muscled thighs, and snapped back to the business at hand.

Just as I reached the wall and dropped my tool bag in the dirt, there was an agonized moan from behind me. I glanced over my shoulder. Linda tried to step up and block my view, but she was too late. I stood and stared.

The largest of the statues had shifted. Where the wet mortar trailed off at the end of a long, misshapen claw, the color had changed. Powder dribbled from the tip, like sand falling through an hourglass. Linda's father stood, staring at it in mute horror. He moved to the trough and tried to dip out a glop of the unused mortar, but it was too thick and grainy. When he applied it to the tip of the claw it clung, and then fell away like gobs of wet rice.

"What..." I said.

"The faucet!" Linda said. She gripped my shoulders and turned me toward the wall. As I spun, I'm certain I saw the end of that claw vibrate. It was like it was trying to shake off the mortar.

Sweat broke out on my forehead. I wished I'd had less to drink the night before and more sleep. I fumbled with the zipper on the top of the bag and jammed my hand inside. I needed a Phillips head screwdriver. Suddenly, what had seemed a quick fix was looking like a major undertaking. The sun was rising toward noon, but I felt clammy. I wanted to look back at those statues.

Linda's hands dropped to my shoulders, and she began to knead the tight knots out of them. I started to tell her to stop, and then wondered what the hell I was thinking and bit my tongue. She wasn't making the job any easier, but I suddenly didn't care quite so much about what might be happening behind me. Probably her intention.

"Just fix the faucet," she said softly. Her lips were so close to my ear her breath tickled over my skin. She smelled wonderful, some mix of spice and vanilla. I felt my erection press into my jeans and nearly dropped the faucet handle.

"Christ," I muttered.

I slid the round handle over the square tip of the faucet. It slipped on so easily that I stopped, and for the first time looked closely at the faucet, and the handle. The end of the faucet valve was a square post that protruded about an inch from the valve itself. The handle had a square hole in the center, and this slipped over the protrusion, held in place by a single screw. That's how it was supposed to work.

I don't know how I missed it up until that point, but the handle was broken. One side of the inner square was broken away – or melted? One of the adjacent sides was only partially there. I gripped it and turned. It tried to catch, but there wasn't enough of the square left to grip the edges of the valve, and it slipped.

"What in the hell happened to this thing?" I asked.

I turned and held it up to Linda, not really angry, but very confused. It was a mistake. Over her shoulder, I had a clear view of the spiraling statues. The first two or three, the largest, had shifted again. They were no longer in the same position they'd been carved in, and I was not quite able to believe – in that moment – that they'd actually *been* carved. One claw had opened, and it was raised over Linda's father. Those farther down the line had begun to drip powder, as the larger ones had moments before. The damage rippled in toward the center.

"Please," she said.

I glanced at the handle again, then tossed it aside and dove for the tool bag. I cursed myself inwardly because – even though I knew I had vice grips, I didn't know whether I'd put them back in the bag. I dragged out a hammer, a tape measure, a set of drill bits and a handful of assorted nails and bolts. There were pliers, and I briefly considered giving them a try. Then my mind filled with the image of that monstrous claw with its impossible extra appendage. I waited, expecting to hear a scream as I dug into the bag again.

I found the vice grips at the very bottom of the canvas bag. I turned to the faucet and snapped them shut over the valve, but they were set too wide. I heard Linda moan, and I wanted more than anything to look back at those statues. I also wanted to turn and run, screaming, into the street….but Linda still leaned in close behind me, her perfume confusing my senses. What *was* that scent? It made me think of the beach, and the sand, though I knew that was crazy. The beach only got bottled as a scent on Seinfeld.

Behind me I heard a sound like something soft and wet sliding over a rough surface. I heard a barked scream and something clattered to the ground. Sweat dripped into my eyes, and I closed them tightly. I fumbled with the vice grips, found the wheel that loosened and tightened the grip and started spinning it. I forced my eyes open with a gasp – I wasn't sure in my panic if I was loosening or tightening it.

"Hurry," Linda hissed. "Oh please…Daddy…"

I stared at the vice grips and almost laughed. Somehow I'd gotten it right. I leaned in too quickly, smacked my head on the wall, nearly toppled over and felt her hands on my shoulders, steadying me. I saw the valve and I reached for it. My knuckle smacked into the concrete wall and I cursed, but I dragged it down and found the metal rod, clinging to it dizzily. I wrapped the vice grips around the end of the valve, gripped the handle, and heard the loud CLICK as they locked in place.

Blood joined the sweat trickling down my face, oozing from a cut where my scalp hit the wall, but I blinked and focused. I'd gotten lucky the first time, but once again I found my mind blanking. Which way should I turn the valve. The stupid rhyme my father had taught me years before tried to surface, but my head pounded.

"Righty, tighty," I gasped.

"What?" Linda said.

"Lovely Lucy," I muttered.

I spun the valve. My knees had gone rubbery, and when I wrenched on the valve stem, Linda let go of my shoulders, leaving me to find my own balance. I never had a chance. The world lurched, and I toppled. For just a second, I held onto the vice grips and pressed my hand into the wall, but it was no good. I fell, dropping slowly. That moment stretched into a surreal eternity.

As I turned, the lot behind me came into view. I couldn't
see any of it clearly, but what I did see wasn't possible. Linda
held the hose, her hand on the metal spray nozzle, gripping tight.
Water arched up and over the spiral of statues, except, something
was wrong. They were moving, and they weren't …white. Not
exactly. Some still were, in near the center, but the others were
moving. The spiral hadn't broken—but spun. The larger statues
—creatures—moved steadily inward. The smallest, in the deep
center, were still solid, and the larger ones, moving in, crushed
them to white dust.

The water slowed them. Just as I hit the ground I saw Linda's
father, like a professional wrestler bursting out of a pile of bodies,
press to the surface, coated in white slime. He fought through
the sliding, chattering horde toward the trough of mortar, now
overflowing with water.

I wanted to scream. I wanted to tell him to look out, as one
of the creatures turned on him and lifted a huge claw. Water
splashed into the thing's face, and I remember hearing Linda's
voice.

"Daddy!"

The throbbing in my head hit a crescendo, and darkness
swallowed me whole.

When I woke, I was in my apartment. Light streamed in from
the window, and my head felt like it had been used for a drum.
I heard something move, and it all came back to me in a flash. I
scrabbled back, hit my head on the headboard, and cried out.

"Hey! Take it easy!"

Linda was sitting on the edge of my bed. She'd changed
clothes, and she was smiling.

"What happened?" I asked. "Your father?

"Everything is fine," she said. "You were wonderful."

I sat up a bit straighter, shook my head, regretted it, and
frowned. I swung my legs over the side of the bed and staggered
to my feet. I realized in that instant that I was only wearing
boxers, but I wasn't in the mood to worry about it. If she was
there, she'd probably been there when I was brought in—as
likely as not she'd stripped me. I left my room, and I heard her
following close behind.

"Really," she said. "Everything is fine."

I hurried to the back door, flung it open, and stepped out onto the back steps. Then I stopped and stood very still, staring. I felt Linda's hands rest on my shoulder. I started to shrug them off, but couldn't find the strength.

"How?" I asked.

The back lot was empty. The trough stood right where it had been, but it, too, was empty. There was a light misting of white powder on the ground, and there were heavy tire tracks, as if a truck had been backed down the alley and in on top of the ground when it was wet. The statues were gone. All of them. There was no sign that anything odd had happened. The hose lay on the ground like a dead snake, and no one was in sight. There was a large pile of canvas bags piled against the wall beside the back of Linda's apartment. Small mounds of white powder had leaked from the torn corners of a few.

"What is that?" I asked, uncertain what else to say.

"Mortar," she said. "It's mortar. Daddy will have to go back to work soon."

I turned to stare at her. She didn't take her hands off of my shoulders. We were very close.

"Tell me you're kidding," I said. "He almost died. *We* almost died. What were those things? Why were they in that spiral, and what happened with the mortar, and the water? Jesus, I…"

Linda leaned in and kissed me full on the lips. The scent I'd been unable to identify wafted around me – something with a hint of trees and the ocean. Something damp, but compelling. I tried to speak. I really did. I tried to pull away and ask again about that horrible spiral, those crustacean monstrosities crumbling, chittering, rushing in around the back lot toward the center where…what?

I felt Linda's hands slide beneath my shirt, and I made a last attempt to push her away. I saw her father's face, the wild terror in his eyes as the white powder sloughed off the largest of the lobster things and they lurched inward over their smaller brethren, scrabbling inward toward that obscured center. How small had the innermost statues been? What would have happened if those larger ones had forced their way to the center? Where were the statues now?

I remembered the truck tracks. I thought about the trough, and the bags of mortar.

"What about the faucet?" I gasped.

Linda paused for just a second. She pulled back, and her smile widened.

"We sent for a plumber," she said. "Daddy is paying. I told him…you'd be busy."

Keeping the tenants happy is my job, and it was obvious that only one thing was going to work at that particular moment. I intended to go back to the rear of the building to inspect the faucet. I meant to check out that mortar and the tire tracks, and see what I could find out about my psycho Maine tenants… but somehow it seemed less important than my new business connections.

I spent a lot of time with Linda after that day, and with her father. I met the drivers of the truck, strange pale men with heavy New England accents who showed up like clockwork once every three months. There was a lot of work to be done, keeping the apartments in good repair, and working out back. The spiral had to remain complete, after all, and mortar isn't an easy medium – even if you have a latent artistic streak.

Someday I'll walk the spiral to its center and see where it leads. I feel drawn to it. For now, I'm happy with Linda. She's a bit of a tart, but she's very affectionate. I even get up early on Saturdays. After all, as building superintendent, I set my own schedule.

AUTHOR'S NOTE: I have always loved poetry. From a very early age, I've been fascinated with Samuel Taylor Coleridge, and in particular with the unfinished poem Kublai Kahn. An old poetry book I got from my aunt told stories about the poets along with presenting their work, and it always itched at me – not knowing the rest of the story. Then I read a fantasy novel (I have no idea what it was titled) where the hero was drawn into another dimension because he was to finish that poem and save the universe. And he did, and I remember reading what that author wrote and thinking...there's still more. It stuck with me for so long that I knew I'd have to address it. Then along came an anthology (that was never published) with a theme of Absinthe, and I wrote this story. When the anthology failed, I sold the story to a magazine called CITY SLAB... The rest is altered history... There is a partially completed screenplay for this that is destined one day to reach the hands of director Rosanna Jeran.

The Milk of Paradise

The flick of a thumb, bright sparks and the faded Zippo lighter with the Grateful Dead emblem emblazoned across its front came to life. The scent of lighter fluid mingled with Sandalwood and hemp. Shadows slid along the floor, wavering and dancing as long slender fingers raised the lighter, bringing the flame to rest beneath a dangling metal ball. The ball was perforated, an old tea ball – an infuser—Art had called it—dangling from a silver chain, suspended about a foot beneath an arching wrought iron frame. Beneath it, glittering and green, sat a glass, half-full of a liquid too odd in coloration to be taken seriously. Art had a name for it. He called it Flubber.

Leaning in close, long dark hair dangling over her wrist,

Belle watched the ball intently, holding the flame to its base. The heat from the lighter set the chain in motion, buffeting it ever-so-slightly as the point where fire met metal grew hotter. Or maybe it was her breath. It didn't matter—not as long as the pendulous motion didn't carry the ball beyond the boundaries of the glass beneath it.

The sickly sweet stench of burnt sugar wafted across the room like the aftermath of a bad caramel, but Belle paid it no notice. She watched the ball spin in lazy arcs over the glass, and, at last, the sizzle of thick brown liquid as the sugar inside melted and slipped through the infuser. Dripping.

Art watched, though not as closely as Belle. He sat back in an overstuffed faux leather armchair with one hand curled around a bottle of beer, and the other holding a slender pipe between thumb and forefinger, angled carefully away from his face, as if anything could have prevented smoke from burning his eyes in a room so full of fumes. Incense. Tobacco. The hash that was charring to ash in his small bowl. The sugar in the infuser, dripping, each drop splashing into the green liquid beneath with an odd sizzle as heat met room-temperature liquid.

Art had played a game much like this with his high school buddies. A baggie, a glass of water, and flame. The dripping, molten plastic made a distinctive sound when it hit the cold liquid. ZILCH! He heard that sound now, drifting through memory as he brought the pipe to his lips again.

In the glass beneath the infuser, the green shifted with each zilching drop, growing more amber – less flubber. Art grinned at the thought. He imagined the glass rising and floating about the room as Belle, irritated, grabbed for it with long fingernails, trying to keep it from spilling.

"It'll never get off the ground," he said to no one in particular. Belle either didn't or wouldn't hear him, and no one else was in the room. The image of Robin Williams, tiny fists pounding against the inside of the glass as the molten sugar dropped around his head like lava and the glass drifting toward the ceiling momentarily captured his attention, and he snorted, barely containing the laugh. Barely containing the last hit off the pipe. No smoke wasted.

Belle had been at it for hours. Hell, she'd been at it for fucking *days* – maybe her whole life. Chasing the green. To Art she looked like some sort of demented alchemist trying to will her lead into gold.

"It's just a fucking drink," he said at last, irritated by her inattention to anything but the glass. He watched a few moments longer, the silence echoing more loudly as the sound of his voice faded, ignored. He stood, downed the rest of his lukewarm beer in a single swallow, and slammed the bottle on the table.

Belle turned to him for just a second, tilting her head at an inquisitive angle, her eyes deep in some other place. Fevered.

"It's just a fucking drink." Art repeated. He turned away and slipped out through a set of green plastic beaded curtains that separated the room they were in from the dingy kitchen.

Belle turned back to the glass. On the floor to her left a spiral notebook lay open near the center. A pen lay atop the pages where lines were carefully filled with letters and numbers. Many of these were rubbed out, erased, or, in a single instance, scribbled over with such force that the page had torn. There were stains on the page as well. In the dim light, they might have been from tears, or the dripping of sweat – the condensation from a bottle of beer – or the deep green, shifting-toward-amber liquid in the glass.

1885 - France - Incomplete
.025 kilograms of dried wormwood
.05 kilograms of anise
.05 kilograms of fennel
.95 liters of 85 percent ethanol
.45 liters of water
.001 kilogram of Roman wormwood
.001 kilogram of hyssop
5 grams of lemon balm
(All original numbers divided by 100)

Let the mixture steep for at least 12 hours in the pot of a double boiler. Add water and apply heat; collect distillate. To approximately half the distillate, add Roman wormwood, hyssop and lemon balm, all of which have been dried and finely divided. Extract at a moderate temperature, then siphon off the liquor, filter, and reunite with the remaining distillate. Dilute with water to produce approximately 1 liter of absinthe with a final alcohol concentration of 74 percent by volume. AND – SOMETHING – FUCKING – ELSE ...

The lettering grew deep and frustrated at this point, slashing across the lined paper at angry angles. Words were scrawled, then marked out and replaced with other words, also marked out. In the center of the page, about three lines beneath the recipe itself and underlined so deeply the page was scored, the word Peppermint remained. Alone, of a small battlefield of herbs and obscure terms, Peppermint survived.

Belle leaned closer over the glass. She'd removed the flame from the tea infuser and was watching the liquid intently. Where globs of molten sugar had struck, whirling tendrils of yellowish hue spun down into the thick liquid. Belle's hair dangled dangerously close, interwoven with several feathers and a small chain of beads. Her eyes glittered – green eyes so dark they hinted of black. Her tongue slid back and forth across her teeth, touching the cheeks on either side, then swirling.

Belle waited until the peppermint in her mouth had faded to such a thin wafer it threatened to melt over her lips and disappear, then she bent quickly and slipped her tongue into the absinthe, letting the ghost of the mint slide into the green depths. Her eyes closed, just for an instant, as she made contact with that slick, wet surface, then she drew back. Peppermint. Ghosts and hints in books she'd spent long hours poring over claimed that this was the secret. She'd been told it soothed the stomach. She'd been told that slid round and round a lover's cock with the tongue, it could bring hallucinations. She'd been told it belonged in the Absinthe—told by voices long dead, preserved on parchments and the leaves of tattered books. Recipes penciled into the margins of notebooks and tucked into unlikely hiding places in diaries and family bibles.

Absinthe was the key, but it had to be *the* Absinthe. *His* absinthe. Was it right? Were the caves of ice raised from stalagmites of peppermint? Did they tingle with too-clean, too-bright taste, or would that fail as it blended with the wormwood's bitter kiss? What did *he* see?

The mint drifted slowly, so thin it resembled a coin-shaped shard of ice. Belle watched, waited, as it fluttered down to the bottom of the glass. Fluttered and melted, flew and flown and – gone. The absinthe had swallowed it completely.

Art shuffled back into the room, but she paid no attention to him. She was staring into the green depths of the glass, mesmerized. He watched her, sipping on a fresh beer and frowning. Her hair dangled over and around the glass, and with the dim candlelight flickering, he caught green glimmers. The wink of some huge, forgotten emerald. The eye of a great cat. Spider webs of dark hair shimmered around it, slender pale arms braced against the floor.

"Found the Flubber, then, did you?" he asked softly, tipping the bottle up again. He tasted the beer, but he remembered the bite of the Absinthe. He remembered her concentration, and how it shifted. He remembered long fingers and curved nails wrapped around a different glass, a slightly different green. He remembered the taste, and the burn. He remembered.

Art turned away and lurched from the room, down the hall that branched left, and right. He turned left, not bothering with the lights. Two doors ignored, the third entered and he stopped, tilting the bottle up and closing his eyes. It was there. He knew it was there, didn't need to see to know. Moonlight streamed in the window and glowed on the surface of a canvas, reclining on an easel and watching him in return.

To one side, on a dresser that had been recruited as a workbench, his palette sat, paint dried on the surface in careless blobs, brush dry-tight in the deep blue. The palette itself was a work of art, a reflection of pain. Art stepped closer and tipped the bottle back, gazing at the canvas. He turned, grabbed a candle from the dresser and lit it with a match pulled from ratty jeans.

The light flared. The Heineken bottle gleam lit the surface of the canvas with a dim, yellow glow. Art drank, and stared, and drank again. He reached out with one hand and traced the brilliantly hued parapet of a domed cathedral, drawing down to rings of lush trees, their branches heavy with brightly colored fruit, rooted in beds of flowers. Ice coated the surface of the cathedral-like doors. Behind, rising up and up, the mountains disappeared into clouds that shimmered with color—a cotton-candy treat for the gods.

The temple was an entrance; doors swung wide to reveal a jeweled cavern within, lights placed strategically so that every brilliant beam reflected and refracted, then reflected again, dancing from surface to surface. Ice. It was a cave of ice. Art drained his beer and wished it was something stronger, something with ice he could swirl around in his mouth as he had when he painted. Cold, biting, distant. Footsteps drifted in, quiet and rhythmic, but Art didn't acknowledge them.

The scent of jasmine teased his nostrils. Art felt a small shiver run up his spine, but still, he didn't turn. It was Sammy. She made little sound, even when she was in the room you had to concentrate to realize she wasn't part of one of the tapestries on the wall, or an over-sized doll. Sammy was an afterthought to the world, so paper-thin, frail and pale she shimmered and sometimes, if you didn't look closely enough, she wasn't there at all.

"It's like she's made of ice," Belle had said one day, watching Sammy flit about the room. "The ice you see, just after it freezes, so thin on top of the water you know that if a wave rose up from inside, it would shatter."

Art set the empty beer bottle beside the dried palette on the dresser and placed the candle in the top, dripping hot wax around the rim to hold it in place.

"Pretty," Sammy whispered, standing very close to his side and staring at the painting, as he knew she'd stared a thousand times before, when he was there, when he was out. When he was sleeping. Sammy was fascinated with the painting, and when she wasn't playing her music, she was staring at it.

At first, Art had been jealous. He liked Sammy, and he loved the painting. Both meant a lot to him, but neither would share. Sammy didn't ignore Art, but she didn't adore him. She adored the painting, worshiped it, and that was supposed to have been Belle. The painting was not for Sammy. The house, its walls dripping thick with images and angst, dreams and nightmares leaking into them, all of it was an extension of Belle. The painting was a failure. Art had failed, and for his pain, a woman he quietly and privately loved had fallen in love, instead, with his failure.

He turned, pinched the wick of the candle between his thumb and forefinger, relishing the heat as he held tight. The burn. It took his thoughts away, for an instant. He turned and headed to the door. Sammy didn't move. She stared at the painting as if the light had never shifted. As if seeing the same image she'd seen by flickering candlelight. As if she had never seen what Art had seen at all, or what he'd painted, but something more.

Head pounding, Art paced back toward the kitchen for another drink. Stronger, and more final. Something tall and amber and clinking with ice that would burn his throat as the candle had burned his fingers, numbing the pain.

The night had deepened. There was no light save that of the candles circling the room. On the floor in the center of the patterned carpet, Sammy sat quietly. On her lap, a wooden dulcimer rested. Art sat slumped deep into the depths of his old armchair, cloaked in shadow. Invisible. Occasionally the soft clink of ice on glass could be heard, accompanied by a quick flash of reflected gold tossed between whiskey and candle through a lens of smudged glass.

Belle knelt on the rug before Sammy. In Belle's hand was a crystal goblet, glittering with ghosts of light from the candles. The goblet brimmed with dark liquid. The light was yellow. Shadows loomed. Art knew what was in the goblet, despite the lack of color. He knew the deep, emerald glitter, and the scent, crusted sugar and licorice, the hint of something more. Different, each time, and yet the demon's breath called with the same voice. Words rose unbidden to Art's lips, and he whispered them, then downed another wet-hot gulp of whiskey.

"As e'er beneath a waning moon was haunted
By woman wailing for her demon-lover!
And from this chasm, with ceaseless turmoil seething,
As if this earth in fast thick pants were breathing."

Belle swung her gaze around, catching Art's eyes as he spoke. She smiled, nodding slightly, then returned her attention to the goblet, and the girl before her. Sammy gazed straight through Belle's eyes. She didn't see the glass, or the long, slender fingers that proffered it to her. She saw what she saw, and Art wondered, if his painting had been in the room, whether she would have stared into its depths in that moment. He shivered.

"Drink," Belle whispered. Beseeching. Commanding. Neither of them had ever seen Sammy drink anything alcoholic. She seldom ate, and when she did, it was the picking of a bird, the brush of butterfly proboscis over nectar-soaked petals. No substance. Now, as they watched, Belle entranced, and Art aching, half with the need for this moment to end badly. It would leave him the one elevated moment, the knowledge that, thoue had failed, he had come closer to success. Even if his offering had fallen short. The othe rhalf of him needed to know what would happen. She would drink, or she would turn away.

Art did not share Belle's dream, her deep encroaching need. But he still wanted to know. He held his breath.

Sammy took the goblet, staring into its depths as though seeing it for the first time. Her concentration was absolute. She held it reverently, and Art knew the scent that reached her nostrils. He knew the taste that would burn against her tongue, the numbing, intoxicating sensations to follow.

Art had bought plenty of absinthe since Belle had offered her goblet to him, but his purchases, steadily more covert and in-depth in their inception, had proven themselves to be nothing more than a series of well-crafted lies. They had gotten him drunk. They had a similar taste, and, in a few cases, similar effects, but they were miserable re-creations. They were the work of a thousand clones, repainting over and over the work of the masters, vending their wares on dingy street corners and dreaming of castles of ice. Belle was a master. Belle might be the last master of a dead art. Art had not painted since the night she had him drink.

Sammy drank. One last second's glance into the depths of the clear crystal, brimming with the green, and she shifted. Everything shifted. The glass tilted, Belle leaned back onto her heels, eyes glittering brightly, fixated on Sammy's face. Her form. Her eyes, now closed, head drawn back and long hair dangling behind as she drained the glass. No sipping. No tasting. No hesitation.

Art expected her to spew.

Sammy only smiled. On her lap, the dulcimer sat silent. Potential sound embodied in curving wood and twisted strings. Gut strings. Strings that had once been the inner workings of a cat or a horse. Strings that had been part of the fabric of some living, breathing being, woven now to the wood, and to her fingers. Sammy didn't speak. She didn't even seem to breathe, though Art stared at her breasts. She fascinated him.

Then she moved. Pale hands tipped by wraith-fingers slid to the strings, pressed against the frets, exploring. No sound at first, only a flicker of motion that caused her nails to reflect the candlelight.

Somewhere in the past moment Belle had reclaimed the goblet without insinuating herself into Sammy's vision. Like a snake. A dark snake, swaying in front of the one she would hypnotize, the one who hypnotized her. Art lifted his drink, but it did not reach his lips. Eyes still closed, lips parted slightly, Sammy began to play.

There was a shift in the room. Subtle, hard to pin down, and so complete that every detail was skewed. Art held very still. His fingers trembled, wrapped around the icy glass, slick with condensation, but he didn't risk draining it. He might make some vulgar, slurping sound that would break the spell. It would be his fault. His mind snapped into focus on his painting. It had been his fault that time, not again.

Belle paid no attention to Art and his frozen mime-with-a-whiskey-glass pose. Sammy paid no attention to Belle. The music soared. Pale fingers flew, dancing down chords and melodies with quicksilver speed and liquid grace. The notes didn't fade. Not for Art. They hung before him, pixelating the air. He somehow found the coordination to set his glass on the table beside his chair. He did not see the table. He felt nothing.

The image of his painting grew before him, each color blending to the next, woven from a tapestry of threads that never existed in the center of the room. Incense smoke and candle light? Too much alcohol and flashback images? Sammy played, and the questions faded to meaningless white noise in the back of his mind.

The painting grew, hers now, his as well, but altered. More vivid. The notes danced along the iced parapets and flowed around the base of each tree, gushed from the geysers and taunted him with all that had remained just beyond his clouded vision. He heard the birds. He heard the rush of water and the echoes from within the caverns beyond the massive doors. He heard the echo of drums, marching feet, a horde. A heartbeat.

The image shivered, and Art held his breath. The music reasserted itself, and the room flickered into focus. He wanted to shake his head, but he held the urge in check. The notes weren't stopping, merely shifting, and the smoky air coalesced once more. A face twisted and writhed, fighting its way through the gloom, drawing strength from the sound. The eyes flashed with emotion. Anger? Lust? Rage? Desire? Art gripped the arms of his chair and leaned back. The features snapped into focus for one long, lingering moment. The eyes focused, not on Art, but on Belle, who lay back now, knees spread wide and back arched, long hair flowing over her shoulders to the floor scant inches beneath. Her gaze was locked on that face, her lips parted and her breath came in heaving gulps.

Art stared, the image forgotten, the music lost as the motion of her body called out to him. His body reacted with stunning force and he gripped the chair arms more tightly still, hips arching, jerking. Her flesh was coated in a hot sheen of sweat. Her eyes were wide and her taut nipples strained against the loose fabric of her blouse.

A string broke.

The silence that followed this jarring sound was deep,

molasses thick and cloying. The scent of the incense flowed in. The dim light of the candles drew back, dragging shadows across the floor and into the corners. The image snapped from existence so suddenly that breath stilled. Nothing moved. The room was a still life, each of them frozen in disbelief. In loss. In pain.

Belle broke first. Her carefully arched body, still stretching to the air above Sammy, curved like a tightly strung bow. Her eyes rolled back and Art saw her hands slip to her hair. Her shoulders slumped to the floor as she tore wildly at the long, silky locks. Her lips parted, but no sound emerged. Not at first. She drew breaths too deep, too full for any lungs and her jaw worked so fiercely that he feared she'd bite through her own tongue.

He started to rise, to go to her and pull her close and bring her back, to be the anchor that bound her to reality, despite the fuzziness in his own head. He nearly made it to his feet before she screamed.

The sound pierced Art to the core of his soul. He slapped his hands ineffectually over his ears, but it had no effect on Belle's tortured wails. The sound vibrated through his skin, seeped into his pores and resonated deep within his senses. His nails dug into the flesh of his cheeks and he pressed his hands so tightly to his ears that the pressure threatened to burst his skull. He heard her as if he were kneeling beside her, ear pressed to her soft red lips. There was no escape.

Art slid from the chair and dropped to his knees. The screams slowly died to silence. The dulcimer was silent as well. Art eased the pressure of his palms on the sides of his head, and very gently opened his eyes. Belle had not moved. She lay back, arched against the floor, eyes closed and her hands tightly gripping long handfuls of her own hair.

He leaned closer and slid his arms beneath her, one hand in the small of her back, the other behind her head. He held her there, afraid to lift her free of the floor. Afraid of her anger.

So quietly that it was difficult to be certain she'd spoken at all, Sammy's voice broke the silence. Art glanced at her, shocked again and unable to react in any way other than to listen.

"A savage place! as holy and enchanted
As e'er beneath a waning moon was haunted
By woman wailing for her demon-lover!
And from this chasm, with ceaseless turmoil seething,
As if this earth in fast thick pants were breathing,
A mighty fountain momently was forced:
Amid whose swift half-intermitted burst
Huge fragments vaulted like rebounding hail,
Or chaffy grain beneath the thresher's flail."

Belle's eyes flickered. Opened. Art turned to her, watching her face. She barely breathed. Her entire frame shook, trembling with the strain of holding the position she'd contorted herself into as she screamed, but she was unwilling to shift. Art held her very still, and very carefully, not daring to speak. The air was a miasma of silence. Sammy had returned to her mute scrutiny of things unseen. Her fingers lay limp on the strings of the dulcimer.

The glass, only a short time before brimming with liquid emeralds and alive with promise, lay canted to one side on the floor, a very thin trickle of absinthe feeling its way tentatively over the rim and seeping into the carpet.

With excruciating care, Belle released her grip, letting her hair slide back and down over the carpet. Over Art's hand. She closed her eyes, relaxed, and breathed. Very softly, she spoke.

"Help me," she whispered.

Art needed to hear no more. He slid his arms under Belle's shivering frame more fully, braced himself, and lifted. She came easily into his arms, slumping against him, and the nearness of her nearly buckled his knees. His mind shot back to the way she'd looked as those eyes that could not have been there, floating above Sammy in the half-light, had devoured her form. Art banished the images, and staggered from the room.

Laying Belle gently on her bed, Art sat in a chair beside her. She looked up only once, catching his gaze, holding it, then looking away and curling into a fetal position. Art reached down, drew her blanket up over her thin shoulders, smoothed her hair gently, and stood. As he left the room, he glanced back at her. She was asleep.

With his mind awash in impossibilities, Art walked down the hall to his own room and did the same.

Belle was up, scribbling furiously in her notebook when Art staggered out of his room. Her hair was wild, and he noticed with appreciation that all she wore was one of his old shirts, buttoned about halfway. She was seated cross-legged on the floor.

Belle glanced up. Without a word, she turned back to her work.

Beside her on the floor she had arranged a number of things, a bottle with the latest recipe minus the peppermint and still intact, some vials, a sheaf of yellowed paper, and other implements so familiar Art paid them little mind.

Apparently satisfied with whatever she'd been figuring, Belle dropped the notebook suddenly and grabbed a small mortar and pestle she had set aside. With deft, sure motion she plucked two peppermints from a bag and dropped them into the wooden bowl. With quick, decisive strokes she crushed them to powder, working well beyond the point where Art would have considered them to be dust. Belle carefully inserted a small funnel into the mouth of the bottle and poured the peppermint through. Art watched, fascinated, as the fine powder whirled in the green depths of the bottle like a small tornado, then faded.

"That was it, then?" he asked softly. "The missing link? The big mojo? Some peppermint?"

Belle glanced up at him, more sharply, and gave her head a shake.

"Not all," she said. "Almost. Very close."

"It wasn't the broken string?" Art asked. "I thought..."

Belle shook her head. She didn't look up, but she replied. "The string broke because it wasn't right. If it had been right, she would not have broken the string."

Art frowned. Strings broke all the time. How could the mixture of a drink have any effect? He might have bought it if

Sammy had been trashed, but she had one drink, and only one drink, and she had been playing beautifully. It had been real. Too real, in fact.

"Who was he?" Art asked, shifting subjects.

Belle did not look up. She did not answer. Her cheeks colored, and Art's brow furrowed.

"He wasn't real," Art said at last. "He was a hallucination, Belle. A dream."

She ignored him, but the muscles in her neck tightened, and she leaned more closely over her work.

"He wasn't real." Art mouthed the words, but did not breathe them to life. He turned away.

Three deep green sprigs of parsley sat on a napkin at Belle's side. She pored over her notes. There was enough in the bottle for one, maybe two more attempts, and she'd have to start again. The process was slow and tedious, bringing the mixture back to the point she'd already reached would take weeks. She had narrowed the possible missing ingredients dramatically, but there were still unknowns. Secrets were never easy to steal.

Her mind drifted. She could still feel the sharp tingling sensation of his gaze, probing her, commanding her. She felt the heat rising and drew in a quick breath, gritting her teeth and clamping her eyes closed hard enough to send dancing spots across the inner screen of her eyelids. She curled her leg back and pressed her heel tightly between her thighs, rocking against it for a moment and shaking. The moment faded, and she breathed more slowly, not trusting herself to move for a long moment. Everything she did had a price attached to it, and to spill the bottle, or ruin the mixture, would be more than she could bear. She was so close.

Sammy's voice lingered in the background of Belle's thoughts. She'd heard that voice so seldom, and never the poetry. It was a soft voice, rich in timbre, but subtle. The room had resonated with each verse, but Belle knew that the silence that had been the backdrop was largely responsible for the illusion of volume.

Belle's thoughts were clouded with the memory of heat. Her body had reacted, held and stroked by each note from the dulcimer, bent and nearly broken by the words. She had felt his breath, had shivered with the beat of something so alien, so powerful and erotic, that if she had died in that instant, the only thing she would have regretted was the incompletion. She'd been aware of Art, as well, had known his need and felt it funneled through her into the moment. The hint of licorice burned on her tongue, coated in peppermint and soaked in deeper flavors. So different from where she'd started, the green bottle with the white label, bought at an off-the-street liquor store for too much money and releasing only the slightest hint of the magic within.

That same day, the day she'd found the forbidden drink, she'd found the bookstore. Shelf after shelf of words coated in dust and forgotten. She'd tasted the absinthe moments after purchasing it, slipping into an alley and taking a too-long draught from the neck of the bottle. With her secret treasure tucked deep in the depths of her purse, she'd run her fingertips along the spines of novels and histories, biographies and collections, leather and cloth, some covered in brightly colored dust jackets, and others with gilt lettering stamped deep.

Then she was discovered as a squat, balding man with one eye much larger than the other suddenly appeared around the end of one bookcase. Belle, too startled to speak, backed away, her fingers gripping the first book that she touched and drawing it free, holding it out in penance for stolen moments of deeply clouded thought. Money changed hands, money she could not afford, and the book was hers, as much a stranger as the man who sold it and she was off with her bottle, the book, and her dreams.

Sometime that night, she'd begun to read.

The parsley was more difficult than the peppermint. The recipe was meant for a much larger batch than the single bottle Belle had concocted, and it took her more than an hour of teeth-gritting and mumbled curses to complete the calculations. Even when she had the figure in her mind and on the paper across her knees, she agonized, going over each number one at a time as if afraid they'd shift and rearrange if she didn't pay close enough attention.

At last she clipped the top of a single sprig of parsley and dropped it into her mortar. She knew the faint dust of the peppermint remained, but it didn't matter. She ground at the leaves with the pestle, pressing tightly and feeling the faint release of juice, the smearing. She made a mental note to be very careful in removing it. Pouring some of the absinthe into the mortar, stirring, and then pouring it all back through a funnel was the best way to be certain. Her measurements were very exact, and if she left anything out, she would not be able to calculate the difference later. She would have to start over. Her shoulders sagged, just for an instant, at the thought. So close.

She worked the parsley slowly to a paste, tipping the bottle now and then to drip a trickle of green liquid over the top, then grinding patiently to blend the paste to a thick syrup. Finally, wrists aching from the effort, she set the pestle aside on the napkin and reached for her funnel. She inserted it in the neck of the bottle and with practiced grace, she poured the contents of the mortar through. There was no discernible change. Green to green, soft rush of bubbles and the bottle stood, still steeped in mystery. Drenched in dreams.

She corked it carefully and stood, holding the bottle in both hands and carried it to the altar. It was actually a bar, or had been, but Art had renamed it the altar when Belle began insisting that nothing but her bottle be kept there. The bottle, and the book. Pressed beneath a sheet of glass in an old picture frame, it remained open to the same page that it had been open to for nearly three years.

Belle whispered softly to herself as she placed the bottle reverently on the bar.

"In Xanadu did Kubla Khan a stately pleasure dome decree,
Where Alph the sacred river, ran,
Through caverns measureless to man ...
Down to a sunless sea...."

She shivered and the bottle nearly tipped as a moment of vertigo shivered through her. She righted it quickly and stepped back. The book and its frame seemed to watch her as she retreated, as she stumbled among the ingredients and tools and notes, as she tripped, finally, dropping to her knees. She cried out at the sharp contact with the floor, but bit the sound off quickly. She wanted no one else in the room. Not yet. Maybe not ever.

This time, she knew, it would have to be her. Art could not paint this moment. Sammy could not draw it from the strings of her dulcimer, or whisper it from her silent lips. The bottle glittered, and Belle looked away. She fought the urge to drink now, to soar and burn with the deep green liquor sliding through her system. It wasn't time. If she drank now, he might not come. He might never come. He might come, and leave her. It had to be the afternoon. She had to be alone.

She stacked her papers as neatly as her trembling hands would allow and gathered her tools. She needed to clean up, and to ready herself. The others would have to be told, warned away and far from the bottle, and her space, when the time came. Belle had work to do.

Without a backward glance, she slipped from the room and into the kitchen. Behind her, the bottle continued to glitter, as if that flickering, captured light dancing along the green glass could watch, or think. Or dream.

Art didn't want to leave, but he knew from the expression on Belle's face that it was not a request. It was her house, after all. It was her gig, her dream or dementia or whatever you wanted to call it. As much as Art liked to see himself as the other half of a couple involving Belle, he knew it was never going to happen.

Sammy only nodded, packed up her dulcimer and donning a long, shapeless jacket, slipped out the back door and into the alley beyond. Neither Art nor Belle knew where Sammy went when she wasn't with them. Just that moment, Art would have liked to know. He would have liked to have been invited to follow, to belong somewhere during the period when he didn't belong in his own home.

It was silliness, he knew, this jealousy he felt toward the bottle. Pointless and foolish. Any other night of the week he would have been up and out and gone without a word, but the thought that he was forbidden changed it all. He hated it, chomped against the invisible bit it implied, but, in the end he grabbed his coat and stomped out into the streets without a word. As he moved steadily down the street and away, he felt the vague flicker of something familiar and distant, and he stopped frowning. He glanced at his hands, then back over his shoulder.

Very suddenly, he felt like painting. The urge came over him from nowhere, slipped into his thoughts and displaced his anger. He stood, undecided, the scents of oils and canvas wafting enticingly from his memory.

"Damn," he breathed softly. He knew he couldn't go back. Not yet. Not now. Belle wouldn't even open the door, and if he grew more insistent, she might go to his studio and his rooms and throw his things out the windows. Images flickered through his mind. Belle prostrate, lying back across the floor. Sammy, fingers poised near the broken string, speaking softly, her words palpable in the incense-thick air. The green bottle, pulsing, growing and winding in a coil that reached to circle Belle's prone form. He wanted to capture it, but was forced to memorize, eyes closed, gripping tightly each sinuous roll of what he had seen and refusing to let it fade.

He would paint. Not now. Not tonight probably, but he would paint, and when he did, he would bring that image to life. If he couldn't give Belle her magic, he could record their combined failures. He could make it so real that the music and the lust burned the edges of the canvas.

He couldn't shake the image of the coils.

"Weave a circle round him thrice,
And close your eyes with holy dread."

Art whispered the words, and again he shivered. He pulled his jacket more tightly about himself and headed off for Sid's, a club where the music was dark and dreary and the lighting was more so. He wasn't in a mood to dance or mingle, but the nightly call of alcohol rang in his ears.

"Fuck it," he muttered to no one in particular. "Just fuck it."

Belle poured the absinthe into a tumbler and placed it upon the altar. She knelt before it, trembling, feeling the weight of the empty house heavy on her shoulders. Now that she'd sent the others away she felt vulnerable, fragile and inadequate to the task she had set herself.

With the concentrated reverence that regularly brought scornful comments from Art, she opened her journal. In the pages of this book she'd documented her quest, her dreams, each and every mistake and small success. She had also recorded her research, and it was to this she turned for strength. The words that had dragged her into this surreal otherworld. The history of Xanadu.

"The following fragment is here published at the request of a poet of great and deserved celebrity [Lord Byron], and, as far as the Author's own opinions are concerned, rather as a psychological curiosity, than on the grounds of any supposed poetic merits. In the summer of the year 1797, the Author, then in ill health, had retired to a lonely farmhouse between Porlock and Linton, on the Exmoor confines of Somerset and Devonshire. In consequence of a slight indisposition, an anodyne had been prescribed, – Here Belle had scribbled a furious note, drawn from other sources - letters and fragments, notes of Lord Byron himself. She had crossed it all out, including the word anodyne, and replaced it with absinthe – from the effects of which he fell asleep in his chair at the moment that he was reading the following sentence, or words of the same substance, in 'Purchas's Pilgrimage':

'Here the Khan Kubla commanded a palace to be built, and a stately garden thereunto. And thus ten miles of fertile ground were enclosed with a wall.'

The Author continued for about three hours in a profound sleep, at least of the external senses, during which time he has the most vivid confidence, that he could not have composed less than from two to three hundred lines; if that indeed can be called composition in which all the images rose up before him as things with a parallel production of the correspondent expressions, without any sensation or consciousness of effort. On awakening he appeared to himself to have a distinct recollection of the whole, and taking his pen, ink, and paper, instantly and eagerly wrote down the lines that are here preserved. 'A person on business from Porlock' interrupted him and he was never able to recapture more than 'some eight or ten scattered lines and images.'"

Belle closed the book. She had read the words so many times she could recite them as litany. She had researched and delved into the letters of Coleridge and Byron, certain she would find the answers she sought. Hundreds of lines, reduced to a snippet of rhyme, and still so powerful that movies had been centered around small quotes from the verse, and novels written in the attempt to finish the work. To close the portal, or open it, as Coleridge had seen it. To present to the world the quality that inspired Byron to insist on the publication of a broken poem, as if it were a key. As if, beyond the inspiration of Coleridge himself, Byron alone could see.

On the altar sat the fruit of years of labor. Belle believed that she knew more of the essence of Absinthe than any living being, and still she quaked at her ignorance. It was a gamble, each time, pouring the product of each long-dead master's work into her bottles and vials, crashing into the walls of their failures and seeing, just beyond her grasp, the essence, the purity of form that would show her what he had seen, what he would have written. The essence and completion of Xanadu that would make it real.

Art had made it surreal. He had grasped the tenuous threads of all Belle had striven for and woven them into an incomplete tapestry that teased her with its borderline truth. She loved him for his devotion and cursed him for the failure, but she knew that the failure was really hers. Sammy haunted her. There was more to the tiny, frail musician than met the eye, but there was no history, no record of things gone and those to come to measure her against. Sammy was as she was, and she, in the end, had failed as well. This one, also, on Belle.

Now came the final, acid test. No conduit. No half-truth or interpretation. Belle, the glass, the deep green magic, and the words. She would find the caves of ice and prostrate herself on their cold, sharp edges until she was accepted, taken or broken, but one with what had been lost. Dark, powerful eyes haunted her, tracking each motion and each thought, seeing through flesh and bone and soul. Waiting.

She took the tumbler gently into her hands. Candlelight flickered about her, and the incense, ever-present, grew cloying and thick, a taste that lingered in the back of her throat, drying her out and reaching to the absinthe for succor and warmth. Belle shivered a final time, so deeply that she nearly spilled the thick green liquid over her hands and the floor. Her knees rattled on the floor, and she gasped.

Throwing her head back, she brought the drink to her lips and upended it. The heat was intense, the burn glorious and excruciating and powerful all at once, washing through her in a burst of fire a part of which dripped down behind the initial fire, a secondary sizzle to slowly singe her throat. She did not move, fearing it would be too strong, that she might vomit or pass out, that she might fail herself as so many others who had gone before. The truth was, they hadn't failed, because they hadn't been reaching for anything. Only Belle had failed, and as the hot liquor burned down her throat, she knew it was her courage that had been lacking, not the ingredients, or the mix, not the strength of will of another, presented as her sacrifice. Placing the glass on the altar, she glanced at her book—her notes —in scorn. She had been hiding in the research, hiding between the pages, lacking the courage to see. To know.

She closed her eyes, and the words came unbidden, slowly, then with growing force. She recited in a steady, throaty voice that purred with strength and resolution.

"In Xanadu did Kubla Khan
A stately pleasure-dome decree:
Where Alph, the sacred river, ran
Through caverns measureless to man
Down to a sunless sea.
So twice five miles of fertile ground
With walls and towers were girdled round:
And there were gardens bright with sinuous rills,

Where blossomed many an incense-bearing tree;
And here were forests ancient as the hills,
Enfolding sunny spots of greenery..."

Belle closed her eyes tightly, her hands out to her sides for balance. The absinthe leaked into her thoughts and drew her deeper, thickening her tongue as she fought for completion. Images opened in her mind. Art's painting flashed into view, but with details he had never seen. The ice rippled with fire. The ground shook with the marching cadence of a horde of booted feet. The landscape surged with greenery, and huge spouting geysers splashed into the air and fell to the earth, all to the rhythm of a resonating heartbeat, drawing her inward.

Her body arched once more, a bow, head pressed against the floor, the altar before her and her knees spreading wider, inviting. She wore a short, soft linen dress, nothing beneath, but it didn't matter. The sensations that washed through her had nothing to do with clothing, or the room surrounding her, or the world where she lived and breathed and lusted for ... what?

"For he on honeydew hath fed,"

The words seeped up from beneath her, hands fashioned of letters that lifted her and offered her…

"And drunk the milk of paradise."

She saw a young man, long flowing dark hair and a broad nose, dark eyebrows furrowed in concentration. In his hand he held a quill, black with ink. He seemed to see her in that same instant, studying her, every inch and curve, eyes bright. His hand trembled, and a droplet of ink threatened to fall to whatever surface he penned upon.

Beside him a bottle sat, aged and crusted with sugar crystals, the cork removed. A crystal tumbler rested beside it, and Belle felt his fingers as he reached for that drink, felt them stroking her flesh and drawing her up, her hips rising to meet the fall of his lips. His eyes never left hers, and the hand that did not hold the quill slid beneath her, curling into the small of her back.

Belle cried out, trying to close the eyes that had opened when she clamped her own shut, trying to avoid the intensity, the absolute pleasure and terror and impossibility of that touch and that moment, but she could not give voice to the sound, or, if she did, she could not hear it. Nor could he.

He leaned closer, and she knew him, from portraits and descriptions, from the twist of the lips that would one day sneer at his own work, questioning its value and releasing it only at another's whim. Those lips so close his breath, hot-sweet with absinthe, brushed her thighs. Belle's entire being clenched.

The air shattered with a sharp sound. Belle clamped her eyes more tightly still, concentrating, but the moment was crumbling around her, falling away. The sound repeated, and she cried out. She arched so violently that her back crackled, spine rearranging to try and compensate. She ground her head into the floor, felt the tug and tear as the motion pulled against her hair. His face had faded and though the heat remained between her legs, the touch had never come. The ice had faded to molten carpet that burned her as she stroked against it, and again, the sound, and again, blaring and bursting through her thoughts.

Then there was nothing.

Art turned his key in the lock at last, determined, if this was his last night in the house, that he would spend it painting. He could not block the images, and though he'd poured drink after drink down his throat, doubling the shots when the first few rounds failed him, his heart pounded and his head spun, not with drunken stupor, but with the images, leeched from the memory of Sammy's music and the faces floating in air, the words and the incense, and the failure. He had painted, but now he knew that he had not been true to himself, or the images. He hadn't failed, he'd been a coward. He knew, and he wanted to share that knowing, but the only way to do it was the painting.

He opened the door and burst inside, and he found her,

Belle, prostrate on the floor, bent nearly double and writhing against the carpet. The incense was so thick he could barely make out the bar beyond the altar. He saw the bottle sitting there, and a glance at the floor showed the empty tumbler.

Belle was unconscious. He didn't know why, or how, but he knew she was breathing. He lifted her in his arms and carried her to his room. He placed her on his bed, covered her tortured features with his sheets and blankets and turned away. She was alive. She was safe. He had to paint.

Art never knew when Sammy returned. One moment he was lost in the painting, and the next he realized he was lost in both the painting, and the sound. She had entered, opened the case, pulled out her dulcimer, and she was playing, matching the notes to his motion, or was he matching his motion to the sound? It didn't matter.

As he neared completion, he was aware of something more. Belle had risen, first to sit on the bed, staring at him in wonder, then to rise and slip closer, molding herself to his body and pressing tight. Other times, other worlds, and he would have worried that she would jostle him, drive him from the images or vice versa, but it was right. Each counterbalance she caused brought the brush closer to perfection, and she held tightly. The eyes glared back at them from the canvas, the ice glistened, and the heat throbbed.

Sammy began to sing along with the tune she was playing, the words distant and familiar, though neither Art nor Belle had ever heard them spoken. The final words of the poem passed, and the milk of paradise ran green in rivers flowing from Art's brush. The eyes of Samuel Taylor Coleridge glistened with longing as he watched them, lost in a corner of the canvas, as they passed. Beyond, seated in a garden, beneath lush fruit trees and near a fountain another sat, also watching. Again they passed, and as they did, the man's tortured eyes slid over Belle and he whispered:

"She walks in beauty, like the night."

But no one heard them spoken..

The words, so long forgotten, whispered over Sammy's lips, softer and lighter, fading to the sound of traffic passing on the street beyond. The smoke of incense wisped about the room. On the floor, heavy with deep green paint, the brush lay still, soaking its contents to the carpet. The painting was spectacular, image torn from image, blended to other worlds and back.

The room stood empty.

In the next room where she'd left it closed, Belle's book fell open silently. The candles burned low, but the light was bright enough for reading. Leaning low, a long-haired, oddly dressed man gripped the volume, holding it up and apparently marveling at the binding and the lined paper within. The book had fallen open to a page etched with verse, and he read. His eyes filled with an odd pain, then he placed the framed book on Belle's altar.

Before him on that altar, sat the bottle. One final shot remained within. He lifted it, took a whiff of the contents, and smiled. He knew that scent, one thing very familiar in a world suddenly gone mad. Without thought, he poured the last of the absinthe into the tumbler, closed his eyes, and poured it down his throat.

Lifting the pen, he stared at the paper, mouthing the final words.

"And drunk the milk of paradise."

Slowly, mind awash with images, he began to write.

AUTHOR'S NOTE: Once, long ago, I was keynote speaker at a writer's conference in the Lehigh Valley up north. I didn't really know what I was going to talk about. I felt a little overwhelmed, because, at that point in my career, though I'd sold several novels and a handful or two of stories, I wasn't sure I had the experience to speak on a subject that would prove useful. Then...I started talking (it's a recurring theme...) What I talked about was the fact that my ideas don't just come to me. Often – I live them. I told them this story – it didn't happen exactly as I wrote it, but it was closer than reality should have allowed. The house – the church – the guy who looked like Charles Manson ... so much of this I did not make up. Then I wrote in my buddy Wayne Allen Sallee – who was present that weekend, a weekend where I'd come to author Elizabeth Massie's house for something we called Pseudocon – a writer's retreat of sorts – a gathering of friends that I have to this day, though at least one has passed from us. Many of these people are authors I now publish. All of them have influenced my life, and my work. We recently visited Waynesboro, and Beth took us to the site of that house. It has collapsed in on itself, but you can look in through the ruins. The piano is still there...

You Lookin' For Herb?

It was getting dark, and the road ahead was fading quickly to shadows. Dave looked about himself nervously, hoping against hope that he'd see something familiar, something that would let him know he was on the right track. For about the thousandth time that hour, he cursed himself for forgetting to bring Beth's phone number.

The Virginia mountains were no place to be lost at that time of night, especially when the only landmarks you could remember that might make everything all right were three giant grain silos off to one side of the road when you could barely *see* the side of the road. It was not starting out to be the best night of his life.

In the seat beside him, Jo was squirming uncomfortably, trying to look unconcerned, but not doing a very good job. All things considered, she was taking it like a trooper. It was their first time away together, and they hadn't been dating very long. His first fear had been that she'd be furious, and that their weekend would be ruined, all by his own ridiculous mistake.

The roads that turned off to either side were all numbered with identical signs. He knew that the one he needed was eight hundred and something, and since he couldn't make out a thing along the roadside, he opted for the one that seemed to ring a bell. 813. It might not be the right one, but it was a place to start.

"I'm sorry about this," he said, turning to Jo with a lopsided grin. "I can't believe her phone is unlisted!"

"It's okay," she said, returning the smile, if a bit nervously. "Is this the road?"

"I'm not sure, but it looks familiar. If this isn't it, we'll come back out here, make our way into town, and I'll figure something else out."

She nodded, and he drove on down the dark, deserted road, paying close attention to the many potholes and the steep ditches. She had offered up her car for the trip, even letting him do the driving, and he had no intention of taking advantage of that trust.

On either side they passed farm houses, some showing lights, others seemingly deserted. Nowhere was there a sign of life or a familiar landmark, and after a couple of short miles, he had to admit that he was lost.

Just as he'd begun to look for a place to turn around and head back the other way, he spotted one last house on the right side of the road. There was a car parked in the front yard, its door open and the dome-light on.

"I'm going to pull in and ask whoever that is for directions," he said with relief. "It looks like they just got home!"

Jo didn't say anything, but he noticed that she was gripping the armrest on the door tightly and her lips were compressed in a very, very poor imitation of a smile. It didn't help that there was an old abandoned church in the lot across the way from the house.

He stared at it, realizing almost immediately what seemed out of place. There was a "FOR RENT" sign on the door! A church for rent, and it came with its own small cemetery out back. Swell. How many gods could be in the market?

He pulled into the driveway behind where the other car was still parked, and he turned off the ignition.

"Wait here?" he asked.

Jo didn't look enthusiastic about being left alone, but it was obvious that she'd rather be near the ignition and the gas pedal than walking into some strange country homestead and chatting up the locals. That was fine. Alone, he could hurry it along, find out where that damned road with the three silos was, and they'd be on their way. Once they'd finally reached Beth's and gotten settled in, he was certain things would be fine. At least he hoped they would.

Crossing the unkempt yard quickly, lips twisted in a friendly smile, Dave approached the car. It was obvious now that, though the door was open, the dome light and stereo on, the occupant of the vehicle had no intention of getting out and going inside. Judging from the two flat tires on the closest side of the vehicle and the flowers growing up through the fender in front, it was more of a home addition than a vehicle these days.

Just as Dave was beginning to think that maybe Jo was right, maybe they would be better off just finding the place on their own, an arm slipped out from the car's shadowy interior to dangle loosely over the door, which was slightly ajar, and a face appeared in the window.

If he hadn't known the man was in prison, and that the idea was ludicrous, he would've sworn that the face belonged to Charlie Manson. Long, greasy hair dangled past thin, emaciated shoulders, and the eyes that stared out from the shadows of that car were feral – like those of a rodent, or some wild predator, gleaming at him through the darkness.

"Yeah?" the man said, and the dry, rasping sound of his voice, followed by a rattling cough, brought things back to reality. It wasn't Charlie Manson, that was for sure.

"Excuse me," Dave began brightly, holding out a hand that the other man ignored pointedly, "but we're looking for the Lindbergh place – it's a farm near here. I think we must have taken a wrong turn off the main road back there."

He pointed vaguely back the way they'd come, trying without success to remember just which number turnoff they'd actually taken.

"You lookin' for Herb?" the man asked, his eyes slightly unfocused. He acted as though he hadn't heard a word Dave had said, and it was obvious that he was drunk, or stoned, or both. At least Dave *hoped* he was.

"No," he answered slowly. "I don't know any Herb – is he a relative of the Lindberghs?"

The man looked at him as if *he* were crazy. "Nope, don't think so. He'll be here in a little bit, though, you could wait."

"But I don't *want* to see Herb," Dave burst out, exasperated. "I'm just looking for directions to my friend's farm."

"I don't know these parts too well," the man told him slowly. "You might go inside and ask – someone ought to be able to help you."

Dave turned, giving Jo a "what can I do?" kind of shrug, and looked about himself quickly. He saw the church next door, its graveyard pointed directly at him and the "FOR RENT" sign hanging at an ominous angle on the door.

"Shit," he said under his breath. He thanked the man quickly and headed for the front door of the place, hoping against hope that someone with half a brain would be inside, and that they could get out of this madhouse and back on the road quickly.

Just as he reached up to knock, a breath of fetid air washed across his shoulder, and he realized that the man had slipped up behind him. An odd sound was filling the air – at first he thought it was just his head buzzing with the sudden burst of adrenalin brought on by the man's sudden appearance – but it was more than that.

A piano. It was a tinny, off-key rendition of some sort of jazz tune, and it was coming from inside the house. Without a word, the man reached around him and pushed the door open, letting the music escape into the night.

Dave coughed quickly, backing up as the scent of the inner rooms hit him. There was a moldy, yellowed sheet hanging from the door frame like a curtain. The place smelled musky, like a huge litter box, or an abandoned barn that rodents had taken over.

Moving ahead of him, and thankfully pushing the nasty, rotting sheet out of the way, the man preceded him inside. With a deep breath, which he held as long as possible, Dave followed. There was a light just to the right—another doorway, similarly curtained to the first. It was from beyond this that the music was rolling forth, much louder now, still filled with so many discordant notes that he knew the instrument must be horribly out of tune.

Parting the "curtain" of the second room, he stepped inside and stopped. Across the room at a run-down, lop-sided old piano, sat what appeared to be a very greasy Little Richard impersonator. Dreadlocks hung down to shoulder length in back—greased or extremely dirty—and the man's bony black fingers danced quickly over the chipped ivory of the keyboard. He swayed from side to side slowly, lost in the music—such as it was.

Then, with a sudden lurch, he stopped playing and spun his head over his left shoulder in a single, fluid motion, catching Dave staring and meeting his gaze flatly. There was no emotion in those eyes—no life of any sort, for that matter. No color. They were white, empty, blind eyes. Dave shivered involuntarily and glanced away, but when he gathered the courage to turn back, the pianist was gazing at his own fingers again. Dave couldn't be certain what he'd seen, but the image of those milky-white orbs strobed in his mind.

"You looking for Herb?" the man asked quickly, not looking back again, or seeming to really care what Dave might be looking for.

Shaking his head, Dave answered. "No. I'm up here to visit some friends, the Lindberghs. They live down one of these roads, eight hundred something. I think the address is 870-B."

The man continued to stare at him as if he hadn't spoken at all. "You aren't lookin' for Herb?"

Holding his anger in check, Dave started to tell him again what he was looking for, but the first man cut in again.

"I know a guy named Wayne Lindbergh."

"Great!" Dave cut in quickly. "Where does he live? Maybe he lives nearby, or he's related?"

"Lived in Richmond," the man said flatly. "Never been around here."

Now anger was passing off into nervous fear. This was going from bizarre straight into late-night horror movie reality way too quickly.

"You don't know where 870-B might be?" he asked, starting to turn for the door.

"This here's 111," the man at the piano told him slowly, as if dredging the numbers up from far, far back in the abyss he'd once called a mind.

About 555 short, I'd say, Dave thought. Aloud, he said, "Well, I guess we'll just go and see if we can't find it ourselves, then. The road has three grain silos off to the side." He threw this in as a final hope, but no sparks flew.

"You can try the trailer park," Manson said, pointing down the road one further than the turn off Dave had already taken. "Someone there can probably help you."

"Great," Dave said, backpedaling quickly and pushing aside the curtain over the door. It was time to get out of there and hit the road – quick. Next would come the chainsaws, or the axes.

"You sure you don't wanna see Herb?" Little Richard asked as he turned away. "He'll be comin' by here later ..."

That was it. Dave turned and lurched toward the front door, pushing the tattered sheet aside and slamming the outer door open with his palm. Somehow the Charles Manson-looking grease-ball had made his way back to the door at the same time. He leaned in close as Dave barreled out into the night and said, "We are a commune of musicians."

Right, Dave thought as he hurried to the driver's side of the car and slammed the door behind himself. *Little Richard in there plays the piano, and you play the stereo out front, right?*

"Did you find out anything?" Jo asked, taking in the expression on his face and the hurried, nervous movements he kept making as he started the car and backed out into the street.

"We aren't staying for drinks, let's just leave it at that," he said, trying for a grin that never quite made it to his lips. He turned and concentrated on the road ahead.

He drove to the next road, turned down it and headed toward the lights of the trailer park. Swell. More of the same, he was sure, but he had nothing else to try. In the distance he saw two figures walking down the road, both with hair down halfway to their asses. Shrugging, he pulled to the side of the road and asked about the silos.

"Oh, you mean 870?" the first of the two boys asked. They were both dressed normally enough – rock-group t-shirts and jeans, boots and leather belts. "That's two roads back, you can't miss those silos, once you turn off."

Thanking them, Dave turned around once more and headed back the way he'd come. He found the Lindbergh farm easily enough, pulled in behind the other cars – everyone else, it seemed, had found the place in the daylight – and he and Jo went inside to join the party.

Everyone that was gathered there was a writer or an artist. They were the "Guests of Honor" at Out-in-the-BooniesCON, or some-such thing, a local SF gathering that would begin the next day.

After everyone was settled, Dave told the story of their harrowing experience on the next road down, and Beth's eyes widened in horror.

"You don't mean the '"Green"' house, do you? God, everyone wonders whether those guys are axe murders, or what."

"One and the same," Dave countered. "Not axe murderers, though, I don't believe. They claim to be a commune of musicians."

Everyone laughed, and after a few more drinks and a few more stories they all turned in for the night, the old house and its eerie inhabitants all but forgotten.

The convention had ended early, and after everyone had

gathered back at the farm, Wayne and Mark convinced Dave to go back to the old Green house.

"Let's go see those guys, man," Wayne said. "What's the harm? A beat-up piano, a few old sheets – maybe we could take a guitar with us and jam?"

"You've *got* to be kidding," Dave had grinned at him in exasperation. He was not kidding. Insane, probably, but not kidding.

So there they were, the three of them, the women having opted for something a bit less adventurous, like horseback riding, walking down the road toward the old house and its neighboring churchyard. Dave wasn't sure whether he wanted to go there at all, but he wasn't going to back down if the other two were going.

They made the expected wisecracks about the "FOR RENT" sign on the church, wondering which ancient god would take the owners up on it. Mark did a pretty good rendition of the slinking, clubfooted pace of a Romeroesque zombie, pointing at the graveyard and saying, "New God moved in, made us leave, He did. Said, no Christian God here, no Christian dead here, left us just like that, homeless."

Dave's laughter cut off midway through the first chuckle when they rounded the corner. The car wasn't there. The weeds weren't even pressed down where it might have been there before. He turned, eyes wide, and just stared at his companions, who were looking back at him like *he* was the lunatic.

"Maybe it wasn't this place," he said dubiously. He knew that it was. The angle on the old graveyard was just as it had been the night before. Moving as if he were in a trance, he made his way to the front door and reached out, as if to knock on it. There was no need. The door stood a few inches ajar, hanging from one broken hinge that was half-rusted through.

Inside the sheets hung, just as he'd said, and he brushed his way past them both in a rush, heedless of the many spider's' webs and scuttling things that shot out in all directions as he passed.

The piano was gone, too. There was nothing in the house at all, in fact. Nothing but the smell, which he remembered only too well, dust, and a family of sparrows that shot out the window in a burst of sound and feathers, nearly stopping his heart.

"Telling the tall tales again, eh?" Mark observed, looking around the place and brushing a cobweb off his arm. "Commune of musicians?"

Dave staggered to the window, his face ashen, and stared across the lot outside at the church. Something else was wrong. The sign – the ludicrous, cockeyed "FOR RENT" sign was gone.

Then he heard it. It was faint, at first, winding its way through his senses so deceptively that he thought at first he was imagining it. It was the music, the awful, discordant piano music. The piano was gone, but the music lived on, it seemed.

"There!" he cried, turning wildly to where his friends were examining some dusty relics in the back corner of the room. "Do you hear it?"

Not waiting for an answer, he rushed back out into the yard. The music was louder there, coming from the direction of the old church. There were lights on, too, he saw, coming from the windows between the cracks of the old boards that held them shut. He stopped, his eye caught by a small pamphlet lying on the ground at his feet.

Picking it up, he peeled it apart carefully where the morning dew had glued the pages together.

The First Church of Light and Vision, learn the wisdom of the stars.

There was more, but he couldn't quite make it out. It said something about the coming of a God, or a savior, or perhaps just a traveling evangelist. He couldn't quite make out the name. It looked like HE..B. He turned to show his find to Wayne and Mark, but they were nowhere to be seen. Frowning, he returned to the old house, looking carefully through each room. Gone

"All right, man," he said aloud. "This isn't funny." He figured they were outside, hiding and waiting for him, and he was in no mood to play their game. "Let's just get back to the house, okay?"

No answer. He made his way into the yard again and

something drew him back toward the church. Maybe they'd just gone over there to check out the music. It could be that the graveyard extended to the other side of the building, that there was another house, which would explain the music. He started forward, watching every shadowy nook where his two friends might be lying in wait, and approached the old church.

As he drew nearer, it became obvious that they had somehow managed to get that piano into the church itself during the night. The music was coming from inside, and, against his better judgment, he moved to the door at the end of the building. There were plenty of cracks in the old wood, he could just look inside and see what was going on for himself.

Before he could bend down to have a look, however, the door burst open. Light flowed out and around him, surrounding him on all sides. Charles Manson stood framed in the doorway, his greasy hair actually combed back and braided and his arms spread wide. Where there had been dull, mindless oblivion in his gaze the night before, now they burned with a strange, wild light.

"I knew you would return," he said, grabbing Dave's arm and propelling him inside.

Across the room, Little Richard sat with his back to the two of them, dancing his hands over the keys of the ancient piano. This wasn't what had captured his attention, though. There was an altar at the front of the room, and on it a feast—or what appeared to be a feast—was laid out. Mark and Wayne stood there at the table, turning to meet his confused gaze with wide, feral grins. He saw that their eyes were alight with the same odd spark as Manson's.

Wayne waved to him, and he saw what was in his friends hand. It was a leg-bone—a human leg bone—and the skin was rotted and flayed from it, black with dirt and maggots. As he tried to pull back, retching violently, Mark called out to him, slipping back into the odd, Monty-Pythonesque accent from earlier.

"I was wrong, Davey, so wrong. Herb don't want the Christian dead to go, we have to get rid of them ourselves!"

As his head hammered to the wild, incomprehensible

banging of the piano, Dave heard the doors crash shut behind him. There was another figure behind the altar, taller, darker, blending into the shadows themselves. As the light began to course through him, eating its way to his eyes, he felt the first pangs of hunger, and he moved forward, moved to the combined beat of piano and stereo—the car had somehow been parked to the left, behind the pews, and Manson had resumed his seat.

As he reached for a rotting hand, he began to wonder. He wondered what instrument *he* would play.

AUTHOR'S NOTE: I grew up in a small southern town. That period of my life has had a powerful influence on the settings, and the characters in my books and stories. Since we've come to live in Eastern North Carolina, this place has seeped into the blood between the lines. I love the old country feel, the abandoned buildings, The Great Dismal Swamp – all of it. One thing, though – the people here are just different. Sometimes you can't understand them when they talk. Some of the families here stretch back to the days when there were British governors running the show. A lot of history stretches much farther back, even, than that. What I did in this story … a bit redneck, a bit funny, a little Lovecraftian… It's one of the tales of Old Mill, North Carolina, where I've returned time and again… I can imagine these two, this place, and this very story being true… It should scare me, but it only makes me smile. This is the revised, author's preferred version, by the way, and will be appearing in an anthology soon titled **Tales of the Al-Azif**, *edited by Matthew Davenport and C. T. Phipps.*

Cockroach Suckers

Near the Great Dismal Swamp, everything grows. Bugs thrive. Plants barely hesitate between frost and full, pollen-bearing bloom. A warm winter week can produce things that should sleep until summer. It's in the earth. Birth, rebirth, and death.

Whatever grows must decompose. That is truth. As the sun set in a splash of deep violet and dark purple above the tree line, Jasper Winslow was contemplating that truth. He was rocking slowly in an ancient pressed back chair, watching the road crumble and brushing flies from his sweat-slicked brow.

Jasper wasn't an old man, but he was no pup. He'd been running his father's farm pretty much on his own since he turned twenty, and he'd been selling the excess produce at this out-of-the-way, run-down stand for just as long. The boards were gray, warped, and without a sign of peeling paint left to indicate they'd ever been white. The swamp was a ways down the road and across a field, but its creeping, encroaching presence worked its way closer every year. The road had nearly washed out in the last flood, and only a dump truck or two of gravel and half-a-dozen lazy state highway workers had prevented it.

In the opposite direction, spitting up a shower of dust and stone in its wake, a pickup truck turned off the freeway, bouncing and weaving down the two-lane gravel road. The back of the truck was covered with a blue tarp that flapped in the breeze. Something poked out from beneath that tarp, but it was still too far away for Jasper to see. The truck was Bobby Lee's, a grimy green-colored Ford as old as Methuselah and twice as cantankerous. Whitish smoke billowed from the tailpipe, and the truck listed heavily to the left, obviously struggling under an unfamiliar load.

Jasper reached down to his left, flipped up the lid on a rusted old metal cooler, fished in the ice and water until he found a beer, and pulled it free. He twisted off the top, slammed the cooler closed with a practiced motion, and leaned back again. He drained a third of the bottle in one quick drag, then sat, resting it on the bulky expanse of his belly, and watched Bobby Lee park.

The truck wheezed, gasped, and died with the rumble of an engine that doesn't want to quit running, despite its dubious ability to do so. The belch of smoke that erupted from Bobby Lee's pipes was so reminiscent of a giant fart that Jasper broke into a grin.

"You runnin' that thing on beans?" he hollered, not getting up, but raising a hand in greeting. Bobby Lee was Jasper's best friend in the world, but it was hot, and Jasper Winslow rose for no man, once he'd started rocking.

Bobby Lee clambered down from the driver's seat, slammed the door without looking back and grinned. "Got one a' them nitro bottles up front," he said, nodding. "Filled it with Hall-a PENYAS just yesterday. You ought to see her run when I punch that chili button."

Jasper laughed. With an uncharacteristic flash of energy, he opened the cooler again, grabbed a second cold beer, and flipped it through the air. Bobby Lee caught it neatly, brought the bottle to the brim of his faded Catfish Hunter baseball cap with a flourish that resembled a salute, and twisted off the top.

"I just bet," Jasper commented. "Day you waste a Hall-a Penya on that truck is the day I quit drinking."

Both of them laughed at that.

"What you got in the truck, Bobby Lee?" Jasper asked, eyeing the oddly draped tarp and the still-listing rear end of the truck. "Some sorta tractor?"

Bobby Lee grinned. He took another pull on his beer, and then shook his head. "Nope. I got me a gold mine, is what. I got the answer to all our problems." He sipped his beer and his grin widened.

Jasper frowned. When he frowned, his brow furrowed, and the expression never ceased to widen Bobby Lee's grin.

"Don't think *too* hard," Bobby Lee advised. "I know you've been conservin' that gray matter all these years—be a shame to waste it now."

Jasper considered getting up. Bobby Lee needed his ass kicked, and there wasn't anyone else around to take up his slack, but for the moment, he held his peace. He was rocking, and that was important. So was the beer, and it was only half empty.

"What's in the truck?" he asked again. This time, his eyes narrowed, and his voice had taken on a cold, empty tone.

Bobby Lee watched him a moment longer, still chuckling, then he spoke.

"You still got that old tin shed you had stored behind your mom's place?" he asked, ignoring Jasper's question. "You know, the one you never put together?"

"I got it," Jasper answered. "So what? What's in the fucking *truck*, asshole?"

Bobby Lee hesitated a little less this time, but his smile had darkened. "Hold your horses," he said finally, "and I'll show you. You don't have to be an asshole about it—I'm lettin' you in on a good thing."

Jasper just rocked. He was one step closer to rising from the chair and doing what had to be done, but he let it ride a last time.

Bobby drained his beer, tossed the bottle aside and turned back to his truck with a curse. "Ought to just leave you here and keep it for myself," he growled. When he got no response, his shoulders sagged, just enough to be perceptible, and he stepped to the truck. There were three ties holding the tarp in place on the near side. Bobby undid them quickly. Then he stepped to the back of the truck, gripped the blue plastic tightly, and with a flourish, he yanked it free.

Jasper stopped rocking. He drained his beer, reached around to set it on the cooler, let go of it and missed by six inches. He gripped the arms of his chair tightly, half rising. "What the f…"

What rose from the bed of the truck took his breath away. Jasper fell back with a thump, setting the rocker in motion again and nearly tipping over backward. He gasped, tried to speak, fell silent, and gasped again. Without thinking, he reached down and retrieved another beer. It was half gone when Bobby Lee, grinning again, stepped closer, leaned down, and winked.

"What do you think of her? She's somethin', ain't she?" he said.

Jasper gulped more beer, rocked forward, and gained his feet. He staggered forward, reached out a hand to steady himself against the truck, and then reached up to run his hand over polished wood that literally swam with tiny intricate detail and what appeared to be words, or letters, or symbols. Who knew? Who the fuck knew and who *cared*?

"It's a … double-D goddam COCKROACH," he pronounced in amazement.

"The world's largest," Bobby Lee agreed, cackling. "Ain't she a beaut? I picked her up down at the flea market. They tried three weeks to sell her, but nobody knew what they was lookin' at."

"They didn't know it was a cockroach?" Jasper turned, his face a wrinkled map of confusion. "How they hell could they not know that? The fucking thing's seven foot tall, Bobby."

It was all of that. Rising so that its antennae floated above the cab of the truck, the gigantic wooden vermin leaned to its left, apparently off-balance, making the truck list crazily. The detail was amazing, like some sort of ART or something. Jasper scratched his head and tilted his hat back to facilitate the motion. Who in HELL would go to that kind of trouble for a goddam cockroach?

"She's an antique," Bobby continued. "Feller said he didn't know how old it was. Picked it up at an Indian camp about ten years ago. Had her in his barn ever since, but his wife said it had ta go. They don't make a Raid can big enough, so here she is."

Bobby was still grinning. Jasper was still frowning.

"But," Jasper formed both thoughts and words carefully, and this one was a corker. Nothing in his experience had prepared him for it, and so he had to figure it out, one word at a time. "Why?"

"Why what?" Bobby asked. "Why did his wife want him to get rid of her, or why aren't there giant Raid cans?"

Bobby had sense enough to back up at this, raising his hands and laughing.

"Easy, hoss," he said. "Hear me out. You ever been out west? I have. I traveled out to Kansas once with my Pa. There's some mountains over there where … well, anyway, I went there. You know what we saw along that highway?"

"Fields?" Jasper guessed, trying to follow.

"We saw fields, for sure," Bobby grinned, "but there was something else. We saw the world's largest prairie dog. We saw the biggest ball of string ever, and we saw the footprints of dinosaurs, preserved in the mud. Every time we saw one of them things, you know what we had to do? We had to pay. You know what Pa said every time, just as we left? He said we was suckers. Didn't stop him from wanting to see the world's largest sausage link, or from payin', but he knew. I know too. That ain't a cockroach, ol' buddy. That's a goldmine."

Jasper was still staring up at the wooden monstrosity. Its

eyes glittered in the sunlight, polished and seeming to glare down at him from their cocked, off-kilter angle.

"What the fuck are you talkin' about, Bobby? It's a damned roach. A BIG roach, no mistakin' that, but still a roach. A goddam, filthy, infest-your-house-and-eat-your-chicken roach. Where's the money in that? Hell, anyone sees it now, they won't buy my fruit."

"That's your problem, Jasper," Bobby said with true sorrow in his voice. "You ain't got the VISION. That's why I'm here— why I'm gonna share this good fortune with you. I'll tell you what we're gonna do."

Jasper listened, staring up at the roach, a tickling, creeping sensation transiting his spine as he did. He didn't like it. The damned wood was slimy to the touch, and no wood that wasn't growing mold should feel that way.

"We're gonna get that damn shed of yours," Bobby went on, "and we're gonna set it up right out yonder." He pointed to the back of the produce stand. "We're gonna put ol' Papa Roach here inside, and then we're gonna make some signs. All up and down 17 we'll have advertisements: 'Ten miles to the World's Largest Cockroach', 'Don't MISS THIS—5 Miles to the Vermin from HELL', '1 Mile to Go—Exit 16A—Produce and souvenirs'. You get it?"

Jasper didn't. He was still staring at the roach.

Bobby leaned in close, whispering conspiratorially in his friend's ear. "It's simple, Jasper. We sell tickets. Folks stop to see, buy a ticket, maybe buy some tomatoes and some corn, and they drive on. They won't be able to help themselves."

"You have got to be fucking kidding," Jasper said, turning to meet Bobby's earnest gaze. "I mean, who would PAY to see … THAT?"

"They won't see it," Bobby said. "Not right off. It will be in the shed. That's the key. And the answer is simple. We make our money," Bobby looked around, as if there were someone to see him, or to overhear a great secret, "off suckers. *Cockroach* suckers."

There were no words for how Jasper felt at that moment, so he turned away, sort of tripped back to his chair, and reached for another beer. "Cockroach suckers," he muttered. "Jesus fucking Christ on a Popsicle stick."

Bobby Lee trailed after him, reaching in to get his own beer this time, and Jasper didn't stop him. There was plenty of beer, and it took too much effort to think and yell at the same time.

"You really believe," Jasper said at last, "that folks'll pay good, hard-earned money to see the world's largest cockroach?"

Bobby Lee's grin was full wattage again. "I know they will, partner. I know they will. Hell, if I didn't OWN it, I'd rather see the thing myself than the world's largest link sausage, and I paid for that."

"How long you think it'll take us to get that tin shed up?" Jasper asked.

"Not more'n a day," Bobby Lee speculated, getting serious. "I helped my Pap put one up in his yard last spring. Not much to it, once you get started."

Jasper nodded, and the nod worked itself naturally into a slow rock. He stared up at the truck and met the multi-faceted gaze of Martha Stewart's worst nightmare steadily. He wanted to tell Bobby Lee to take the thing and hit the trail. It was a damn-fool idea. He knew it, and Bobby Lee should know it, but... damned if it didn't sound as if it might actually work.

"Shit," Jasper muttered.

Bobby Lee let out a whoop, knowing he'd won.

"You be here first thing in the morning," Jasper growled. "Be ready to work, no hangover. If we're a' goin' to do this, we're a' goin' to do it quick. I still got fields to plow, and produce to get in. If I let it go, we won't have a thing to sell except tickets, and I doubt that's gonna work out too well."

"I'll be here," Bobby Lee promised. Then he turned back to the truck and grabbed the ties on the tarp, pulling them tight and cinching them to the truck bed.

Once the huge bug was covered, Jasper felt a little better. There was something in the smooth, wooden surface of the thing's eyes that was unnerving. He knew it was silly, but that didn't change a thing.

"Damn thing gives me the willies," he said, reaching for another beer and staring at the blue-draped figure.

"Hope it gives everyone the willies," Bobby Lee commented. He reached into the cooler and fished out another beer for himself. "I'll have this one more, then I'm gonna hit the road. SmackDown is on tonight, and directly after that I'll be gettin' me some shuteye. I feel destiny callin'."

"That ain't destiny," Jasper chuckled, "it's indigestion from all them Hall-a-Penyas you *ain't* feedin' to your truck."

The two laughed and drank their beer in silence. Both of them kept giving the truck sidelong glances, but neither of them mentioned the thing in the back again. Not much later, Bobby Lee climbed in behind the wheel and, honking like an idiot, backed up in a cloud of dust and trundled his huge cargo off down the dirt road toward the highway. Jasper cleared his produce, locked what he could in his makeshift office, and stacked the rest in the back of his truck. He didn't have far to go. Two backroads turns and he'd be on his own road, tucked back up in close to the swamp.

Just before he left, he hefted his cooler onto the tailgate of the truck and slid it in, closing up behind it. He glanced at the road, thought about it for about ten seconds, then grabbed a last beer "for the road" and hopped in behind the wheel. He wasn't likely to meet one of North Carolina's finest between the stand and his home, but by his way of thinking, he was drunk enough already to get the ticket. No reason to deny himself a pleasant drive by leaving all the beer in back.

A white tail of dust and gravel spitting out behind him, Jasper gunned the truck into the growing twilight.

When Jasper pulled up in front of his stand the next morning, he saw Bobby Lee's truck already parked over to one side. There was no sign of his buddy, but around back of the shack, dust was rising, like there was a herd of something rushing past. Jasper parked, hopped down from his truck, and started around the side of the building to see what was what.

He stopped at the corner and stared. Bobby Lee was going to town on the ground behind the stand with a rake, clearing away brambles and bushes like there was no tomorrow. He'd already cleared a space about twice as big as the metal building in the back of Jasper's truck would need, and that ground was bare, scraped even, and squared off with perfect edges like Jasper had never seen.

"Bobby!" he called out. "Bobby Lee what in HELL are you doin'?"

At first, Bobby didn't seem to hear him, just kept right on a rakin' and shuffling around that rectangular patch of cleared ground. Jasper leaned down, picked up a rock and whipped it through the air to collide with the seat of Bobby Lee's pants. That got his attention.

"Wha…" Bobby Lee whirled, his rake held high in a comical parody of a martial arts stance. Then he saw Jasper.

"I said," Jasper repeated, "what in HELL are you doin'?"

"Just wanted to get me an early start, that's all," Bobby Lee said, grinning sheepishly. "I stayed up kinda late last night. Guess I talked a bit too much about her," he cocked his head in the direction of the wooden behemoth still tarp-covered in the back of his pickup truck. "Irma got tired of it and chased me out. I slept in the truck until the sun came up, then I came here and got started."

Jasper blinked, glanced down at the ground, and at the rake in his friend's hand, then back up to Bobby Lee's eyes. "Just how much coffee you had, Bobby?" he asked at last. "I ain't seen that much work out of you in the last year, and you don't even look like you broke a sweat yet."

Bobby Lee glanced down at the ground as if noticing the cleared patch for the first time. He leaned on the rake, reached to his back pocket for the bandanna tucked into his hip pocket and brushed it across his face. It was more out of habit than necessity. Jasper could see the man was as cool and fresh as if he'd just gotten up after a long night's sleep.

"Hell of a job," Jasper commented. "Gonna make settin' up a durn site easier."

Bobby Lee nodded. Now that he'd stopped working and started seeing what he'd been doing, he'd taken on a sort of glazed expression. He heard Jasper fine but didn't seem to really be paying any attention to him. He was looking at the earth he'd cleared, and glancing up now and then at the truck, as if there was something he couldn't quite make sense of.

"We have to put her here first," Bobby Lee said at last, tossing his rake aside. "I ain't seen the door of that shed, but I'm betting it's not big enough to take her in through. I brought us some pallets I had out back of my place to keep her out of the dirt."

Jasper blinked. He hadn't thought about it, but damned if Bobby Lee wasn't right. They'd have to build the shed around that thing, and even then it was going to come close. The peaked roof of the shed would top out at around eight feet in height, and the roach ran over seven. Jasper shook his head.

"We're damn fools, is what we are," he commented, turning away. "Damn fools."

Bobby Lee didn't answer. He was already headed toward his truck, the tarp, and the giant wooden body beneath. While Jasper unpacked his own truck, setting up the tomatoes and beans in neat rows on the bench out in front of his stand, Bobby unfurled the tarp, rolled it, and tossed it to one side. Then he got in behind the wheel of his truck and very slowly backed it toward the space he'd cleared, being careful not to catch the edge of his tailgate on the corner of the produce stand.

Jasper paid him no mind. He knew there'd be a short rush on the vegetables just before noon, and he needed to get them out and in place to be inspected, detected and selected, as his ol' Pap had used to say. No time for cockroach nonsense, nor for Bobby Lee, if it came to it. That boy needed any help, he'd have to holler for it.

That call never came. Jasper plunked down into his old rocker, kicked up his boots like he'd done a thousand times before, and started rocking. Mrs. Tefft dropped by on her way back from dropping her kids at school and picked up two pounds of fresh tomatoes. Edna Johnson came by for her regular order of green beans and potatoes, and Sheriff Ben Grouse pulled up in his cruiser to grab a small basket of strawberries for his Missus. Jasper never charged the sheriff for small things like the strawberries, and in return Jasper never got charged with anything himself. Like drunk driving or illegal parking. Or running a produce stand without a business license. Things in the country had a way of working themselves out.

All that while, Bobby Lee was out of sight back behind the stand. None of Jasper's customers commented on it, though Sheriff Grouse eyed Bobby's old pickup suspiciously while he perused the strawberries.

A couple of times Bobby Lee walked past to Jasper's truck, grabbed parts of the shed out of its long, corrugated box, and headed back out of sight, but he didn't say a word. He was moving fast and he kept his head down, mumbling to himself all the time. Jasper figured it for cursing, but the one time Bobby Lee came close enough for his friend to hear, all that came across was some sort of rhythmic mumbo jumbo.

"What you doin', Bobby Lee?" Jasper called after him. "Takin' up that rap music?"

Bobby Lee didn't answer, and Jasper wasn't inclined to raise himself out of his seat and follow after to insist on it. Truth be told, he didn't rightly care what Bobby Lee was sayin' as long as he didn't say "Come on back and help me, Jasper."

The noon rush passed, and Jasper was popping the top on his second beer of the afternoon when he finally started to feel guilty. Bobby Lee had been working quietly all morning long, since before Jasper himself had even arrived, and not a finger had been raised to help him. It was true that Jasper had provided the land, the shed, and all the moral support a fella could want, but it was also true that he'd agreed to be part of this cockamamie project. The least he could do was make a solid effort to pitch in and do his part.

Besides, the pile of shed parts still left in the truck was getting pretty small, and Jasper was beginning to wonder just what the hell Bobby Lee was doing back there. They'd agreed to move the cockroach into the cleared spot first, and then build the shed, but it seemed like Bobby Lee had changed his mind somewhere along the way and just started building. Hell, from the banging and clanking Jasper had heard, the damn thing must have been just about finished, and that was a job. Jasper had built one just like it out back of his house for storing lawn tools and making home brew.

Shifting his weight forward, he sat up, drained his beer, reached with practiced ease into the cooler and brought out two more. Then, with a long, drawn-out burp, he stood and headed around back of the stand.

For the second time that day, Jasper Winslow stopped dead in his tracks. He felt the bottle in his left hand slipping free and gripped it very suddenly, stumbling back. Bobby Lee's truck stood off to the side again, but it was empty. The damned roach was nowhere to be seen and standing smack-dab in the center of that cleared plot of land, the shed had taken shape. More than that, it was perfect. Jasper had had two cousins and his old lady helping, and he had not managed to get his shed up in near the time or manner that Bobby Lee had done this one by himself.

Bobby Lee was nowhere to be seen, and Jasper, taking a deep breath for courage, stepped forward to the door, slid it aside, and stepped inside. The building's interior was shadowed. There were no windows, and even the sunlight that slipped in behind him through the door did little. Jasper stepped forward, blinking, and ran smack into something hard after the second step. Something jabbed his cheek hard, something smooth and cool. Something sharp.

"Damn!" he grunted, stepping back. "Bobby? You in here? What in hell did you DO?"

There was no reply, but Jasper heard the murmur of voices near the rear of the shed. He reached out with one hand, letting the beer bottle crack gently into the side wall of the shed, and followed the left wall around, being careful not to move too fast, in case any more of the damned cockroach's double-D goddamned appendages felt inclined to give him a whack.

About halfway back, Jasper stopped. The shed had gone deathly cold. And quiet. The shadows, which shouldn't have been very deep in a building with open eaves and the front door open wide, clung to him, blocking his vision. The mumble of voices had shifted to more of a drone, like a bunch of midge flies hovering over the swamp. The tone rose and fell in a steady, hypnotic pattern, but there was no sign of Bobby.

Jasper turned and edged his way back toward the front. He had a big halogen search light in the back of his truck he used for deer spotting. That would light this place up and show him what was what.

Thing was, the farther he slid along the wall toward where he knew that door had to be, the farther it seemed he still had to go. He saw the cleared dirt outside, plain as day, but his breath was coming in short bursts, and he knew, without seeing it, that it was shooting out of his mouth like fog. It was cold enough Jasper felt the frost that suddenly coated the beers he held, and the burn of the cold glass against his skin. His toes were numb, and each step he took toward the door, and the light, was an effort he wasn't sure he felt like making.

Then the sound stopped. A hand fell heavily on Jasper's shoulder and he screamed, jumping back against the pressed metal wall so hard it dented. He gripped the beers so tightly he wondered if they might shatter.

The shed had grown lighter. Bobby Lee stood in front of him, holding out a hand for one of the beers.

Jasper teetered. He leaned heavily on the wall, despite knowing full well it had been erected by the grinning idiot standing before him in about half the time the job should have taken. It held.

"Hell, Jasper, what's wrong with you?" Bobby Lee asked. "You look like you've seen a ghost. Or maybe," Bobby grinned, turning and raising a hand to the wooden monstrosity behind him, "a giant cock-a-roach?"

Jasper heaved off the wall, lurched to the door, and stumbled out into the late afternoon light. He took in several deep breaths, and then turned back. All he saw was Bobby, sipping on his beer and staring back at him. The shed behind Bobby's back had no special characteristics, beyond being extremely well-constructed. There was no way to penetrate the shadowed interior from where Jasper stood, but he heard no soft voices and he saw no deeper-than-normal shadows. The air was warm, moist, and filled with mosquitoes.

Jasper shook his head. He glanced down and noticed he was still holding his unopened beer. With a quick twist, he opened it and tossed down half the bottle.

"Maybe you've been sittin' out in the sun too long, Jasper," Bobby Lee commented. "You don't look so good."

"You didn't see, or hear, or feel anything wrong in there?"

Jasper asked, eyeing his friend suspiciously.

"Like what?" Bobby Lee scratched his head and took a draw from his beer. "I was in the back, tyin' down the straps to hold that big old money-makin' baby in place. I didn't see or hear a thing."

"I don't reckon you want to tell me how you got that thing out of your truck, neither," Jasper observed, his eyes narrowing.

Bobby Lee never blinked. "I backed her up and used the winch. How in hell did you think I got her *in* the truck, Jasper? I ain't no Superman."

Jasper blinked. He hadn't expected such a simple answer, and if he could've gotten his body to contort to the right shape, he'd have kicked himself in the ass for not thinking of it.

"Is there somethin' wrong, Jasper?" Bobby Lee asked.

Jasper turned away and lurched back toward his chair, and his beer. He didn't say a thing until he was seated once more in his old rocker, staring out at the dying sun and route 17 passing in the distance. He reached for another beer, tossed another one to Bobby, and closed his eyes, leaning back.

"So," he said at last. "Just when did you expect we would start drawing in these 'Cockroach Suckers,'" he asked.

Bobby was grinning when he opened his eyes, and the two talked well into the evening, watching the sun dip deep orange behind the line of trees that bordered the swamp. Finally, when the last of the beers had been emptied, Jasper rose shakily and headed for his truck. He left the produce baskets as they stood and grimaced at the expected tirade when he reached home without them, drunk. Didn't matter. For once, Jasper was convinced that Bobby Lee might border on human intelligence, and might actually, God forbid, be right about something. They were going to make them a pile of money, and it was going to start the very next day.

Bobby Lee stood beside Jasper's truck and helped him up into the seat, slamming the door for his friend.

"I'll see you tomorrow, partner," Bobby said. "Bright and early."

"You done a piece of work today, Bobby," Jasper replied.

"Maybe you should sleep in a bit. Won't be any good tomorrow if you're all worn out or hung over."

Bobby winked at him, and something in that gesture, something sparking deep in his friend's eye, sent a cold a shiver through the air, and set the murmur of distant voices caroming off his skull and ricocheting about his mind.

"Don't you worry about me," Bobby said, his voice low. "I'll be here, ready to rock."

Jasper turned the key in the ignition and brought his old truck to life. He punched down on the gas and shot out of the small gravel lot onto the feeder road without a word. He was shaking, and his skin was coated in sweat.

"Damn beer," he whispered, gunning his engine and praying not to see a cop.

Bobby Lee stood, watching his partner depart, and then turned back. He didn't head for his own truck but slid through the door of the metal shed and pulled it tightly closed behind him. Moments later, the night filled with the drone of a thousand mosquitoes, or the grating crackle of cicadas in season. The blood-red sun drenched the skyline and melted to black.

Jasper saw the signs before he was within five miles of his stand. The first one was simple, square and white, black lettering.

"LOOK—5 MILES"

Then they got progressively larger, and more explicit, as he moved along 17. Jasper didn't take 17 very often, but this morning he'd had to restock his beer cooler in Elizabeth City, so he'd come in the popular route—the way his customers would come in.

"DON'T MISS OUT"
"3 ½ MILES TO YOUR WORST NIGHTMARE"
"2 MILES—THE WORLDS LARGEST AND HARDEST TO KILL"
"ONLY ONE MILE, TURN IN ON LEFT"
"½ MILE TO WORLD'S LARGEST COCKROACH! TURN NOW!"

This last sign was subtitled with the words "Fresh fruit and produce, inquire within."

Jasper turned down the side road and gunned his engine, spinning his tires and shooting dust and gravel into the air so thick he couldn't see the road behind him. He saw that even the dirt road itself hadn't escaped the signs. There were small ones and large ones, some proclaiming TOMATOES and others with large brown roach feelers raised high and eyes bugged out, staring at the road.

When he pulled up in front of his stand, he saw that there was a walkway, flat river stones set into the loose dirt of the field, running around back of the produce stand. A huge white wooden finger pointed the way around the corner toward the shed in back. Jasper climbed down out of his truck, slammed the door in case by some miracle Bobby Lee hadn't heard him, and followed where that finger pointed.

The shed was transformed. Sometime in the night, Bobby Lee had brought in paint and turned the drab, beige-colored pressed metal into a gleaming, multi-colored monstrosity. The base was black, but there was orange trim, and there were pictures, cockroaches running this way and that, little roach motels in pastel, Miami-Florida sorta colors, and to the right of the door a large can of bug spray with feet, holding a finger to its button and spraying toward the entrance.

Jasper's jaw dropped, and his legs turned to rubber, but before he could collapse to the newly-lain stone walk, Bobby Lee hurried out the door of the shed and grabbed him by the arm, steadying him. Jasper gaped at his friend, who was wearing a button-down shirt, a clean pair of black pants, a damned *belt*.

"Wha..." Jasper never got it out.

"Mornin' partner!" Bobby Lee said. "I did a little sprucin' up, seein' as how this was our first day in business, and all."

"Sprucin'... but..."

Bobby Lee cut him off again. "Don't you worry about it, partner. I didn't expect you to be here to help. I just got the bug, you know? Get it? GET IT?"

Bobby Lee was shaking him, and Jasper wished it would stop. He couldn't decide whether he more wanted to collapse to the ground or puke, and the shaking wasn't helping him with the decision. Then Bobby whirled back toward the front of the produce stand, supporting Jasper by the grip on his arm, and led him to his rocker.

"You don't worry 'bout a thing, Jasper," Bobby said. "Any customers show up, you send 'em around back to me. I'll handle it from there. You stay up here, sell the fruit, smile at the people, and watch out for ol' Sheriff Grouse. I expect we'll see him before the day's out. I got his paperwork all finished and signed in my truck, but I figgered I'd let him have the satisfaction of figurin' he's got us by the balls before I showed it to him."

Mention of the sheriff broke Jasper out of his fog.

"What papers? What did you do, Bobby Lee? Why would the sheriff…"

"Well, you don't think he'll drive down 17 and miss those signs, do you?" Bobby Lee asked, keeping his voice low and slow, like he was talking to a recalcitrant mule. "I tried to get as many out there as I could. Got to rememberin' those signs for the biggest ball of string I was tellin' you about, and just let my imagination go, you know?"

"When did you sleep?" Jasper asked finally. "My God, Bobby Lee, where did you learn to paint like that …" Jasper waved his hand back in the general direction of the shed and its not-quite-dry murals, "over yonder? And where in HELL did you get a button-down shirt that has all the buttons?"

Bobby Lee's grin never faded.

"I feel like a new man," Jasper, he said. "I feel like this has been my destiny, you know? Everyone has to find them a place in life, and I reckon I walked into mine when I hit that flea market the other day."

"You was born to rip off suckers on a giant wooden cockroach display?" Jasper asked, trying to sort it all out in his head. "That what you're sayin', Bobby Lee? You tellin' me your momma raised you and fed you and tried to put you through school just so's you could build a home for a giant bug?"

Bobby Lee blinked. Just for a moment, Jasper thought he

might be getting through, and then the light in Bobby Lee's eyes faded out, and blinked on again, high beams flashing.

"That's exactly what I'm sayin', I guess," he replied. "You just send them folks around to see me," he added, "and don't forget to sell them their ticket first."

Jasper glanced down to where Bobby's gaze had strayed and noticed a big roll of paper tickets on the old wood table next to his cooler. The tickets said $5 ADMIT ONE. Jasper shook his head. He was about to comment further when Bobby Lee abruptly turned on his heel and marched back around the corner to his shed. Jasper thought about following to press whatever point was forming in his mind, but something made him sit tight. He didn't want to go into that shed again. He didn't know why, would have denied the sensation altogether if confronted with it, but there it was. He remembered those voices. He remembered the chill, the dampness, and the way his steps had slowed as if he were wading through butter.

Jasper got up, set to work putting out his produce and clearing away what he'd left behind the night before. He pointedly ignored the walkway leading behind his stand—until the people started coming.

Over the next week, the produce stand became something of a sensation. It seemed like everyone from the Outer Banks and Kitty Hawk to Raleigh and Durham had heard the news. There was a new roadside attraction, and they were flocking to it in droves. Jasper's small garden had proven unable to keep up with the sudden demand for fresh tomatoes and strawberries, and Bobby Lee worked straight through one weekend to get pavers in to create a real parking lot. The drive coming in from 17, which had been nothing more than a gravel and dirt side-road, more discouraging than inviting to anything with wheels, had been resurfaced by the county, who were quick to see what the new attraction was doing for the tourist trade and local businesses.

The white signs on the freeway had been replaced by a longer series that ran up and down route 17 and onto some of the bisecting and intersecting roads with exits. In the middle of

the bypass on the way to Virginia, there was a huge black sign
with dripping green letters proclaiming:
STRAIGHT FROM THE DEPTHS OF THE GREAT
DISMAL SWAMP. NO KITCHEN IS SAFE—NO TRASH CAN
IS SACRED. SHE'S BIG—SHE'S THE BIGGEST DURNED
COCKROACH IN THE WORLD—18 Miles, South 17. FRESH
PRODUCE—T-SHIRTS—SOUVENIRS—PEANUTS.

The sign featured a giant, comical bug crawling over the
top of the letters, huge antennae blocking the long, flat view of
cotton fields beyond. It was only one of many signs, and it wasn't
kidding about a bit of it. Racks of t-shirts lined the front of the
parking lot. The produce stand itself had grown, incorporating
a double-wide trailer with siding that housed vats and bins of
rubber and plastic cockroaches and giant mosquitoes, rubber
snakes, and bumper stickers that said, "I Saw it and Lived" and
other such things. Jasper's mind was whirling so fast from one
new thing to the next that he nearly forgot the shed out back,
and what lay within.

He sat out front every day, watching them, curious coming
and sort of dazed and glazed going. They bought the shirts, the
produce, bags of peanuts, and handfuls of rubber bugs. Jasper
had never had so much money in his life, and, for once there
didn't seem to be a legal reason he couldn't keep it.

But as things settled into a rhythm, and he had some time
to sit and watch, little things began to itch at him. Bobby Lee,
for one thing. The man never slept. As far as Jasper could tell,
Bobby Lee had not slept a wink since the first day he'd brought
the damned cockroach to the stand. It didn't show. Bobby Lee
was always smiling, always moving, working, and scheming.
The shed out back had grown a foundation of concrete blocks
that raised it a good four feet higher off the ground, for instance,
and it had happened, seemingly, overnight. There was no sign
that Bobby Lee had hired the work done, or that anyone else
had an idea how it might have happened, but the next morning
Bobby Lee was as fresh as a daisy and ready for anything. So
he said.

Jasper had seen the difference the minute he pulled into
his reserved spot at the front of the lot. There had already been

three families in from Raleigh, waiting for the cockroach exhibit to open, parked in the lot. The shed, which should have been, as always, hidden by the structure of the produce stand itself, was clearly visible, rising into the sky to a height it should not have attained. Jasper had nearly run over a stand full of t-shirts staring at it.

Ignoring the calls and questions of the customers, waiting on him to open, he ran around the corner to the shed. Bobby Lee stepped quickly through door, as if he'd been waiting for his partner to arrive, smiling broadly and waving at the new foundation with a flourish of one brawny arm.

"Well, what do you think? I got to worryin' over hurricanes and the like, thought I might get 'er fixed into the ground a little more permanently."

Jasper stared up at the ludicrously tall structure and frowned. His mind was framing all sorts of questions, most of them starting with the words "How in the HELL," but none of them would quite make the journey to his lips. He stepped toward the doorway and reached around to where he knew the light switch was mounted on the wall, but before he could flick it, Bobby Lee grabbed him by the arm.

"You might not want to do that," Bobby Lee said softly.

The touch of Bobby Lee's hand on his arm was cold. Where their skin met felt like ice had been packed in under Jasper's skin. He heard the scuttling of what his mind conjured into a mound of thousands of crustaceous, squirming bodies. He stared into the shadowed interior of the shed, and more tiny glittering pinpoints of light than the stars in a cloudless summer's night sky winked back at him—then were gone. Something huge and hulking centered the shed, larger than the cockroach itself could possibly be, twelve, maybe fifteen feet in the air, instead of seven. The interior of that shed had a cold draft, and the scent of the place was dank and sweet with rot. Like the swamp.

Jasper reeled from the stench, yanking his arm free of Bobby Lee's grip. His partner was still smiling, but the smile was brittle, and for the first time Jasper looked deeper into his friend's eyes. They were bright, far too bright to be natural.

His skin was sun-dried to the point of being leathery—or even papery. And the cold.

"You mainlining ice, Bobby Lee?" Jasper whispered. "What the hell is wrong with you—and—with that place?"

"Not a thing, Jasper," Bobby Lee said. His voice was as normal and pleasant as ever, but there was no mistaking the way he moved in front of the shed door. It was a sidewise sort of shuffle. Like a scuttling bug, or a man working his arms and legs via strings, like a puppet. Too fast, but sort of clumsy and "wrong".

"You go back out front and send those folks in," Bobby Lee said softly. "We don't want to disappoint them."

Jasper turned, remembering the customers gathered at the edge of the parking lot for the first time since he'd rounded the corner. He stepped back, started to say something, then turned and fled to the front—to his chair, and his beer, and the line of folks already stretching halfway around the parking lot, all of them wanting a glimpse of that damned giant cockroach.

Jasper wondered if they felt it. He wondered if they smelled the stench, and heard the scuttling feet—the soft, chitinous voices that never stopped speaking or chirping or chanting or whatever-the-hell they were doing. Maybe he was just losing it. Bobby Lee had sure done him a good turn, letting him in on this deal, and one thing was certain—there was no shortage of cockroach suckers in the world. No sir.

Jasper grabbed the roll of tickets and began doling them out, five dollars a pop, to bright, eager-faced kids and tolerant parents, young couples on long vacations and truckloads of rednecks in for a quick laugh. He only paid them half a mind, but one family caught his eye.

They pulled up in a brand-new SUV, the kind with a million features, such as a Blu-ray player in back and OnStar up front. Mother, father, a boy of maybe thirteen in a black t-shirt with the center of his lower lip pierced and his hair spiked like a damned purple and green porcupine, and the girls. They were twin girls, probably eighteen or nineteen, tall and long-legged with matched honey-colored hair and short skirts. Jasper couldn't have missed them if he tried, and despite his need to vend tickets to the next twenty people in line and price t-shirts for another fifteen visitors on their way out, he managed to keep an eye on them until they wound around the corner and out of site toward the shed.

For the next half hour or so, Jasper was too busy to think about them, and that was a tribute to how hard he was working, because there was absolutely NOTHING Jasper loved better than a cute set of twins. He liked to watch TV Land on cable so he could catch the old Doublemint Girls commercials. It wasn't until that family was winding their way back out, the boy selecting a truly disgusting plastic roach souvenir, and the mother laughingly holding one of the "I Survived the Great Dismal Swamp" t-shirts across her breasts and winking at her husband, that Jasper remembered them at all.

It was later in the afternoon, and Jasper scanned the diminishing crowd quickly for the twins. They were nowhere to be seen, and he grew almost frantic, staring out over the thinning traffic in the small parking lot to see if he'd somehow missed their trek back to the SUV. There was no one visible inside the vehicle, and the rest of the family seemed oblivious. They laughed and joked a little—or the parents did. The boy jammed a pair of headphones onto his head, cranked the volume on some sort of expensive portable MP3 player, and zoned out. They walked away as a group, straight to the SUV, opened the doors, and got in.

Jasper stepped away from his counter, holding up a hand to those waiting on him to give him a moment. He stepped to the corner of the stand and glanced around at the shed. Bobby Lee was there, grinning and waving at him, but there was no sign of the girls. Jasper frowned. He turned to scan the SUV again, but its taillights were already disappearing out the feeder road toward 17.

"What the hell?" he muttered. He turned back to the counter and went through the motions for the next twenty minutes or so, ushering the last of the crowds out and away. Jasper carefully counted out the day's proceeds, which were phenomenal, and packed the bills away into the bank bag he'd taken to carrying in a lock box beneath the seat of his truck. When the shirt racks had been wheeled inside, and the tiny remnants of the day's fresh produce had been stored for the night, he locked up carefully.

He stepped to the corner of the building, as he did every night, and called out to Bobby Lee.

"You done for the night, Bobby?"

"Just about," Bobby called back. His voice floated out from the interior of the shed, and for a moment, Jasper stared. There was no light on inside, and it was growing dark outside. The shadows inside had to be deeper still.

Jasper shook his head and turned, walking deliberately to his truck. He had no intention of going home, but he had a plan, and it involved Bobby Lee watching him leave the parking lot, so he drove on out the feeder road and turned right on 17 toward Elizabeth City. He figured it wouldn't take him more than five or six beers and a shot or two to be ready to come back.

The hulking signs leading toward the world's largest cockroach loomed over the ditches and crossroads of Highway 17 as Jasper passed them, winding his way slowly back toward the stand, and the shed, and what lay within. He had no intention of turning onto the feeder road; that would be too obvious. Jasper had been running his produce stand for a lot of years, and he knew more than one way in, and out. He passed the main road and went about half a mile until a paved road bisected the highway. It bore the same name as a thousand North Carolina roads, Dead End, but he paid that no mind, other than to hope it was just a name, and would not prove prophetic.

The road wound back in along lines of trees that bordered fields outlined by even rows of cotton. Jasper drove slowly and carefully, keeping his engine as quiet as possible. He turned left onto a dirt track and followed the rutted, poorly kept road deeper into the trees. The road grew progressively worse, and it wasn't long before he found a place to pull the truck in under the overhanging branches and off the road. He parked and popped the top on another beer as he stared off into the darkness across the cotton field.

He could make out the imposing shadow of the impossibly tall shack from where he sat. The odd shape of the building reminded him of a giant outhouse, and he chuckled, downing the beer in quick gulps and reaching for another. Made sense, he reckoned, that a giant roach would end up in a giant outhouse. He wondered why he'd never noticed it before.

When the second beer had been sucked dry, he got out, tossed the can in the back of his truck, and stood, getting his bearings. It was still a quarter of a mile through the cotton to the shed, but as long as he was quiet, he was sure he could sneak up on the place. He saw Bobby Lee's truck, and there was a dim glow seeping out along the roof line, and near the bottom of the building. Whatever it was Bobby Lee had going on in that place, it was going on now, and Jasper aimed to see it for himself. If Bobby Lee was holding out on him, partying with those twins and such, Jasper aimed to be part of that, too. If it was something else...he shivered deep inside.

"Partners," he muttered to himself, "is partners."

The moonlight was bright, bathing the back of the shed in cold, white illumination. Though it was unseasonably warm, the closer Jasper came to the back of the building, the colder it grew. By the time he broke free of the cotton and into the area Bobby Lee had raked clear that first day, his teeth were chattering, and he threw his nearly empty beer can behind him, curling his arms around his chest.

"What the hell?" he said to no one in particular.

Moving quietly, he worked his way around the shed on the left side, hesitating as he drew near the corner. He pressed close to the shed, and where his arm brushed the corrugated metal, something rippled over his skin. There was a stench, like rotted vegetation, or some sort of hot mud, but there was no heat. Jasper's heart danced like a bug on a magnifying glass, and for a moment, with the blood rushing to his head, he thought he'd pass out. Then he steadied himself, regretting instantly the contact with the building this required.

The walls vibrated, and the vibration translated to sound in his head. The sound was a drone, as though there were a million mosquitoes humming inside, or the wings of a host of wasps beating against the far side of the wall. Jasper closed his eyes, caught his breath, and in that instant, he saw them, clinging to one another, climbing and grasping and bobbing with black-gold-black-striped stingers primed, dripping poison. And he heard... words.

There were no words he knew or understood—except that on some very deep level, he did.

He opened his eyes with a start and pulled away from the wall.

"Jesus Jumpin' Jehosephat Christ," he whispered. Each syllable of the words came out in a separate gasp.

He wavered between continuing around the corner and turning to run and never look back, moving on to Virginia, or Maryland, and starting over. Then he thought of Bobby Lee. He remembered long, lazy afternoons fishing, hard days on his daddy's farm, Bobby Lee at his side, working until they fell down in the dirt exhausted and then washing it all off with a garden hose to start over and do it again. He couldn't leave Bobby Lee in there, even if Bobby Lee WANTED to be in there.

"Wish I'd brought some bug spray," he muttered, and turned the corner of the shed, moving stealthily toward the sliding door in front.

A sickly, greenish glow seeped out through the doorway. It reminded Jasper of the glow sticks they sold at summer carnivals, or the glow-in-the-dark stars he'd hung on his ceiling as a boy. The droning was louder now, and it covered a wide range of tones—deep and resonant to high-pitched and ear-splitting. Jasper pulled a wad of tissue out of his pocket, hoped it wasn't too dirty, and wadded rolls of it in each ear, blocking as much of the sound as possible.

He thought he recognized two recurring words... "Al-Azif"—he'd heard—felt?—them when he'd leaned on the building outside. Thinking about them brought him a memory of his first glance at the Double-D Goddammed cock-a-roach in the back of Bobby's truck. Words, symbols, that rippled across that slimy surface... like they were moving. Had the thing been talking to him, even then? Was it talking to Bobby?

He stared at the door, trying to think of a compelling enough reason to turn tail and run, but he couldn't shake the thought of Bobby Lee, and those crawling, touching, stinging bugs.

"Ah, hell," he said softly. Before he could change his mind, he stepped inside.

If the air had been cold outside the shed, inside it was frigid. There were lights, but they were soft and green, and buried in the corners near the rear of the building. Jasper couldn't see a thing except the huge, vaguely defined silhouette of the giant wooden cockroach. The greenish glow shimmered around the edges of it like the silver lining on a cloud gone rotten. And that was another thing. The stench was horrible. Every breath had weight, as if he were breathing liquid, or some sort of thick gas, rather than air.

The droning pounded in Jasper's head, and thinking became difficult. Gritting his teeth, he skirted the side wall of the shed, pulling as far away from the statue on its wood pallet base as possible without coming into contact with the wall to his left. He didn't want a repeat encounter with the vibration. As he moved through the cloying shadows, he concentrated on an image of Bobby Lee's smiling face, and whenever that started to fade into the sound and stink, or threatened to be rattled out of his head by his chattering teeth, he thought about those twins.

It was the longest walk of Jasper's life. He knew the length and breadth of the shed; he'd bought the damned thing in the garden department at Handy-Mart himself. Sure, the walls were taller than they'd been, and it was a little harder to walk in this air than it had been last time he'd been inside, but it should have been a ten-step, twelve at the max, journey from the front to the back, and though he couldn't string two thoughts together in a line, he knew he should have already run smack into the back wall. Except, he didn't.

The sound and shadows closed in behind him then, and he saw that the glow was concentrated near the rear of the cockroach and down low. He headed in that direction, sweeping his gaze to the right and left, looking for any sign of Bobby Lee, or the twins, or whatever the hell was making that fucking NOISE... but he saw nothing. Nothing but the glow, and as he drew near to it, he felt a scream bubbling up through his chest that he only barely managed to bite off, clamping his lip tightly between his teeth and grinding. He tasted blood, but it didn't matter. Somehow, he knew that the last thing he wanted in this place, at this moment, was to draw attention.

What he saw was a small pile of glowing orbs. They were roughly the shape of a baseball, and there were dozens of them, clinging in a wet, sticky mass and coated in slimy ichor. Among them, tiny shapes squirmed and crawled, some flitting a few inches through the air but unable—quite—to break free of the mass, plopping wetly back into the others to crawl and tug at the sticky fluid, and then trying to break free once more. Jasper stared, mesmerized. It took a few moments to realize that the droning had increased in volume, and that it was moving.

Breaking his gaze free of the crawling mass at his feet, Jasper glanced up sharply. He couldn't see anything, but he could hear it, and moments later, he felt it as well. The air whirled, driving the image of a tornado like a spike into his brain. He still saw nothing, but his mind formed the images he couldn't bring into focus, and he knew they were there. He didn't know if they were mosquitoes, or wasps, hornets, or something... else. It didn't matter. They were circling, faster and faster, but they were not coming closer. Something else was.

He saw Bobby Lee's shadowed form step from the shadows, moving slowly and deliberately, as he himself had been moving since stepping into the place, only differently. Jasper wanted to turn, run, and be done with it, but he stood his ground. Licking his dry lips, he tried to speak, but the words came out in a rasping whisper.

"Bobby?" he whispered. "Bobby, what..."

Then Bobby was close enough to be seen in the dim, green glow of the orbs, or eggs, or whatever the hell they were, and Jasper nearly fell. His knees, solid and strong a moment before, had taken on the consistency of jelly, and the only thing that kept him from losing a perfectly good six-pack of beer was the thought of those—things—crawling among the scraps and bits and drinking his beer as they fought free... and joined the swarm overhead.

Bobby was awash in tiny bodies. It was impossible to tell

what they were, what color, what size, as there were too many. They coated him like a second skin, moving and chittering, squirming and lifting tiny antennae and proboscises to search and test, looking for—what?

"Jas...per" Bobby Lee croaked. He couldn't speak clearly. When he opened his mouth they crawled out slowly, sliding over and around one another as they crossed his lips, and curled back up over his ears to join the rest.

Jasper wanted to vomit, but he held it. Bobby Lee's eyes were clear and bright. Maybe too bright, but there was no alarm in them. No panic. The insects, roaches, wasps, whatever they were, shimmered over him in waves, but he stood, staring calmly into Jasper's wondering gaze.

"Wha..." Jasper stopped. He didn't want to ask a question. He knew Bobby Lee would answer, but he didn't want to witness the filling and emptying of his friend's mouth a second time if he could help it. Instead of speaking, he shrugged, backing away a step.

Bobby Lee nodded toward the huge wooden cockroach, and stepped forward, laying a hand across the bottom segment of one huge mandible. Jasper stepped back, but something in Bobby Lee's expression held him steady.

Without speaking, Bobby Lee reached into his pocket and pulled something free. A moment later, as Bobby Lee flicked his thumb to free the blade, Jasper saw that it was a Buck knife. Without hesitation, Bobby Lee took a slice off the statue. Jasper watched the splinter of wood float to the floor and followed Bobby Lee's pointing finger to the spot where he'd cut it free.

The wood only coated what lay beneath. It was smooth, as the wood had been smooth, but darker. Bobby Lee gestured for Jasper to step closer, and, not knowing what else to do, unless it was to run, Jasper complied. Bobby grabbed his wrist, and for a moment, that was nearly the end of it. The bugs crawling and shifting and seething over Bobby Lee's arm reached out feelers and legs, pinchers and proboscises to the new flesh Jasper offered. He tried to yank free, but Bobby Lee held tight. In a moment, it didn't matter.

As Bobby Lee pressed Jasper's hand to the cut in the

wood, something shot out from within. It was hard and sharp, round and hollow, and it plunged into Jasper's hand without hesitation. His body spasmed, and he tried to jerk free, but it was too late. He felt his pulse through the palm of his hand, felt whatever it was that had pierced him probing deeper, sucking with incredible force at that small puncture in his hand.

The things that coated Bobby Lee were moving up Jasper's arm, but he couldn't spare them any attention. He was trying to scream and unable to free himself of the muscle-contracting spasm of pain long enough to force the air from his lungs.

Then it stopped. Jasper staggered back, grabbing his wounded hand in the other and then releasing it to swat at the bugs, brushing them from his arm, waiting for the bites and stings that never came, and backing away again. Bobby Lee looked as if he would speak again, despite the danger of the insects swarming his throat, but at that moment, Jasper struck his back on the wall, pressing tightly into the metal and its constant, droning vibration, and the need for speech was erased.

Thoughts flowed in a steady progression through Jasper's mind. He saw things, strange, impossible things. He saw stars, gleaming in the sky. He saw cylinders of sleek, shining metal, gleaming and shooting at impossible speeds among those stars. He saw explosions of fire and light, like a Fourth of July gone mad and he felt the waves of pain as explosions followed the flight.

He saw masses of people and mounds of insects. He saw the giant roach, not solid and carved, but skittering about a mountain slope. He saw stone pillars and a temple, and he saw the people, kneeling, coated in shimmering sheets of exoskeletal motion, kneeling in an ocean of insects.

A man—no, a priest—stood near the top of the tallest mound, a huge book open in his arms. A single shaft of light snaked from the stars above to strike the pages as the man read, slowly, his voice a drone that blended with those of the insects swarming around him. Jasper opened his mouth… whispered… *Al-Azif.*

He saw the swamp, crazily recognizing the fishing hole he and Bobby Lee had been visiting since they were kids. He saw the muck and the rising water, moss and scum, the slither of snakes, and the great crash of gator tails, and always, over and

over, the passing of sun to moon to sun, until, finally, he saw a
fishing pole and a red and white bobber, rising and falling in the
grip of a soft swell on the surface of a still pool. The line grew taut
and the pole bent. Whatever it was, it was huge, and there were
droplets of water running up and down the line ... or ... not water.
The droplets moved up, not down, and Jasper saw them reach the
pole and continue coming. They moved in a solid, lightning-fast
strike up the line and down the bamboo and onto the hands and
arms that waited. Onto Bobby Lee, who stood on the bank, staring
stupidly as they invaded his flesh, taking him before he could cast
the pole away and dropping him to his knees on the bank of that
swampy lake.

Then the statue rose, hung up on Bobby's line and dripping
swamp mud and putrid, rotting vegetation. No way Bobby Lee
was pulling it free of that mire, but he was connected to it, and as
more and more of the insects, or whatever they were, coated his
skin, he rose unsteadily to his feet, shook his head as if freeing it
from something, and watched in wonder.

Then the statue was on the bank, no clear view of how this had
come to be, only that it was. Bobby Lee was wiping it down with
rags, spraying it with some sort of bottled detergent, and clearing
away every indication that it had ever come within a foot of the
swamp. Cleaning and wiping and polishing, he brought it to the
sheen that Jasper had first noted, and then, turning, he walked
away.

The next image was Bobby Lee's truck and somehow,
impossibly, the statue was in the back. Bobby Lee was covering it
with the blue tarp and fastening it carefully to the hooks up and
down either side of the truck's bed.

And then the vision faded. The connection between Jasper
and the swarming, droning horde was broken. Jasper turned and
walked out of the shed. He didn't look back. When he was out in
the fresh, cool air of the evening, he turned around the corner of
the shed and moved toward the parking lot. He plopped into his
old rocker, closed his eyes, laid his head back, and sat very, very
still. A few moments later, he heard the crunch of Bobby Lee's feet
on the walk, and he looked up. There were no bugs. Jasper glanced
to the side, but realized too late the cooler wasn't there. No beer.

"It's not what you think," Bobby Lee said softly.

"I don't think a damn thing," Jasper replied. "I saw what I saw. Where are they, crawling under your shirt, down your damned pants?"

"They're in there with *her*," Bobby Lee said. His voice was still calm. "They never come out of the shed."

"Not just them, neither," Jasper shot back. "I know them twins never come out, Bobby. What did it do, suck them inside like it tried to do to me?"

"No," Bobby Lee said. Then he chuckled.

Jasper snapped his chin from his chest and glared at his friend. "What in HELL are you laughing at? Them girls is gone, and no tellin' how many others, and you stand there grinnin' like a damn fool."

Bobby Lee was actually laughing, and it pissed Jasper off. He rose to his feet and cocked his arm back. "You shut up, Bobby Lee, or giant double-D Goddamned cockroach or not, I'm gonna SHUT you up."

Bobby Lee was still laughing, but he held up his hands in surrender, backing off.

"It ain't that, Jasper," he managed to say at last. "There ain't nothin' wrong with them twins. They's waitin' at the Eagle and Anchor back in Hertford for us. You thought she was EATIN' 'em?"

Jasper's arm fell to his side, and he frowned.

"What the hell are you talking about?" he asked at last. "What do you MEAN they's waitin' on us?"

"Just what I said," Bobby Lee chuckled. "She don't eat folks, Jasper, she just likes to have us near. Those others, the little ones? They only come out at night. That shed is like her temple, now. You saw the temple."

"I saw a bunch of naked folks kneeling in a lake of bugs, too," Jasper countered.

"Well, she has a right to feel wanted, don't she?" Bobby Lee said. He was almost whining. "I mean, she DID bring all them folks in here, just like she said, and she DID help me build that shed, then build 'er up again. She's even talkin' 'bout havin' me bring in river rocks and do it right."

"What do you get for all that?" Jasper asked. "You ain't been home in a month. I know, cuz I talked to your old lady just yesterday. She isn't sorry to see you go, but ... why?"

"Them twins isn't the first to stay at the Eagle and Anchor, Jasper. They won't be the last, neither. Those girls, they'll be back, too. Ever' last one of 'em has felt her touch, and she calls 'em back. For me. There was a book, once. She told me about it. It was destroyed, but she managed to suck enough of the words into her children we might could rewrite it. Bring it back..."

Jasper's mind reeled. Already he was daydreaming of those twins, their honey hair and wide eyes. In the background of those dreams, he could see a stone building rising from the cotton to challenge the sky. He saw cars lined up like soldiers in a huge lot, bright neon signs and banners flapping in the wind.

"Waitin' for us now, you say?" he asked softly.

Bobby Lee nodded. There was a flicker of greenish light around the corner of the produce stand, and then the night went dark. Jasper closed his eyes, and in that darkness, he felt antennae flicking in the night breeze, seeking him, yearning for the salt of his sweat and the heat of his skin. Seeking communion.

"Thank the Lord," he said at last, turning toward Bobby Lee's truck and walking away, "for all them cockroach suckers."

"Amen," Bobby Lee added, grinning.

Above, the stars shone brightly, and Jasper could have sworn, as Bobby Lee pulled out of the parking lot, that the brilliant spots of light re-arranged themselves into a new shape. A constellation he could believe in. Popping the top on the beer Bobby handed him, Jasper saluted the sky, tracing the lines of stars with his graze and grinning.

"Look, Bobby Lee," he said softly. "Ain't that constellation The Twins?"

*AUTHOR'S NOTE: This is an oddball story. I have no idea, really, why I wrote it. It started as a scene I was playing with, some paragraphs of description, and took on a life of its own. It's one of the more clearly Lovecraftian tales in the book. This was first published in my section of the Bram Stoker Award-Winning collection **The Gossamer Eye** – which was – at its heart – a book of poetry. We decided that, along with the poetry, we'd add stories, but only those with a lyrical, mystical quality. We did something right, because we won the award for best poetry collection that year. This is the first reprinting of that story since that long out-of-print collection.*

Darkness – and the Light

The surface of the lake gave new and deeper meaning to the term '"placid."' The water was so still, and so dark, that the very absence of sound and motion drew images from deep within Jonathan's mind that were anything but peaceful.

The shoreline stretched out to his right so far that it disappeared in the gloom, but Jonathan wasn't interested in that dark expanse. His gaze wandered left to where the lake curved around a rocky outcropping that stretched down into the depths beyond. The forest drew within about fifty feet of the shoreline, then stopped. Nothing grew closer. There were stone, sand, driftwood and the sun-bleached bones of dead fish littering the ground, but nothing moved.

From that flat, tide-slicked surface, the tower rose. Brick upon brick of white stone made dark by wind, and rain, mud and slime. Jonathan let his gaze slide up that wall, catching each glimmer as it reflected the moon's pale light. The last of the sun's red-orange glow had faded from the skyline, and the moon rose slowly, silver-lining the damp stone. Three quarters of the way up the wall, a window opened over the forest. From within, Jonathan saw the soft glow of candlelight.

The moonlight dimmed, and Jonathan glanced up sharply. Dark clouds had rolled in, and a ripple of lighting shot between them. In that instant, the entire lighthouse snapped into view, stark against an outline of brilliant light and darkened sky. He took a step back and brought his hand to his heart. A lighthouse— on a lake. No ships to guide. No wreckage lining a coral skeleton of dangerous reefs. Black, dead-calm water and silence.

It was just as he had seen it as a child. Just as the pictures had shown it reborn. It was in the wrong place.

Jonathan tore his gaze from the tower and spun back to the lake. The water rippled, undulating to the rhythm of the moon, oblivious to the tower and it's single, darkened eye. No light flashed from the tower. There was no wind to cause the ripple.

"Why did you do it, old man?" Jonathan whispered. Turning back to the window, he added. "What have you done?"

The wind had picked up with the approach of the storm, and Jonathan felt a sudden chill, despite the season. He stuffed his hands into his pants pockets and strode across the slimy rocks toward the tower. As he reached the rough-hewn wooden door and raised the cold steel knocker in one clenched hand, the beacon in the tower a hundred feet over his head snapped on, flashing in a brilliant, fog-cutting beam across the water.

Jonathan sat at an old wooden table, fingers gripping a steaming mug of coffee. A fire raged in a small recess in the wall, hardly a fireplace, more an alcove with vents set too close to the floor to provide efficient heat, and before that blaze a man stood, hands clenched behind his back, staring into the flame. It could have been a scene from some Hollywood Scottish epic. The man didn't wear a kilt, but somehow the rugged denim jeans and work boots conveyed the effect anyway. Wild locks of deep red hair flowed over stooped shoulders, tinted with highlights of silver gray.

Angus was tall, taller than most men and thin so that his motions seemed to take forever, long, graceful patterns of coordination. He would have seemed ungainly if it weren't for the preternatural grace of each gesture. Jonathan watched, fascinated, as his uncle began to pace before the fire, shadows dancing along the walls like great predatory beasts.

Then, in the periphery of his vision, Jonathan caught another movement. More subtle, more powerful and so close to the corner and the floor that he couldn't be certain he'd seen anything at all. He turned quickly, his own motion a shorter, more slender version of his uncles. If it weren't for his close-cut dark hair, Jonathan might have been a small re-composition of the older man's form. When Jonathan's father had been alive, the three of them had been a positively eerie sight, Angus too tall and wild-haired, Ewan, Jonathan's father, not quite as tall, but very angular, wide in the shoulders and a long, very narrow face – and Jonathan. Smaller, younger, but so closely modeled after Angus as to seem a shadow if he walked behind the big man.

Jonathan stared into the empty corner, started to speak, then kept his silence. Experience had taught him that in such an audience he would get but a certain number of opportunities to question. It was important that the questions be fully formed before he gave them voice. It was important that he stuff his emotions deep inside where they would not taint his speech. Angus would know. Back turned, shoulders hunched against a Scottish wind that no longer sliced through the cracks in the ancient stones, Angus would see through to his soul.

"I carried every stone, Jonathan." Angus' voice cut through the silence suddenly, banishing it as if it had never existed. "Aye, the men, they tore her down, but I carried every stone of her to the trucks, watched them wind into the distance leaving less and less behind each time they came. Those were strong, strapping lads, but for every stone two of them lifted, I carried a second. Bits of my heart, they trucked away."

"Why?" Thoughts of carefully chosen words forgotten, Jonathan half-rose from his seat, then leaned back, gripping the mug so tightly that his knuckles whitened. "Why Angus? You know what she watches...and why. How could you take her away?" Even as he waited for his answer, images of Angus,

huge blocks of stone hefted as easily as Jonathan remembered
the big man shouldering barrels of ale, trudging from the
lighthouse to the trucks, and back, the waves of the lock tossing
foam and droplets of water at his boots and stinging his eyes.

"I've no more to do with it than you, boy," Angus growled,
"If you think you know what she watched, then you must know
that she watches still."

Again Jonathan held his silence. The lake that lay beyond the
tower's walls was ominous in its own right, but it was no Loch
Drummond. It was new, with the taint of a new world, recently
civilized and ignorant in the ways of the older darkness. It was
water, and darkness, cut now by a swath of light that did not
belong. No more, no less. Not so the Loch.

"Word is," Jonathan said softly, "that it is restless."

Angus' fingers tightened until Jonathan could see the skin
turning white, but he didn't turn. "It was not my choice, lad. It
has never been any man's choice."

Jonathan took a long swallow of the hot coffee, feeling it
burn down his throat.

Angus whirled in anger. His eyes blazed, green and brilliant
and alive with sudden accusation. "And what would you be
knowin' of it? Where were you when she watched The Loch,
eh? When your father, rest his soul, and I stood in the tower?
London? Paris? Traipsin' the streets of Las Vegas and tellin'
drunk-boy stories on your crazy Uncle Angus?"

Jonathan stared into the swirling depths of his mug and
held his silence. It was the truth. He'd not seen The Loch since
his boyhood days, when he'd played along her shore, young and
carefree, never questioning why he couldn't sit on the stones
and watch the soft slap of the waves after the sun had gone
down. He'd left with his mother at the age of eight and never
looked back. Not during the waking hours.

"I'm not here to tell you I understand more than you do,"
Jonathan answered at last. "I'm not here to apologize for my
life, either. If mother and I chose to leave, you chose to stay. Or
she chose you."

Angus stared a moment longer, deep green eyes boring
into Jonathan's heart. Spinning back to the fire, the old man

growled. "Damned if she didn't choose me."

No words were spoken for a few moments, but the silence had grown suddenly less tense. Jonathan turned, glancing out the window over the forest. In the distance he could make out the soft glow of the city. There were no windows overlooking the lake. To see that, there was only one vantage point.

"I want to see the tower," he said. Too quickly, courage lost in the space of that breath. The words dwindled to nothing, and there was no indication that Angus had heard them. The old man stood still as a stone statue, staring into the glowing coals of the fire. Then, when Jonathan had nearly given up, the old man turned, slowly, and without a word, strode to the door.

Jonathan rose, following quickly.

The stairs wound up and up, too close-set, as if designed for shorter feet and stronger toes. Jonathan stumbled several times, trying to achieve some sort of rhythm, but whether he attempted one, two, or three of the old stone steps at a time, he could not make the climb more comfortable. All his life he'd climbed stairs, but somehow these presented a new challenge. Angus had already disappeared around the upward curve. Years of practice had acclimated the old man's muscles to the odd dimensions of the stairs.

Jonathan stumbled, cracking his shoulder painfully on the wall, and he hesitated for a moment, laying his forehead against the cold stone. A sudden flash of insight nearly sent him reeling back and down. Who had these stairs been built for? Who would line up thousands and thousands of stairs so – *wrong*?

Long, sinuous bodies flowing upward, losing themselves in the turns and curves, hundreds of feet pounding, slapping wetly on stone, gripping and tugging the corners of the stairs. The dimensions shifted, the windows confronted Jonathan at eye level, and the stairs became handhold after handhold after handhold drawing him upward into the light...

Jonathan shook his head and pressed off the stone. Gritting

his teeth, he began child-stepping up the stairs, no longer fighting the discomfort, but working through it. The rhythm had shifted somehow, and what had seemed impossible grew more or less bearable as he pressed on up to the tower.

The door was just as Jonathan had heard it described. As a child, he could have climbed those stairs a thousand times. He'd seen his father, and his uncle, silhouetted against the brilliant beam of light as it snaked out over the Loch, keeping their silent vigil night after night without fail. Jonathan had loved the mystery of it, but he'd felt no urge to unravel that mystery. Something in the imposing stone walls and the expressions of those who entered had turned him aside each time. No one had ever forced the issue.

Now he wished he'd been stronger. Braver. He stared at the oak panels and the knob, set too low for easy access. Jonathan stopped once more, just short of the final step. The latch bothered him. The angle was wrong. He could see, even from where he sat, that he would have to lean in close to grip the mechanism – very close. Bent nearly double.

Before it could become more of an issue, the door swung wide, and Angus was there, hair a wild halo of grey-white framing deep red angry face, and that framing a deeper scowl. No words, only that stare, but Jonathan looked down to his feet and stepped forward hurriedly, tripping over the last of the close-set stone stairs and tumbling into the chamber beyond.

Angus closed the door behind them with a quickly-spit word that could have expressed exasperation, or contempt. A word that made no sense, and perfect sense at the same time— foreign and familiar. Jonathan tried to place it, but there was no opportunity.

He staggered upright, catching himself against the wall to the right of the door, then nearly tumbled headlong. Instead of watching where he placed his feet, his gaze was captured by the light. It sliced through the darkness with a power that sizzled and crackled. There was no sound, but Jonathan could feel it lifting the hairs on his arms and at the base of his neck.

It wasn't just the light. The illumination was no different from that of any high-powered beam. Nor was it the darkness.

Not exactly. There was no room, in that instant, for any other light. Jonathan was blinded by the brilliance and all else was nothing. Black. Empty and without life or heat. Only that slender, too-white beam, cutting into the deep black heart of the night existed. Around the base, darkness swirled within darkness. Slow, serpentine coils of—something—moved slowly and steadily, and an energy—a power—more than that of the light—shivered through the air.

Jonathan was drawn. He reached out a hand, groping toward the light and took a short step forward.

"Get hold of yourself," Angus' voice crashed through the silence. "Stand like a man and look away from the light. It isn't for you. It isn't for any man."

Jonathan shook his head violently, stumbled away from the light and Angus' hand. As he tumbled toward the stone wall, his vision shifted. He saw coil after coil of dark, sinuous flesh, jointed and then again, and again. Chitinous, whirring sounds filled the air, like a projector's motor, lending a surreality to the beam of light that nearly brought images of dark movie theaters and buttered popcorn before Jonathan crumpled, blacking out cold.

When he woke, the light was off to his right, and Angus was shaking him gently. Jonathan saw the rough-hewn stone blocks of the ceiling, and for a long moment his mind was lost, marveling at the engineering that kept those stones in place, preventing them from caving in on him and deepening the darkness. Angus' face as he leaned down was too long – too narrow, and his huge, broad shoulders had stretched ...fingers elongated and too-thin. Jonathan shook his head again and closed his eyes.

"Wake up lad!" Angus reached down and slapped his cheek lightly.

Jonathan blinked and sat up slowly, levering his hands against the stone until he was seated, staring at the wall, away from the light.

"What happened?" he asked? "What ..."

"If you'd looked for them before, lad, you'd have seen," Angus grated. "They've always been here. Always. Did you think your granda' built the lighthouse? Did you think it was *ours?*"

"I thought she watched." Jonathan whispered.

"And she does," Angus muttered, turning away, "As I watch. As *they* watch, and have watched. As they've taught us to."

Jonathan shuddered. Not a quick shake, or a shiver up his spine, but a deep, soul-wracking quake. If that was what watched, those things, shifting and snaking around the base of the light, so close beside his father, and his uncle, and behind the shield of the light, then what did they watch for? And why did the image of those multi-jointed creatures and Angus, with his too-strong, too-tall frame and deep set eyes fit so easily into one vision? What could be so much more – wrong – that such a bond of vigilance could form? Where did the others watch from – did they share the light, or was there another dimension – so far from Jonathan's own reality it could be sensed, but not seen? And what could they do if the light failed? What could any of them do?

Jonathan rose too quickly. He staggered, bringing both hands to his face as his head throbbed and the blackness threatened to wash over him again. Angus turned away, ignoring him. The old man had stepped to the window beyond the light. Cut glass, beveled and prismatic at the edges, convex, the light shimmering through the very center, magnified and focused by a pair of lenses that hung from an intricate framework before the flame of the tower's light. Jonathan knew that the wick curled deep into the bowels of the tower, and that the oil, filled before it could ever reach a low level, was the heart of the old lighthouse.

He knew this because he had read about it. Over the last year, as his obsession with the tower had grown, consuming his days and haunting his nights, he'd read every word he could find on the old structure. He'd read letters from his homeland and his family. He'd read threats and warnings and words that dripped with fear. He'd seen photographs of the lighthouse as it was dismantled, stone by stone, and he'd read the article in the St. Jiles Virginia Beacon about the crazy old Scotsman and his trainload of rocks. How the tower had been reconstructed to a madman's specifications, to guard a shore that had never seen the prow of anything larger than a motorboat.

There was little that Jonathan didn't know about the old lighthouse. So he'd thought. Now, walking slowly to that glass portal to stand beside his uncle, he realized that there were no words he might have read that could have explained it. There were no waves crashing below. No Scottish wind whipped banshee-strong through the eaves. All was silent.

Jonathan remembered the waves. He'd stood on the shore of The Loch and watched the wind whip them from those dark depths time and again. Even then the villagers had talked. No need for a lighthouse on the shore of the Loch. No earthly reason for that stone monstrosity.

Of his memories, only the storms had followed the lighthouse to its new home. Lightning painted the sky in chiaroscuro shades of brilliance that strobed across the screen of Jonathan's mind after each flash. No color. The lake was black and rippling, but there were no waves.

"Why here?" Jonathan asked finally. "Why this dark lake so far from the Loch that the stars aren't even the same in the sky?"

"I told you it was no doing of mine," Angus muttered. "I brought her to this land, and I followed my heart. When the train passed over the trestle that spans the river leading to this place, my heart nearly stopped. I wanted the light, then. I wanted to be here, looking out. Watching, not helpless and poised so far above the water. It was an empty pit of darkness, and there was no life in it."

"But ..." Jonathan turned, watching the older man's face. "The Loch?"

"They chose to tear her down, lad," Angus answered softly. "I fought them, but I was one man. No one stood at my side, and not a soul heeded my warning. It took every bit of my life's savings to cart her away before they razed the tower to the ground."

Jonathan knew it was true. He'd been to the Loch. He'd heard them, laughing in the pubs and telling tales of the crazy old man and his lighthouse. They'd said Angus had worked night and day, not allowing another to help. They'd called him the bug-man, too tall, too strong, like an ant soldier carting kernels of corn to some dark queen. Jonathan had kept his silence, sitting in the back and sipping his beer, but he'd listened to them all, and he'd wondered at their ignorance. He'd wondered, as well, at the taint of fear permeating their stories. They made fun, but at the same time, a lone man carrying every stone – by hand – was beyond their comprehension. Sipping his ale, Jonathan had been shocked to realize it was beyond his, as well.

"Cormac Duggan was there," Jonathan said, turning to the glass portal, away from the brilliance of the light. He stared out over the expanse of the lake, watching the rippling water glitter brightly. "His father has stood at this same window, at your side. He should have known better, and yet there he was, laughing and drinking as if it didn't matter."

"His father lies five years in the grave, lad, in the same stretch of stone and dust that holds your own father." Angus sighed. "Cormac is young, and the quick money and quicker tongues of those fresh in from the cities have turned his head. He has never stood at the Loch by night. None of them have. Pray they never do."

"It doesn't matter now," Jonathan said softly.

Angus spun, arm slicing through the light and gripping Jonathan so tightly by his shoulder that the younger man staggered and cried out in pain.

"It will ALWAYS matter! Why do you think I'm here?"

Jonathan pulled away violently, staggering to the wall and glaring back, confused now, and more than a little angry.

"I have no idea why you are here," he grated, rubbing his sore shoulder. "The Loch is thousands of miles away across an ocean – the same loch you told me must always be watched. ALWAYS. Now you stare out over this dead-water lake as if it were home. As if you could look at this place and see the shores your father watched, and where mine died. I have *no idea* why you would drag this tower, stone by stone, to a country that isn't even old enough to remember your father's father. None."

Jonathan reached out and grabbed the old man's collar. "We don't *belong* here, Angus, nor does she."

"You have looked out over the waters of the Loch, boy," Angus growled, shaking loose and glaring, "but you haven't watched these. If you think we watch for a thing that can be contained by the shores of a single loch, then you have come with too little knowledge, too late to help."

Angus turned and strode to the portal. "It matters not where the lighthouse stands, lad, only that she does."

Jonathan wanted to scream. He wanted to grab Angus by that wild, white hair, fling him into the stones and make him see. Of course it mattered where. How could it not? If it did not, what would that mean?

Dark shapes shifted near the base of the light and Jonathan flinched. Angus did not. The floor tilted and Jonathan felt the frugal lunch he'd downed on the road threatening to resurface.

"How?" he whispered hoarsely. "How can it not matter?"

"The water is a key, Johnnie," Angus replied, voice softening as he spoke his nephew's name for the first time since seeing him at the tower door. "It isn't the only key, but it is our key. The water is a weakness – and so, we watch. It is our purpose."

Jonathan moved to the portal, laying his fingers against the convex surface of the glass.

"A weakness in what?" he asked.

"If we understood that, lad, we'd not need the light."

Jonathan shifted his attention to the odd structure in the center of the tower. A globe-shaped well rose from the stone of the floor, circled by a short stone wall. From the top of this, a metal framework twisted upward, the center of which was the huge, serpentine wick. It was held in place by a screw-like mechanism worked by a large hand crank. The flame licked up the insides of a clear glass chimney.

Inside the tower, the light was a bright glow, seeping into the corners and chasing shadows about their feet with each flicker. Between the flame, and the portal stood the dual-optic lens system that turned the dancing flames into a concentrated beam, shooting out into the night and cutting through the thick darkness.

"How far is it across the lake?" Jonathan asked. He was

staring out along the beam's path, but all he could see was the darkness, and the light.

"Not two hundred yards," Angus replied, voice low and far away, "by day."

"What do you..."

Jonathan fell silent. Something was crashing into the base of the tower. The sound jolted him. He moved closer to the portal, trying to peer down the side of the tower, but the angle made it impossible. Then he saw it. Rising into the beam of light, crystal droplets of water, and foam—white and frothing. The sound came again, rhythmic and powerful. Waves.

"What is happening?" Jonathan asked, not really expecting an answer. "What kind of weather could cause waves like that on a lake?"

"Not the lake, lad," Angus growled, "nor the Loch. Remember what I said. It doesn't matter what, or where, we watch in the world you entered from – it only matters that we *do* watch. You canna always hear the waves. Sometimes it is the wind. Sometimes it is tremors so strong the very foundation of the tower shivers and it doesn't end until it's wee-stepped up the bones of your back. Sometimes there is only the darkness, and the light."

Jonathan stared out along the light. There was a pinpoint of something—a flickering shadow—moving along the perimeter of the light. He couldn't make out if it were the flap of wings, or a swirl of smoke. His heart skipped, and for a long moment he couldn't breathe. The waves below crashed again, sending foamy spray dancing into the bright beam. Jonathan lost the motion, then darted his gaze to the right as it reappeared, closer and more distinct. It was a darkness moving against a backdrop of lesser darkness. It spiraled, around and around the light. He could see it pressing tighter, repelled, whirling closer. Whatever it was flung itself at the light again, and again, each time failing to bring more than a momentary haze to the light as it spun, visible and invisible at the same time.

Jonathan placed one hand on the glass portal, focusing and leaning in to the glass. Closer. It was spiraling closer, and Jonathan could sense something moving around his feet—brushing his legs. Agitated sound shivered up from the floor to tremble through the air. Every hair on his body stood on end, and it was a struggle to stand against the insistent tug and chatter. Jonathan concentrated. He shuddered at the sensation of those—things—swirling around his legs and gripping his clothing with too-tiny hands. He needed to look down, to see – to scream. He did not. From far away, he heard Angus' voice, calling out to him, then fading, in and out, whirling with the spiral shadow. It was so close—so close he could nearly make out details of ... "Angus," he whispered, "Angus, what ... I ..."

"For God's sake, lad," Angus voice broke through the growing shiver of sound, reaching Jonathan's numbed mind, but too slowly—too late. The old man's body cut a dark swath across the light's beam, breaking up the perfection and sending a wild shadow dancing into the night. As the perfection of that brilliance was marred, the world warped. Jonathan tried to turn away from the window, toward Angus, and the light, but he was too slow. The walls and the window strobed and pulsed between darkness and light, and Jonathan's legs no longer supported his weight, not as they should.

Jonathan heard echoes of Angus' voice, far away and fading. He felt himself falling into the fracture Angus had caused in the perfection of the light. His body stretched, moving oddly, bending and bending and bending in ways he could not—would not. He cried out, but it was not his voice, nor any human cry that joined the frantic, chitinous whirr. Through it all, his gaze was fixated on a dark point shimmering along the edge of the light, and at that weakening of the brilliance of the light, the thing sped closer, flashing as only total black can do, brilliant as lightning and empty as eternity.

Then the shadow melted, washing back, revealing what lay beyond that portal. Jonathan curled away. His body swayed, rearing up and back, just as Angus' heavy form hit him, propelling him beyond the space between the light and the portal. The spiral shadow slammed into the glass, and the tower shuddered. The huge stone structure lurched, threatening to cant to one side and topple, sending the light and those in the tower tumbling to a pile of ruin on the shore below. There was a shiver, sinuous and powerful. The tower whirled on it's base, curling outward along that beam of light, as if reaching for – something. Groping. Failing.

Jonathan didn't feel the shift. His eyes were wide open, glazed and dull. He crashed to the stone wall, Angus piling into him and the shifting of the tower adding to the momentum. His shoulder—what should have been his shoulder—gave way with a sickening crunch and he crumpled to the floor. The others writhed and twisted around him, and though the whirring, chirping voices made no more sense to him than they had before, he sensed their terror and joined it with his own. With a roar, Angus rolled away, fighting to regain his feet and turned wild-eyed to face the portal.

It held. The tower shivered, then righted itself, and with a quick flicker, the flame leaped back to full height, burning brightly and shooting its single beam out into the darkness once again. Angus knelt, one leg to the side, balanced carefully and ready to spring toward the beacon. His breath was ragged, and his hair, white and wild, circled his head like a shifting halo. Slowly, as the tower and the light stabilized, he rose.

Jonathan lay huddled against the wall, dazed. The room shivered, and something snapped. With that snap, the pain drove through his arm and chest unmercifully. He cried out, clutching his one good arm to his chest tightly, instinctively, then screaming again as he pressed too tightly on ruined bone. His eyes glazed, as though he stared through the stone into some other place.

Ignoring Jonathan, Angus took a quick circuit of the beacon, cranking the wick up half a notch and staring out into the darkness. Then, turning slowly, he moved to the wall and carefully lifted the younger man into his arms.

Jonathan wasn't light, but Angus' shoulders bunched, and he handled the burden easily. Another stone. Another solitary trek. Without a backward glance, he headed for the stairs and kicked the wooden door open, disappearing down into the shadows ... footsteps tapping too closely together as he worked his way down the ancient stairs.

Jonathan stood on the rocky shore, the stagnant water no more than a foot from the toes of his boots. His arm was tied back in a sling, holding his separated shoulder in place firmly, but not firmly enough to aggravate his cracked ribs. Wind teased gently through his hair, brushing a single strand up and back over his cheek. His eyes were fixed on a point somewhere beyond the far shore. His back was too stiff, and his lips were set in a grim line.

Angus stood at the door of the tower, watching. He didn't speak. The sun was setting slowly over the horizon, and the water was taking on the sheen of a deep, black mirror. There were no bird calls, nor did an insect cry into the growing darkness. No sign of life existed within the stone circle that held the tower – except the two men. Two generations. Watching the water. Jonathan stared into those waves, studying his own reflection as the sun died on the horizon. He traced the too-long lines of his face, wondering if it weren't a bit longer now, and though there was no one near – nothing within yards of him – he could hear the whirring echo of terrified voices. Not human voices, but familiar.

Jonathan turned, stepping carefully across the slime-coated stone. He made his way to the tower slowly. Before he entered, he glanced up the wall. The cracks in the stones shifted momentarily, rippling round and round the tower, sliding like endless serpents feeding on themselves.

The windows were too low to the stairs. He'd not noticed it before, but suddenly his mind put the pieces of the puzzle into place. The windows were too close to the stairs that were too-close together and too shallow for humans to climb. He felt what it would be to gaze out through those windows, rippling up the stairs. He felt the draw of the light. The tower rippled, then grew still. Still as stone.

"No moon tonight," Angus observed quietly.

Jonathan nodded. "Might have to crank her up another notch, just to be sure."

The door closed behind them, and the sun set slowly behind the line of trees beyond the lake. The lake grew silent, and then, slicing through the fog lifting from the water's surface and the thick, cloying gloaming, the light sliced out. Watching.

AUTHOR'S NOTE: I have written a number of stories that involve scenes in different places, surreal bits woven together into a whole that presents questions, and not all of the answers. This is a story like that. I'm deeply obsessed with ancient myths, with the blending of this world, and others… This story was supposed to be published in a magazine titled Fantastic Stories, but it never happened. It is presented for the first time in this collection.

Death, & His Brother, Sleep

Lady Claudia stood by the bedside and watched her husband sleep. She held a wine glass; another like it stood on the table beside his bed. After a quick glance around to be certain the two of them were alone, she leaned close and let her scented curls brush his face as she placed her own glass on the night stand, and traded it for his. She felt his breath, hot on the skin of her throat, and she hesitated. His eyelids fluttered. He drew in a quick gasp, jerked his head very slightly to one side, and then grew still. His chest rose and fell regularly.

She kissed the tips of her gloved fingers and brushed them over his eyelids, then turned and left the room quickly, the goblet cradled to her breast. The room was dark. Only a single candle flickered in a glass chimney on the dresser, and it was mostly burned away. When Lady Claudia's shadow had passed from sight, and the candle flame had ceased its momentary dance in salute of her passing, the room settled to a deep shadowed gold. Tapestries hung heavy on the walls and beaded curtains filled the doorway. The bed was canopied, its drapes thick and lush. All sound was deadened, and only

Patrick's steady breathing, stirred the motionless air.

Claudia stopped and stood very still in the center of the next chamber. Her heart hammered in her chest. A soft voice whispered to her from the shadows.

"If you press any harder on that glass, Lady, you will certainly crush it."

Claudia did not turn.

She stood in a sitting room centered by an ornate fireplace. To either side of this were curtained alcoves. There was a fainting couch along one wall, and several comfortable upholstered chairs gathered in a semi-circle before the hearth. There was no fire. It was summer, and there would not be need of heat for several months, but Claudia felt a sudden chill.

Lucas stepped from the shadowed alcove to the right of the fireplace and bowed low. She acknowledged this with a slight inclination of her chin. She did not turn to face him, and though she eased the pressure she was applying to the glass between her palms, her legs shook and threatened not to support her. When she did not speak, he stepped forward boldly and took the goblet from her hands.

"The dosage was as we discussed?" he asked.

She nodded curtly and held her silence.

Lucas stood very close, regarding her in silence, and she trembled anew. She wanted to order him away, but could not, and he knew it. Not now. He studied her as he might have a fine painting. To distract him, she spoke at last.

"He sleeps peacefully," she said.

"He dreams," Lucas added, turning away. "Soon the dreams will no longer be his own. He will be quite mad, you know? It may pass, but…"

There was a crystal decanter on a low table in one corner, and he crossed to it. Unstopping the decanter, he tipped a bit of the amber liquid into the goblet and swirled it slowly, coating the inside of the glass and watching as the blood-red droplets of wine that remained within trickled into the brandy leaving slender trails like veins on the goblet's side.

Lucas took the glass chimney from one of the room's several candles and set it aside quickly. She knew it must have burned his fingers, but he showed no sign of pain. Deliberately, he held the goblet over the flame until the brandy caught fire in a liquid wash of blue flame. She watched, mesmerized, as he swirled the burning liquid and turned toward her. His face was lit with the odd glow of that flame, and his eyes glittered cat-like, just for an instant, before he turned and dashed the goblet into the fireplace. The glass shattered into glittering, burning shards and the logs, stacked in place and awaiting the first fire of winter, flared up in the splash of brandy, then died away leaving nothing but white, wisping smoke.

Claudia's hand had come up, fingers pressed to her lips in shock at his sudden motion and the bright, shattering sound. He was at her side in a moment, his hand supporting her elbow. She shook him off and backed away.

"There is no one to hear, Lady," he said. "Perhaps the shattering glass will awake Morpheus, and the dreams will be sweet."

"What have we done?" she asked, backing away another step. She crossed herself and turned from him, staring at the door leading out into the hall. "My God, what have we done?"

He ignored her question, turned away, and slipped through the beaded curtain into the bedchamber beyond without another word. Moments later, Claudia left the outer chamber and made her way down the upper hall to the great stairway. She stood at the balcony looking out into the shadowed, late-night emptiness below her, and a single tear wound its way from the corner of her eye forward and down, crossing her cheek to salt her lip. She rested her hand, just for a moment, on the soft swell of her belly. She was not showing yet, but soon. She bit her lip and held it to keep from screaming.

Then she turned, started down the stairway, and did not look back.

Lucas wasted no time, though it would be hours before Patrick awakened. After a quick check to be certain there were no adverse effects from the drug, he brought a wooden case in from the outer chamber and placed it on the ornate marble surface of the bureau. The lid opened on hinges to reveal an incredibly intricate music box. He wound it carefully and then released the catch, watching as the glittering gears and tumblers rolled into motion. The song was ethereal, harmonies blending and shifting in hypnotically woven patterns. It had been designed to help a lady sleep, but abandoned when that sleep turned out to be filled with odd visions and dreams.

He poured two pinches of greenish powder from a vial into a small bowl and mixed it with several drops of water. When he was satisfied, he lifted the chimney from the single candle and carefully poured the mixture into the well of wax surrounding the wick, just beneath the flame, letting it blend in until it was impossible to make out even a faint green stain on the candle's surface. By the time it had burned away, there would be no trace except the slight, lingering odor of poppy and a hint of sandalwood.

He worked more quickly now that the drugged incense had begun to permeate the still air of the room. He could survive being caught in Patrick's chambers—he was a close confidante and could claim to have only been helping his friend to bed after too much wine. The incense and the music box would be more difficult to explain.

He lifted the corner of the bedspread and peered quickly at the floor beneath. Nothing had been disturbed. The lines of the pentacle were clearly visible, two points protruding slightly from beneath the edge of the bed. There were two concentric circles within the confines of the star, but he could not make them out from where he stood—not in the dim light with the smoke thickening about him.

Lucas pulled a worn leather journal from his pocket and flipped quickly through the pages. There were glyphs and scrawled formulas, short paragraphs, snippets of verse, and, near the rear of the book, the words he sought. It had taken him a year of painstaking research to translate them, and even now, sweat streaked his face and ran beneath his collar as he stared at them and wondered. One mispronounced syllable was all it would take. One verb conjugated improperly, or a name sounded with the wrong inflection, and the result would be skewed. If that happened, he had no idea what the outcome might be. As it was he was depending on the half-mad scrawling of a man

two hundred years dead. Claudia thought he was protecting
her, but Lucas knew the truth. What he sought was power, and
these words could bring it to him across worlds, and across the
ages.

Leaning in, his lips so close they nearly brushed Patrick's
ear lobe, he read softly.

*Thanatos turned, his head cocked inquisitively, as the music box mel-
ody bled through the shadows. He heard the shuffling steps approach
and the words, spoken from far away, echoed through his hall.*

Antonius stared through the darkness. He did not speak, and
if he was aware of his surroundings, he gave no indication.
Something had caught his attention, and that had not happened
for a century or more. His eyes would not focus, and the dry,
creaking rasp of skin on skin that accompanied the opening
of his jaws echoed hollowly from the damp stone walls. In
the distance, the sound of the river's passing whispered with
the voices of others, no more than a name here, or a soft cry
there. He had looked into that river once, watched the faces roll
over and over one another, limbs fading into torsos fading into
waves. He had leaned down to touch a woman's face and found
the surface of the water reflecting his own features, his own
hand, reaching to drag him down.

So close. He had pulled back, turned away, and found
the caverns. He remembered the voice of the river, but until
his eyes opened and his jaws slowly parted, he remembered
nothing else. It had faded to gray, to the color of stone, carved
from his mind by the passing of time and the dead, stagnant
air. Now another voice whispered in his ear. He did not know
the voice, and he did not know the name it called him by, but he
understood the words, and his long silence broke with a dusty
wisp as he breathed the words out once more. They spun from
his lips as silver threads that hung in the air, spiraling toward
the river.

Thanatos watched as the threads wove into patterns above the waves.

He reached out a hand to snare them between his fingers, a strange cat's cradle of dead sound, the skeletons of words so spider-silk thin they clung to his flesh. He brought them to his lips with a flourish. He breathed, and the dead air hanging above the Styx became animated, rolling the threads into seedpods that blew downstream and slipped through the gauzy curtains of time and worlds...

The brick wall of the alley was chilled and damp. A cold, relentless wind worked its way into the cracks and crevasses, drawing whirlwinds of debris from the grit and gravel on the ground to invade the deserted stairwells and shadowed back door exits. Patrick shivered, huddled up in the corner formed by the metal wall of a dumpster and the bricks at his back. He stared into the street beyond the alley in terror.

He did not know he huddled against a dumpster—though the scent of garbage hung cloying and rotten in the cold air— but he felt the metal. The word dumpster would have rung empty and meaningless in his ear. He did not know what the dim glow of streetlights meant—though they gave him light. He did not know what the roar of automobiles on the street portended, but he drew away from it and hid his face.

He was wrapped in rags that stank of sweat and a thousand odors his senses were not equipped to process. The brick at his back and the metal at his side were foreign, and dragons passed the entrance to this roofless cave with hungry growls and bleats. The rich tapestries of his chamber were gone, and the walls of his keep had evaporated into a world of nightmare and dark magic.

It seemed only a moment in time since he'd shared a smile and wine with Claudia. He had stood in his sitting chamber, staring into her dark eyes, but he could not remember what they had spoken of. He recalled her hand on his arm, guiding him toward his chambers. He breathed the memory of the scent of her hair, and felt the brush of her breast through her silk dress when his heavy, clumsy feet failed to move in compliance with his jumbled mind's command and he stumbled. He had steadied himself against one post of his bed as her fingers unwound the wineglass from his own.

She had brushed his hair back from his face and whispered to him. His lips had been sticky, as though gummed with some paste, and though she stood close enough to reflect his features on her eyes, he hadn't been able to focus on her face—or her words.

And the words continued. He heard them beneath the roar of the dragons and the whistle of the wind. Every time he thought he could make sense of his thoughts, or the images surrounding him, the words wound in and out of his mind like a tailor's needle and thread, sound dragging through each hole and drawing the pain tighter, stitching his brain into a wad of tension so taut it thrummed and blotted sanity.

It was not Claudia's voice, but it was familiar as this place was not. The words were monotonous, a chant, or atonal song, perhaps verse. Patrick fought to concentrate and bring them into focus. He blinked slowly, but images assaulting him did not waver. Above the softly repetitive voice, others rose, loud, jarring, and very close. He curled into a tighter ball, drew the unfamiliar rags close, and willed himself one with the shadow of the wall. The voices, accompanied by heavy footsteps, drew nearer, but he understood none of the words.

Lucas spoke into Patrick's ear, his lips so close his breath bounced back to his cheek. He watched Patrick's eyes. The text Lucas had studied for so long gave indicators he must watch for, but the candle smoke itched at his senses, winding its opiate-drenched scent up through his nostrils. He needed to close his eyes and catch his breath, but it wasn't possible. There could be no break once the words had begun, no moment of silent, however brief. And he found that he had no choice. His lips moved, and the words flowed, but somewhere near the middle of the text they had ceased to be his own.

He had a sudden dark vision of his face, drawn back in a rictus of pain and denial, fighting to control renegade lips that repeated the dirge-like litanies helplessly. The process was designed to bring madness to the man on the bed, not to himself. That is what Antonius had written so long ago, and that is what Lucas had believed. Now, since the words had taken on a life of their own, he mulled over possibilities and latched onto an oblique translation.

"Once begun, the chant cannot be stopped." Lucas had assumed this to mean he must continue speaking, no matter what distracted him. Now he wondered. The difference in translation was very subtle, but its impact was not. The chant could not be stopped. He prayed fervently that no other would enter the room—not even Claudia—to see him thus. Patrick's eyelids fluttered, and, detached from the moment, Lucas realized it was the first indicator. The dreams had begun.

Morpheus watched in silence as seeds of sound blossomed, and he smiled. He reached out and plucked them, one by one, pinching them between thumb and forefinger and closing his eyes at the delicious pop as each released its contents into the ether, blending one with another until the sound vibrated with potential – a viol string instant. Morpheus plucked the string. The music was clear and bright, a song not heard in millennia, and he hummed the tune.

Sid opened his eyes and stared. The walls beside and behind him were of stone, not brick. He glanced to his right, but there was no scent of garbage in the air, and he knew he would not see the dumpster. The mouth of the alley was not the mouth of the alley at all—but at least it was there. He ran his tongue over his lips. Something dry and dead crackled, and very faintly—the memory of the concept of a memory—he tasted dust.

Hunger no longer gnawed at his stomach, and his hand did not shake, though it was difficult to move. He had never been so cold, but it didn't matter. Nothing mattered and the taste of dust did not linger. Sid walked toward the mouth of the alley that was no longer an alley, listening for honking horns and loud, brash voices. He heard whispers in their place, soft and sibilant, never completing a phrase and rolling into one long run-on sentence in his mind. The sound was like the surf at the beach, or the hiss of rain in a thunderstorm. White noise, he thought, remembering the concept but unable to apply it against the gray, colorless backdrop of stone.

At the end of the alley he stepped out onto a broad shore. The sand that lined the water's edge was fine, and very white. A gray mist floated above the water, and there was light enough to see, but Sid couldn't tell from what. There were no streetlights, and there was no color. He could not remember why it mattered. His memories were there, but fading, drifting further and further back, and he had to concentrate to draw them forward, to move and to think.

With nothing else to do, he wandered slowly toward the riverbank.

Hypnos heard a single note, clear and bright, and smiled at his son's artistry. He stared out through utter darkness into a world of slumber. He turned slowly, found the one he sought and his smile widened into a laugh. He snapped his fingers sharply and sat back to watch the ripple of that sound wash through into another world.

Antonius' eyes flashed open. He heard his own words through Lucas' lips, pressed very close to his ears. He did not know Lucas. He did not know the bed, or the chamber in which he lay. He smelled the sweet smoke of the poppy and he felt the vibration of the words. He *felt*—and that was more than all the years since his death had granted him.

Lucas did not notice the motion of Patrick's eyelids, but continued to speak in a flawless stream. The ancient words poured from his lips in a voice no longer his own. He had dropped to his knees beside the bed, and his head slumped toward the mattress. He lacked the strength to rise and the sense to care.

Antonius lacked neither. His mind unraveled the cobwebs that had bound it in an instant and he inhaled deeply, letting the opium in the candle ease his tension. He felt a strange lethargy, and then realized he was both drugged and slightly drunk. He smiled. He ran his tongue over his lips and tasted the salt of sweat, and the bittersweet aftertaste of red wine lingering.

There had to be three. It was another moment before he

understood what the words meant to him. Three. One was this new body. Two was his own, standing in the caverns near the Styx, lifeless and drying out like a cornhusk. Who was the third, and where? He turned his head slowly to the side and gazed into the glazed eyes of the man kneeling at his side. Not this one. He was the catalyst—the key—but he was not part of the puzzle.

The doors had been opened; the triptych was painted, but not yet dried on its canvas. He had to apply the seal. Then there would be time to celebrate, and to find out who and where he found himself. He rose shakily. The man kneeling beside the bed continued speaking, but he did not rise. Nor open his eyes.

On the floor by his side, Antonius saw the notebook, and he smiled. He reached down, retrieved it, and began to search.

Patrick fell into fitful sleep. He was terrified of the images that assaulted him when he opened his eyes, and the voices that had passed earlier had been incomprehensible. He had examined himself and found that the body was not his own. It was thin and wasted, emaciated and weak. His hands trembled if he made the effort to hold them up before his face, and he did not trust his legs to support him if he rose.

So he slept. The odd hum and glow of streetlights faded to black, and he dreamed.

He saw the shoreline of a river. White sand stretched out to either side, and a man stood alone on the shore, staring down into the water. The words in his mind had faded to a droning hum, rising and falling but never forming complete words. He heard the whisper of other voices from the direction of the water. He walked out onto the sand in the direction of the lone figure on the bank of the river. As he drew nearer, the voices grew louder, though no less confused.

Sid turned from the water with an effort and watched himself drawing nearer, striding across the beach with more poise and grace than he'd possessed in years. He wondered how he could be walking toward himself, but he gave the matter only a moment's thought. With a shrug, he turned back to the river.

A woman, tall and slender, swirled beneath the waves with her arms outstretched to him. She rolled across the nearest wave, and he took half a step forward. The water lapped at the soles of his boots, but he did not reach out, and she washed away, replaced by a hag with rotted teeth.

Another voice joined that in his head, and he felt something snap into place. The sound was the turning tumbler of a lock.

Thanatos felt the feather touch of Morpheus' chord, riding the ripple of Hypnos' finger-snap revelation. He rose and turned to welcome his brother and his nephew as harmonies formed and sound deepened. Each spoke at once, voices blending in a singular understanding. They stood, side by side, as Patrick walked up beside Sid and stared into the rolling currents of the Styx. The chant continued, and they felt the third, though he was not bound by death, or sleep, or dream. He spoke, and the sound shifted realities like stacked dominos, readying them to topple in symmetrical patterns. The fabric of worlds had twisted, but it would snap back. He spoke again, and it was pinned in place. He spoke again, and the twist became a fold.

Thanatos flicked his hand toward the Styx, and a wave rolled across the surface, gaining strength and rising above the dark surface as it undulated toward the two figures standing on the shore. The three waited in patient silence on Death's shore.

The words continued to pour from Lucas' lips, but Antonius no longer heard them. He had managed to slide off of the bed and stand, though he was weak. The opium clung tenaciously, and he could not snuff the candle.

"Once begun," he breathed, leaning heavily on the bedpost, "the chant cannot be stopped."

He clutched the leather journal in his hand. He had found the final incantation. The man leaning on the bed had translated it to some tongue Antonius did not understand, but it did not matter. Both the translation and the original were intact, and he had only needed to see it to remember. Years peeled away from his mind and his thoughts cleared slowly. He woke from a pitch-black dream into a hazy fog and fought for clarity. At the proper moment, when the chant reached its apex, he would insert the words, one by one, rhythmically counterpointing the other man's voice and creating the rift that would place the seals. The chant could not be stopped, but it could be broken.

Then he heard it. He shook his head, trying to clear the sound, but the motion shifted the opium more quickly through his veins, and he was not yet comfortable with motion. The sound rippled up from recesses deep inside him, growing in strength as it approached the forefront of his thoughts. He tried again to shake it off, but it was no use, and he slumped against the mattress, closing his eyes.

He heard the rush of water and whispered a negation that no one could hear. He knew there were things that he had to remember, but they were slipping away. He heard the words and moaned, as crucial cadences were lost to him. He fought an inward battle, scrambling to redesign the pattern before it slipped away, to patch up the crumbling walls erected by the words he'd penned so long before, in another world and a distant time.

He dropped to his knees beside the other man, but he did not feel the floor beneath his knees. He felt sand, gritty sand that cut like tiny diamond shards of glass and worked itself through his skin, seeking blood. He glanced up, and he saw himself. He saw another, standing at his side, and he rose, stumbling forward without thought to where the bed might have gone.

He saw himself leaning close, listening to the whispered siren words of the Styx. He saw the ripple as the river's surface raised and rolled forward, and he knew in that instant that he would not reach the shore in time to stop himself. He cried out but the words stuck in his throat and held, and he fell silently, hand outstretched to himself – and his hand outstretched to the rushing water.

Sid saw a face reflected in the water, but it was not his own. Other faces continued to ripple across that surface, and he watched them in fascination. They spoke to him, implored him, screamed mindlessly into the silence of his mind, but he did not reply. He leaned closer and held out his arm, and watched in fascination as that of another man was reflected. A thin man with only bones and skin to keep him erect. The sunken eyes and mummified lips were morbid and appealing at once, and Sid wanted only to touch them, to feel the cool water brush over his suddenly desiccated skin.

He was aware of another leaning at his side, but he did not glance over at him. If he had, he would have seen that the face reflected his own familiar features, his own thin, but living hands. He would have seen himself leaning to a reflection that beckoned, even as Thanatos' wave bore down on them both.

Neither heard the snick of Antonius' knees as they sank into the brittle sand.

The wave rose and touched their fingers in one moment and the sound burst free of Antonius' borrowed lips in a mournful, dirge-toned wail. Hands with fingers hooked like talons broke the surface of the water and took Sid and Patrick's wrists. The two tumbled forward in unison, drawn on and down by the wave and disappearing beneath the surface quickly, blending their forms with those beneath the water without a sound, lost in eddies and swells. Gone. There was a swell in the sound as the swell in the Styx subsided, and then silence.

Morpheus strode down the sand to the body on the shore. Leaning close, he pressed his lips to the man's ear and breathed dark harmony into the sleeping mind.

Hypnos snapped his finger a last time and Thanatos contemplated the waves. It would amuse him to see when the two rippled across the surface, their fresh anguish giving the dark waters new sheen.

Patrick's eyes fluttered, and then opened with a snap. He rose in confusion, nearly tangling himself in the sheets and covers of his bed. There was an odd scent in the air, but he dismissed it quickly. His head pounded, and beside him, kneeling against his bed, was Lucas. The man's cheek lay damp in a pool of bile and his lips moved in some silent speech.

"Mad," Patrick whispered.

His head throbbed, and he tried to remember what he'd had to drink, how much. His mind was blank. The last thing he remembered was standing in the outer chamber.

In that instant, Lady Claudia stepped timidly to the door and stared.

Patrick staggered to her, placing an arm on her shoulder, as much for his own support as her comfort.

"Call someone," he choked out. "Lucas has gone mad…"

As Claudia's hurried footsteps echoed down the hall and through three worlds, and Patrick fell heavily back onto the fainting couch in his sitting room, a hand reached from the death cold waters of the Styx. Thanatos gripped Lucas by the hair and dragged him down the sandy beach to meet that grasping claw, whistling a dirge.

AUTHOR'S NOTE: I have had the distinct honor and pleasure of collaborating with a number of talented authors. In this one, the author is not only amazingly gifted, but also the love of my life. It will come as no surprise to those of you who know me to hear that Sherlock Holmes is a hero of mine. When you combine that brilliant, analytic mind with the dark, dimension-shaded wonder of H. P. Lovecraft, you get something special. This story was published in Shadows Over Baker Street, *and was inspired partially by Robert Louis Stevenson. When Trish and I started thinking about the story, the idea that hit hardest and stuck with us was...what if Watson was the client?*

Death Did Not Become Him

With Patricia Lee Macomber

It has been many years since the events I now record took place, and even now, running through them in my mind, I'm uncertain if I should continue. There is a question of privacy involved, to be certain. There is more. I fancy that when all is said and done, these words will one day find their way into the hands of others. Still, my purpose over the years has never been to further my own reputation, and certainly I've been brutally honest when it comes to others.

Let me begin by mentioning the most glaring oddity of all. In this case, when my friend Mr. Sherlock Holmes admitted his newest client to 221 Baker Street, it was none other than myself, half-crazed and shaking like a scared dog.

Upon my arrival, the clock in the church tower chimed eleven. It was later than I had thought, and far too cold for a sane man to be about. All but one light was out in Holmes' flat and I assumed him to be asleep. It did not matter. The burden of that night was too much to bear alone, and at the very least I needed the comfort of my old friend's solid intellect.

I paced, until my shoes threatened to wear ruts in the sidewalk. I wanted desperately to turn around and return to my own home, have a brisk shot of brandy and slide between the cool sheets of my bed. What I most emphatically did not want was to see my relationship with Holmes tainted by the appearance of insanity. Still, there was nothing for it but to plunge ahead, and I finally dashed for the door in desperation, wanting to reach it before my traitorous feet turned away yet again. Before I could raise my hand to the door knocker, the door swung inward, and I found myself stumbling to a clumsy halt, staring into the grinning countenance of Mr. Sherlock Holmes.

"Do come in, Watson," Holmes said with a twinkle in his eye that set my cheeks burning with embarrassment. "Another few paces and you'll wear the leather from your soles." As he took in my expression, Holmes grew more serious, and he closed the door quickly behind us, taking my coat.

"I'm terribly sorry about the hour, Holmes," I blurted, "But the matter simply can't wait."

"I gathered from the odd slant of your hat and the mismatching of buttons that this was a matter of some importance," he replied. He turned and disappeared into his study, and I hurried to catch up with him. When I reached the dimly lit room, he was already in his chair, legs stretched out before him and his fingers pressed together under his chin. "So tell me what brings you out so late on a cold night."

"I've come to offer you a new client, Holmes."

"But you've come alone. Who, then, would your client be?"

I watched him for a moment, steepling his fingers and staring at me, eyes twinkling. I knew he had already deduced my reply, but I made it anyway. "It is I, Holmes. This time, it is I who seeks your aid."

The skin around his eyes drew taut and his lips pursed. "Very well, Watson. Why don't you sit down, take a brandy, and tell me your story."

I sat back, closed my eyes, and let the events of the evening flow back into my consciousness, telling the tale as best I could. I knew any detail I left out, or forgot, might prove the one thing Holmes needed to see through it all as nonsense, so I was careful. The brandy helped. This is the tale I told.

It was but a few hours ago when a knock came at my door. It was later than I was accustomed to accepting callers. I immediately assumed it to be you, Holmes. Who else would call on me at such an hour? My heart quickened at the thought of adventure, and I hastened to open the door.

The man who met my gaze was gaunt, tall and weathered as if he'd spent long years on the deck of a ship, or working a farm. His complexion was dark, and his coat clung to him like a shroud. I could make out two others standing directly behind him in the gloom.

"Dr. Watson," he asked, his voice sharp and edgy.

"You have me at a disadvantage," I countered. "I'm Watson, and you are? My God, man, do you know the time?"

"I am well aware of the time," the man answered. "My business with you cannot wait."

The man held forth a sheet of paper, pressing it toward my nose as if I could read it in the dark. "Did you sign this?" he asked sharply.

"I can't see what it is from here," I said. "Step inside Mr..."

"Jepson," he said, stepping hurriedly through the doorway. "Aaron Jepson. My companions are Mr. Sebastian Jeffries and ... well, read the paper, and you may see who else accompanies me."

I knew I should have told the man to return by daylight, but I'd invited them in, and the deed was done. I glanced at the other two, who remained silent. The first was a white-haired old chap with ruddy features and wide, bulging eyes. His cheeks were overly full, making his lip drape oddly downward. I didn't know him. The third wore a dark coat, as did Jepson, and a hat pulled down to hide the features of his face.

I glanced back to the paper and began to read. It was a death certificate. I had signed it only a week before, pronouncing one

Michael Adcott dead of a knife to the back. Mr. Adcott had been out too late in the wrong part of town, and apparently someone had fancied his wallet a bit more than he himself.

"What has this to do with any of you?" I asked bluntly.

"Mr. Jeffries," the first man explained, "is my solicitor. I should say, he is my cousin's solicitor. I'm not certain if you would have been told, but there was a sizeable investment—a tontine—involved in the death. Michael was one of only two surviving members of the tontine, and upon the declaration of his death, the courts moved to deliver the tontine's assets to a Mr. Emil Laroche."

"I knew of no tontine," I said, "but I see no way I can help you in such a matter. Mr. Adcott died, and as I understand such arrangements, that would indicate that the courts were in the right."

"So you say," Jepson said, "and yet, you would be—for the second time this week—mistaken."

I blinked at him. "Mistaken? How ..."

Jepson held up a hand, then turned to his third companion. "Michael?"

My heart nearly stopped. The man removed his hat slowly, staring at me through eyes I'd seen glazed and closed so few days in the past. He didn't seem to see me, not really, and yet he reacted to Jepson's words with perfect understanding. The dazed, haunted expression of those eyes burned into my mind, and I had to shake my head to clear the sensation of—something—something dark and deep. Something wrong.

"This is quite impossible," I stated. "There is no way this can be the same Michael Adcott that I examined earlier in the week. That man had sustained a direct stab wound to the back, penetrating a lung, and he lay dead in the street at least an hour before I arrived on the scene. There was a constable on the spot, Johnston was his name."

"And yet," Jepson said, holding up one hand to silence me, "Michael Adcott stands and breathes before you, a very alive, and suddenly destitute man. Only your intervention, Dr. Watson, can prevent a horrid miscarriage of justice."

This was a strange situation, to be certain, but I fancy that

I've acquitted myself well in any number of odd happenings over the years. Without hesitation, I stepped closer and stared at the man before me. He wavered back and forth, as if his legs barely held him upright, and I squinted, trying to find some fault between my memory of the dead man, and he who'd disturbed my evening.

"Impossible," I muttered, stepping back. "Preposterous."

Jepson eyed me coldly. "And yet, a fact that is difficult to deny, I suspect," he said shortly.

At this, the plump man, who'd remained silent until that moment, stepped forward, fumbling a monocle from his breast pocket and perching it on the bridge of his nose with a palsied hand. The lens teetered, and I was nearly certain it would drop from its perch before he could steady it, but miraculously the man got it under control. He lifted a small sheaf of papers, bringing them closer so he could glance at them through the lens.

"It would seem," he spoke, the words slow and forced, "that we have a situation before us requiring the utmost in haste and discretion."

"You would be Mr. Jeffries," I stated, not waiting for an answer. "I would expect, sir, that of all gathered here you would be first to note the absurdity of the claim lain before me. Dead men do not pry themselves from the grave, no matter the fiscal windfall it might provide themselves or others. This man cannot be Michael Adcott."

Jeffries glanced up from his papers quickly, nearly sending the monocle flying. "I assure you, Dr. Watson, that he is. I have served the Adcotts for the past twenty years as solicitor, and I know my client when he stands before me."

"Which would lead me to believe, sir, that you have mistakenly pronounced Mr. Adcott dead." Jepson folded his hands in front of him and peered down his nose at me.

I must say that I would rather admit to an error in judgment than to the possibility of the walking dead. All evidence and proof aside, I needed them gone just then.

"Return here tomorrow at four sharp and I'll have the answers you seek," I told them, shoving the papers at Jepson and marching them forward.

Holmes had grown contemplative, his eyes were focused, but not, I think, on any point in the reality we shared. Leaning forward in my chair, hands on my knees, I gazed at him anxiously and finished.

"With the house again empty and my heart still beating a savage rhythm in my chest, I could think of only one thing to do, and that was to bring the matter to you."

Holmes eyes shifted, and he rose suddenly. "And well you did, my dear Watson, well you did indeed."

He was already walking toward the door, wearing an uncharacteristically distracted expression.

"I must see to some things, Watson," he said suddenly. "And you must rest, old friend. When the sun has risen a little higher in the sky, we shall see what we can find."

"But, have you no thoughts on this matter?" I cried.

"Thoughts are often all that we have, Watson. There is nothing that I can say for certain, but I do have – thoughts. That is for tomorrow. Go and get some rest."

With that, he opened the door, and I could think of nothing to say or do, other than to stumble out into the night and off toward home, wondering if my old friend now thought me daft. The sky had already stained a deep, blood-red with the sunrise.

Jepson glanced furtively to either side, then slipped through a massive wooden door and into the depths of the squat, monolithic building beyond. The exterior was dingy brick, even the soot and grime seemed soiled, and there was an oily sheen to the place, gleaming sickly in the early morning light.

He carried a case under one arm, and he'd come on foot. No coach waited outside that door, nor did any spot his entry. There had been precious little traffic through those doors in recent years, and what there was, men tended to ignore. Such knowledge was best left to others, or to no one at all. It was a dark place, and the screams of those who'd entered and never been freed echoed through the air surrounding the place like a hum of electricity. So it seemed to some.

The Asylum of St. Elian had been closed for reasons never

released to the public. There were rumors of dark experiments, of torture and sin, but they were not often repeated, and usually died before reaching the level of a good story. There was nothing good in the building, and if it hadn't required actual contact with the place, most would have been happy to wield one of the hammers that brought it down.

Jepson had found no trouble at all in renting a portion of the fading edifice, and with Jeffries handling the legalities and paperwork, had managed to do so with near anonymity, the solicitor having been granted the right to sign on Jepson's behalf. The laboratory of St. Elian's, and the ward nearest that foul place, had come under Jepson's control easily and without contest. Even the homeless and the drunks avoided the place. It was empty and lifeless as a tomb, and that suited Aaron Jepson just fine.

Now he made his way down the dark main corridor and fumbled a large skeleton key from one pocket of his jacket, balancing the leather case precariously under one arm. He'd cleaned up as much as possible – or necessary – but the old lock ground it's metal tumblers together in a sound near to disbelief at the intrusion of his key. St. Elian hadn't welcomed him gladly.

Once inside, Jepson wasted no time. He moved about the room, bringing the dim lights to life and placing the wooden case carefully on a bench just inside the door. The laboratory was much as he'd found it. There had been a great deal of equipment left behind when the building closed, and none had felt the urge to return and clear it away. The thought of the use it might have seen was enough to slap away even the greediest of fingers. Jepson had carted in, late at night and under cloak of the deep London fog, the last remaining bits of what he'd dragged from his father's home – his inheritance.

Despite the hum and glow of the lamps, shadows clung like swamp lichen to every surface and bit of furniture. Jepson shivered, then, irritated with himself, drew forth a box of matches and lit the large oil lamp on the table beside his case. Turning up the wick, he watched as the flame licked upward, flared, and settled. Standing in the pool of light this created, he felt a little of the spell of the unease lifting and drew a deep breath.

There was little time, and there was no room for delays or hesitation. Jepson flipped open the case and stared down at the contents. The interior was lined in rich velvet. In slots manufactured to accommodate their exact shape and size, a line of six vials rested. The first three were empty. In the next two slots, a greenish liquid roiled. It was not quiescent, as it should have been, sitting still on the table. It swirled and curled toward the edges of the vial, reaching up the sides and falling back down—as if trying to escape. The third and last of the vials contained a flat, red powder. Jepson stared for a few moments longer, as if mesmerized.

Then, as if recovering his senses, he reached for the next full vial and drew it forth, along with the third vial, containing the powder.

With one deft, tandem movement of his thumbs, he uncapped both vials. Inside the first, green, liquid and light, the solution ceased its movement. He tilted the second, angling the lip of it toward the first, tapping gently, mentally ticking off grains of the powder. The green liquid devoured it, changing color slightly, then regaining its normal appearance almost as though the powder had been digested. He re-capped both vials, and returned the sandy substance to its place in the wooden case.

To the right of the case, further along the bench, sat an open carton. Jepson carefully laid the vial down beside the box and reached inside, drawing forth a small leather bag. It might have been easier to work had he unpacked his things, but there was something about the old laboratory, and the asylum walls surrounding it, that made even Jepson want to avoid a deeper connection with the place than was absolutely necessary. The less he unpacked, the less he'd have to pack when his work was done.

He opened the bag and pulled out a small kit. It contained a syringe, a bottle of alcohol, and a small pouch of glittering blades and tools. He grabbed the syringe, which sported a hideously long needle, picked up the vials once again, and turned toward the door.

At that precise moment, a low moan echoed through the

corridors beyond that door, and Jepson froze. The sound was deep, rolling up from the stone bowels of the asylum and rising to a banshee wail that reverberated and echoed back onto itself, forming waves of sound without rhythm or reason. The sound was drenched in pain.

Jepson staggered, bringing one hand to his brow to brush away the sweat and nearly poking out his own eye with the syringe. He cried out and cursed softly.

"Damn you," he said softly. "It's too soon. I should have hours." He stared at the doorway, and the dark, shadowed hall beyond. "I should have hours," he whispered.

The moans rose again, louder than before, and there was a deep metallic clang. He could almost believe the solid stone floor shook.

Under his breath, Aaron Jepson began to pray. He prayed in the ancient Hebrew, the words he'd committed to memory, the charm his father had brought to him from the mind and faith of his grandfather and his grandfather's father. He thought of the ancient, torn shred of canvas, soiled and worn, the spidery lettering etched into that cloth. With his eyes closed, he could see those letters burning brightly – as if they had a life of their own. He could sense the madness behind the verse, could almost see the wild, skewed eyes. He had heard them described so many times they seemed part of his own memory, and not that of his father's father.

Jepson spoke slowly and very softly, trying not to blend his voice with that other – that horrible, hate-filled sound.

Entering the hall, he took a single deep breath, released some of the pressure he was putting on the vial before he crushed it in his hand, puncturing his skin. Fresh sweat broke out on his brow at the thought of that green, glowing slime slipping into his veins. He had a sudden image of the case in the laboratory behind him, the vials and the thick velvet. This led to further memories, journals and stories—stories that would be impossible to believe – were the proof not waiting one floor down in a stone room barred with iron.

Jepson shook it off and stepped into the hallway, moving quickly and purposefully toward the sound. Nothing mattered but the vial in his hand, the syringe that would empty it, and the words. He had to speak the words, had to repeat them from memory, just as he'd learned them, or it would all be for nothing. The madness that echoed through the halls would become his own, and the money... all that money.

There were dim lights strung along the hall, leading down a wide stone stair, and into the shadows below. Jespon took the steps at a trot, ignoring the sounds, which had grown to a constant shriek of madness and a grinding rattle of metal. As he went, he grasped the syringe tightly and plunged it into the lid of the vial. His footsteps grew quicker, and the heaving of his breath threatened to steal the words from his lips, but he couldn't wait any longer. It had to be now, and it had to be quick.

He hit the bottom step, stumbled, righted himself and hurried down the hall. The sounds were close now, immediate and maddening. To his right, barred doorways loomed, cells that had lain empty for long years, their iron doors latched and rusted. He passed the first two cells without a glance, but as he came abreast of the third, he slowed, backing toward the center of the hall. Fingers gripped the bars of that third cell, long and sinewy—strong. The bars shook again.

Jepson took a step closer, raising the syringe like a dagger over his head. The words flowed from his lips, but he had no more control of them now than he did of the tremble in his wrist, or the rubbery sensation that threatened to deny him use of his legs. He slipped toward the barred door, and suddenly a face slammed into it, too-wide eyes glaring at him, framed in wild, unkempt hair. The skin was sallow and pale and the bars shook harder than they had before, threatening to tear loose from the stone of the walls.

With a cry, Jepson plunged the syringe down and slammed it into the flesh of one of the arms groping through the bars, fingers wide to seek his throat. He felt the needle bite and brought his free hand down on the plunger, jamming it home with a grunt and stepping back, leaving the needle deeply imbedded in it's target, watching in horror as the arm was jerked inward, catching the syringe on the bar and snapping it off near the center of the needle. Green liquid glittered in the air, splashing the walls and floor in droplets that glowed and hissed. Jepson stepped back further with a gasp. His heart slammed too quickly – too violently – in his chest, and he feared it would stop. He couldn't get breath to slip past the knot in his throat, and only the intervention of the wall at his back prevented his toppling to the stone floor.

The screams tore through the air at inhuman volume. Jepson slapped his palms to his ears and closed his eyes. Nothing could have blocked that sound, but he muted it, and, blessedly, within moments the sounds began to fade. The screams receded slowly to wails, the wails to moans. His eyes snapped open wide, and he pushed off the wall, moving toward the bars of the cell. His voice rose instantly, returning to his chant, bringing the ancient Hebrew to life through his voice, and trying to imagine that he was in control of the situation.

He stepped closer. The light was very dim, and the bony wrists and yellowed, skinny arms no longer groped between the bars. In fact, the cell's occupant had retreated to the far wall and slid down to a sitting position on the floor, knees drawn up and head back.

Jepson spoke more clearly, enunciating carefully. There was no reaction within the darkened cell. No motion, no sound. He grew calmer, gaining confidence, and he stepped to within an inch of the bars, staring down fixedly at the man cowering against the back wall. The final words of the chant tumbled from his lips, resonant and strong. For just an instant, as the hall fell silent, Michael Adcott raised his head, staring into the eyes of his captor. The captive man's eyes blazed with something beyond insanity, beyond rage or pain.

But only for a second. Then those eyes were dead. Blank. Nothing more reflected in their dull black depths but the dim light of the torches in the hall. Jepson watched a moment longer, letting his breathing catch a normal rhythm and straightening his jacket, running one hand back through sweat-soaked hair.

Reaching into one pocket, Jepson retrieved a ring of keys and inserted a large iron skeleton key into the cell's huge old lock.

"Come along then," he said, his voice cracking once, then steadying again. "Come along Michael. We have work to do, and I've had enough nonsense for one day."

Adcott didn't move. Not until Jepson's fingers gripped his upper arm and tugged. Then, with slow, mechanical motions, he levered himself from the floor, leaned against the wall for support, and found his feet. The man did not turn to Jepson, nor did he answer. When Jepson turned toward the door of the cell, Adcott followed as if drawn in the other man's wake.

It was nearly three o'clock by the time Holmes made his way to the door of my flat. He stood outside the door, and when I invited him in, he shook his head impatiently.

"Your coat, Watson, and hurry. Timing is crucial, and we have several places to be before evening."

I didn't hesitate. Long years as Holmes' companion have removed several layers of my natural hesitation. There were only two choices, follow as best I could, or be left behind and miss whatever was to come. My coat over one arm, my hat in the other hand, I slipped out the door, and Holmes pulled it tight behind me.

Just as I was turning to go, I saw him bend at the waist, reaching down to run a finger along one of the cracks in the sidewalk. Straightening, he removed a bit of paper from his pocket and carefully folded whatever he'd scraped from the ground inside. I thought to ask what he was doing, then thought better of it. All in it's time, he'd say. Why force the words?

There was a carriage waiting at the curb, and Holmes slipped inside. I followed, and without a word the driver was off. I should have liked to have asked where we were bound, but experience told me the words would be wasted. Holmes had the predatory, hunter's gleam in his eye I'd seen so many times before, and I knew he'd speak to me only when he was ready. I contented myself with slipping into my coat and leaning back to watch the streets as we passed.

The carriage headed into the center of the city, and it was only a short time before we pulled to the curb. A quick glance out the window confirmed my suspicions. We had pulled up in front of the morgue.

"Why have we come here?" I asked in surprise. "I've told you the man was in my flat, alive and standing as you, or I."

"If, indeed, the man you saw was the same Michael Adcott you pronounced dead," Holmes replied, exiting the coach and motioning the driver to wait, "then I would expect without a doubt to find that body here. The fact you met a man you believe might be Adcott does not mean the Adcott for whom you signed the death warrant is not dead."

He fell silent then, leaving me to follow the trail of his thoughts to their obvious conclusions. A brother? A close cousin? Why hadn't it occurred to me? My ears were burning with the sudden realization I'd acted the fool, but I followed Holmes into the morgue entrance nevertheless. What had I been thinking? That dead men walk?

It was late in the day, and it was unlikely that many would be walking the halls of that dark place, but Holmes entered with familiarity and confidence. There was nothing to do but to follow.

It took a good bit of cajoling on Holmes' part, but the clerk behind the desk, a dour little man with too-thick glasses and a perpetual frown that creased his brow with deep wrinkles, finally agreed to escort us to where the body of Michael Adcott had been stored. The body was, he assured us, right where it had been left, tagged and recorded.

"I sent you a report earlier this very day, Mr. Holmes, did you not get my message? Do you think he's up and walked away then?" the man asked. His voice was grave, but now there was a twinkle in his eye that had not been present as he argued with Holmes at the front desk. "They do that, you know. One day here, the next up and gone, and days later wives and mothers, daughters and friend are here, telling how they've met the corpse on the road and asking after the remains. Sometimes, they're just not there."

I didn't much appreciate the clerk's levity, but Holmes paid the man no mind at all.

"You saw the man, then," Holmes asked, watching the man's face with keen interest. "You verified the information you sent personally?"

The old man cackled. "If he's in my book, Mr. Holmes, he's in my morgue. There are papers that must be filled out to remove a corpse, and permissions to be granted. No such papers have passed my desk for the late Mr. Adcott, and if there are no papers, there is no reason to look. He is here."

"Then let us wish him Godspeed on the road to the next world," Holmes replied. "Let us see Mr. Adcott for ourselves, and then we shall see what we can make of the rest of this business."

Unfortunately for my own sanity, the remains of the late Mr. Michael Adcott were indeed missing from their slab. No note, no papers of explanation or permission. The numbers and documentation lay neatly in place, but nobody accompanied them. The small man was less talkative now, and a sight less sure of himself.

"Perhaps he's been moved?" I suggested.

The man shook his head, not turning to meet my gaze, only staring at the empty spot where a dead man should be. "There were no papers. No one moves without paperwork. No one."

"And yet," Holmes observed mildly, "Mr. Adcott seems to have been in the mood for an afternoon stroll."

"Shall we search for him?" I asked, ready to button up my sleeves and get to the task at hand.

"There's no time," Holmes said, his expression shifting in an instant to the old, familiar intensity of the hunt. "I didn't really expect he would be here, but without knowing ..." He trailed off, and I followed him out the door. Without a word he was back in the cab and holding the door impatiently, as I made to enter.

At just that moment, there was a cry from down the street, and I turned, startled. A young man darted from around the corner of the morgue, tousled hair waving about a roguish face and a scrap of paper clutched tightly in grubby fingers. I recognized him at once, as did Holmes, who rose and exited the carriage, calling to the driver to hold.

"Mr. Holmes," Wiggins cried, coming to a halt and holding

out the paper. "We've found him, sir, as you asked."

Holmes didn't say a word, but took the paper from the boy's hand, eyes blazing. He read quickly, then folded the paper and slipped it into one of the pockets of his coat. "The others are posted?" Holmes asked quickly.

Wiggins nodded. "He'll not slip past, sir. Count on it."

"I do," Holmes replied, almost smiling. Shillings changed hands and Holmes had turned away and re-entered the carriage before I could ask what was written on the paper, or who the 'irregulars' were watching.

I knew better than to ask. I'd seen that expression on Holmes' face too many times. He was on the trail of something, and until that thing was in his grasp, he'd not share it with anyone. Best to keep to his side, watch his back, and wait until he was ready to speak. The carriage took off without a word from Holmes, and I realized suddenly that he'd already anticipated our next stop. Either the note Wiggins had brought him had confirmed his suspicions, or it was related to another matter.

I watched out the curtained window as we passed deeper into the city, trying not to think of the scrap of paper in Holmes' pocket, or the pallid face of Michael Adcott, staring at me from heavily lidded eyes.

Jepson walked briskly down the street, hands pressed deeply into the pockets of his coat. At his heel, Michael Adcott followed more slowly, his gait forced and clumsy. Jepson paid his companion no mind. They had to meet Jeffries at the court before the last of the judges left chambers, and that left little time indeed. Time was slipping through his fingers too quickly, and things he'd expected to have accomplished had evaded him.

The Doctor—Watson was his name—was a problem. The man should have seen what was obvious, feared what was less so, and signed off on the paperwork by now. Without that signature, they would be forced to let a court decide Michael's state, and at the very least, he'd be found unfit to speak on his own behalf. That wouldn't do. Michael Adcott would not be speaking to anyone, and that was another problem.

For the moment, things were under control. The serum

—alone—was not enough. That much had been clear in the sketchy notes that had been included with the case that lay waiting in the laboratory at St. Elian's. Only fate—a bottle of wine—and a loose tongue had given Aaron Jepson the information he needed.

"There was a time," his father had said, head drooping toward the table and fingers loosely gripping his wine glass, "when we had ways to deal with our problems. There are things we know," the old man had glanced up to see that his son knew the "we" in question. "We have always harbored our secrets, Aaron. There was a time when we kept them less guarded— when a Rabbi could walk the streets with the respect of those around him. They knew. I know."

Several glasses of wine later, and a lot of cajoling and flattery on Aaron's part, and those secrets had begun to surface. Men from clay. The Kabbalah. Patterns of words and form, rhythm and breath that emulated the formation of the first man. A mad Arab poet who spoke as if he were in another place and time and stared into distances that were not there. Those words, copied onto the canvas corner of a tent and guarded, studied— shifted over the years and recombined. Alhazred, the man had been called, and though he'd been mad, he'd been a prophet, as well—a prophet of power. At first the notion had seemed ludicrous. A clay monster controlled by he who gave them life, born of the proper words, the proper earth—the prayers—the faith of the Rabbi, and the vision of a madman.

Sworn to secrecy, Aaron had left his father's home and set out to find a use for his new secret. Money wasn't everything, he reminded himself often, but no money was certainly something to be avoided. Money was power, and if you were not the one with the power, you were under that man's thumb. Aaron Jepson would feel the pad of no man's thumb.

A chance encounter had landed the wooden case in his hands, won from a drunken, reeling fool at poker. The man had wagered it against a five pound note, holding it close to his chest and announcing drunkenly that the secrets to life itself were contained within, and that this being the case, it certainly qualified as collateral against a five pound note. The case had been found floating, he claimed, off the shore of the island of Eucrasia after the explosion that destroyed it's culture and its ruler. It had been handed from man to man since, and nothing was known of its contents save that they came from the laboratory of one Dr. Caresco Surhomme. Jepson, who knew of Caresco's work, had agreed impatiently, the four threes in his hand itching to be slapped to the tabletop, and he'd walked away with all the other man's money, and the wooden box. He could still hear the fellow's words, echoing in his mind.

"You'll find more than you bargain for in there. I'm glad to be rid of it. God bears a very heavy burden my friend – don't be too quick to shoulder it."

It had taken years of poring over correspondence and articles, diatribes about and against Caresco and fictions written about the man and his work, to realize what it was that he possessed. It had taken another five years to analyze the serum and attribute it to one small corner of Caresco's work. The reversal of aging. The shaving away of the ravages of time. Taken to the extreme, and with certain additions of Jepson's own device, reversing the process of death.

Jepson shook his head to dislodge the memories of what had come before. More important to see to the needs of the moment. He led Michael around a corner and disappeared into the fog. Jeffries would know what to do, and they would have to set about whatever it was with haste. Both the serum, and the incantations and amulets his father had reluctantly provided him, were proving less stable than he'd anticipated. The row in the cell earlier had been a near miss that Jepson didn't want repeated.

The asylum brooded over the street beneath, giving off a sensation of density, immovable and old as time. When the carriage stopped in front of that place, and Holmes stepped out, tipping the driver, I was sure he must have lost his mind. The Asylum of St. Elian had been deserted since I was a young man, still pursuing the degrees and education that would lead me to a career in medicine. The stories I'd heard had seemed laughable enough at the time, but faced with the reality of the place, they came back to me full force, flickering across the years of my memory with chilling speed.

Holmes didn't hesitate. He moved from carriage to door with purposeful steps, reached up and rapped his knuckles against the door sharply. I stared at him, then at the building before us. I would have bet my last pound that no one had passed through that door in ten years. Holmes knocked again, then turned to me with a purpose.

"No one seems to be about, Watson. We must hurry."

"Hurry where?" I inquired.

Holmes was already trying the door. It was, of course, locked, but I noted with amazement and some alarm that Holmes had pulled a small tool from his pocket and inserted one end into the lock. A few deft movements of wrist and finger, and I heard the sound of tumblers sliding into place. The latch gave way, and Holmes pulled the door open, slipping inside. There was nothing to do but to follow him into the shadows, and to pray that most of what I'd heard back at university was the hogwash it had seemed. The heavy door closed behind us with a loud *CLICK*. Holmes fiddled with it for a moment, then turned away.

"Locked," he whispered.

There was no light, but Holmes moved quickly and easily, making his way to the first set of doors to his left. He pulled out a box of matches, lighting one and holding it up as we entered the room. It was a crude, antiquated sort of laboratory. On one of the benches, a few crates lay open, packing material and other items strewn about as if opened and gone through quickly and without much care.

I moved up beside Holmes, glancing over his shoulder as the light from the first match flickered, then died. The quick glimpse had been enough.

"Medical equipment," I said softly.

"As I suspected," Holmes replied, turning to the other bench. He lit another match, and this time he slipped along the wall and found the light switch, flicking the power to on.

"Someone will see," I hissed.

My friend ignored me, and, with a quick turn about the room, I realized my error. There were no windows. We were encircled in stone as surely as if entombed. The light was dim, but Holmes made use of it quickly, making his way to a wooden case flung open on one of the bench tops.

The case held two vials, and I saw that Holmes had looked past the greenish, glowing liquid and the other – full of something that looked like sand. He plucked it from the case and held it to the dim light. Then he removed the folded paper he'd brought away from the doorstep of my flat and opened it. He held the two objects together, and I saw that what was on the paper was a bit of clay. Red clay, unlike anything near the city. The dust, or sand in the vial had the same reddish hue.

"Watson, have you heard of a man named Caresco?"

I started violently, nearly toppling into the nearest of the benches. "Caresco Surhomme? ""Caresco is dead." I replied, a bit more calmly. "His island was buried in volcanic ash. That Caresco?"

Holmes held up a hand, and I fell silent. The greenish contents of those vials had taken on a new reality for me. I had heard of Caresco and his hellish experiments, and I knew the end he'd reached. Playing God with the human anatomy, enslaving the mind. Seeking a cure for death and time.

"I know of Caresco, as well," Holmes assured me. "I was fairly certain his work was tied up in this, but there is more – something vital that we are missing."

He returned the card to the case and began pacing the room, rooting through the remaining cases and tossing paperwork and equipment aside without a thought. Clearly, he had no intention of trying to keep our illegal entry a secret. Holmes turned and lifted the vial in his hand so that I could see it more closely.

"Clay?" he asked. I didn't believe that he expected an answer, so I remained silent as he replaced the vial and continued to stare into the case.

Then, just as I was certain he would turn in disgust and leave that accursed place, Holmes laid hand on a small leather-bound volume. Pulling it nearer to the light, he flipped open the covers, which had nothing upon them but a few characters rendered in Hebrew. Holmes' brow furrowed, and he flipped the pages rapidly, grunting under his breath.

I glanced over his shoulder as he flipped through the pages. The script was coarse, and though I'm no linguist, I saw what seemed to be alternating lines of Hebrew and some antiquated form of Arabic. There were notes scribbled in the margins. I could make out none of it, but Holmes seemed to be devouring it all.

"There's no time to waste, Watson," he said at last, replacing the book where he'd found it and tidying up the room just enough so that a cursory glance would show no evidence of our presence. "We must hide ourselves."

We moved none too soon. Holmes had just switched off the lights, and dragged me down the hall and through another door when we heard the grate of an iron key turning slowly in the lock. We could just make out the cursing voice of Aaron Jepson through the solid wood, growing louder as he pushed the door inward and stepped inside.

"I curse the day I first laid eyes on you," he was saying.

There were two sets of footsteps, and I guessed that the second set must belong to Michael Adcott. There was no answer to Jepson's ranting diatribe, but the echo of shuffling feet followed his hard, sharp strides into the hall. The door closed once more, and Jepson moved into the laboratory, shoving things about roughly. I held my breath, but he seemed to notice nothing amiss.

"I suppose there's nothing to do but to put you back in your cell and go in search of Watson," he said at last. "There is more than one way to get a paper signed, and if Jeffries can't straighten this out without the good doctor's input, then input he shall have."

Only silence was his answer, and the two sets of footsteps moved closer to us once again, passing into the hall and by our door, moving into the gloomy interior of the old asylum. Holmes hesitated only for a moment, then followed. I trailed behind, moving a bit more slowly, dragging the tips of the fingers of my right hand along the wall beside us as we went. I didn't want a chance misstep to alert Jepson to our presence. Indeed, I had no idea what Holmes planned to do, and I wanted to be as ready as possible for any circumstance.

We followed the pair down into the bowels of that wretched structure, and at last I felt Holmes' hand on my arm, and came to a stop. Just ahead, around a final corner, there was a stationary glow, as if a torch or a lantern were being held. I could still hear Jepson's muttering voice, and I heard, as well, the clatter of keys on a ring. Holmes was moving ahead again, very slowly now, and I followed, keeping well back, not wanting to cause my companion to stumble.

Jepson's words came into clearer focus. He was agitated to a state that his voice quavered. If I'd been seeing him in my office, I'd have prescribed a stiff brandy, and a few hours rest, but Jepson was as far from being prepared to rest as a man could be.

"I'll find him, don't you worry," he was saying. "I'll make him sign those papers, show him the error of his ways. He saw you, plain as the nose on his face, walking about. Alive. No reason he shouldn't sign, and by the Gods he will."

There was more. His lips never ceased their motion, the words flowing in an endless stream. There was the solid CLICK of a key turning in a lock, and the creaking of rusted hinge, followed by the shuffling of feet. I started to inch forward, not wanting to miss a word of what was being said, but I felt Holmes' hand gripping my shoulder tightly, and I grew still.

He leaned in close and whispered into my ear. "Something is afoot, Watson. Listen!"

I did—and there were two voices. The second, far from coherent, began as a low moan, shivering up from some deep darkness I could not equate with human consciousness. I heard the scrape of shoes on the stone floor, but they weren't measured steps. The sound was random and wild, quickly drowned out by the wailing voice. It rose from a moan to a banshee screech so rapidly that I was physically stunned by the blast of sound. There was a crash, and a loud cry, followed by a volley of crazed curses.

"Now, Watson," Holmes hissed. "We must hurry."

Without looking back, Holmes rounded the corner and stopped. I came up short behind him and stared over his shoulder.

Aaron Jepson was shoving Michael Adcott toward the door

of the cell frantically, cursing with each breath, fighting to avoid the other's flailing arms. Adcott's hands were clasped to his head, fingers twined in his thin, wispy hair, ripping, then gripping again, and ripping more, tufts drifting about the two in a slow-motion counterpoint to their struggle.

"Get in that cell, damn you," Jepson screeched.

Adcott either didn't hear the words, or ignored them. Backpedaling, he rammed Jepson into the stone wall, spun to the side and began slamming his own head into the stone with such force it made me sick to watch. Jepson, momentarily stunned, took a step toward Adcott, then seemed to think better of it. He reached into a pocket and pulled out a wrinkled sheet of paper. With trembling voice, he began to read, or, at least I believe he was reading. The words were unfamiliar to me, and his entire frame was shaking with such frustrated rage that he couldn't hold the paper still enough to read.

Adcott stilled, just for a moment. The man turned toward Jepson, who stood between Holmes, myself, and Adcott, providing a face-on view. To the day of my own death – may it be more lasting and complete than poor Michael's – I will never shake the image of those eyes from my mind. They flared with inner light so intense that I could imagine worlds within, arms flailing and voices crying out for salvation. Those eyes were windows straight to hell, and in that second, they burned full force into the soul of Aaron Jepson.

Jepson began to back away. He tried to continue the chant, but the words failed him, and his voice faltered, then fell silent. Adcott was moving with quick, purposeful strides that slipped from a walk to a full sprint in seconds, propelling his slight frame with alarming speed toward his tormentor. The madness of moments before had blossomed into an intense concentration of anger.

"My god," I whispered.

Adcott hit Jepson at a full run. One of Michael's hands gripped the other man by the throat and drove him backward into the stone with a sickening crunch. Jepson tried to speak, but no words or air made it past the iron grip at his throat. His legs buckled, and as Adcott continued to drive forward, squeezing ever harder, Aaron Jepson fell to his knees, eyes bulging.

In a voice so clear and pure that it washed over the scene like the water of a mountain stream on a flame, Adcott spoke. He spoke three short words, and as he spoke them, Jepson struggled a final time, eyes widening further, if that was possible, and then went absolutely limp, the life crushed from his body.

Adcott staggered back. The effort of concentration had drained him, and the otherworldly rage and strength with which he'd propelled himself vanished. He turned, noticing us for the first time, and raised a hand toward Holmes, as if asking for something. Seconds later, I saw Michael Adcott die for the second time in a single week, and I nearly fainted away on the spot.

Holmes had me by the arm and headed toward the door before I had my wits fully about me, and we were out and into the waiting carriage without a word, closing and locking the doors of St. Elian's behind us firmly. Holmes stared out into the night, and I collapsed into the seat and my own thoughts as the carriage hurried into the fog.

We were seated in Holmes' study, sipping brandy and watching the fire that very night. Holmes was staring into the flames, not offering any explanations, and at last I'd had all I could stand of it.

"Holmes," I said, "back in that laboratory, you said there was something we were missing. I'm familiar with Caresco's work, and the abominations he is purported to have created. I have heard that he managed to reverse aging in some subjects, though at the cost of the mind – this is beyond me. I never heard that he had cheated death, and in any case, Adcott showed none of the madness reported of the earlier experiments. A great number of very learned men have pored over the bits and pieces that remain of his notes – they found the research to be an abomination, and the process beyond repair. Was Jepson a mad genius?"

"He was not," Holmes replied, turning to me at last, steepling his fingers and taking a long breath. "Aaron Jepson was a Jew."

I stared at my friend, wondering if something in the night's business had addled his brains. He returned my gaze with his usual frank, half-amused expression firmly in place. I waited and, finally, cracked.

"What in the world," I asked slowly, "can that possibly have to do with this mess?"

For the first time since we'd left that accursed asylum, Holmes smiled.

"How much do you know of Jewish history?" he asked. I shrugged, and he continued. "There are legends," he said. "Legends that trail back to the Holy Land itself, and that are known to only a select few. When you first spoke to me, I was nearly certain that Adcott must have a twin that no one had been aware of, or a cousin who bore a striking resemblance to the dead man that they were trying to pass off as Adcott to win the funds from the tontine. There were obvious answers, but the obvious answers caved in, one by one.

"I then began to explore the less obvious, and there was something that bothered me from the start. Jepson's name. I knew it was familiar to me, but Aaron is hardly an uncommon name, nor is Jepson, so I set out to see if I could find what it was that itched at my mind.

"My search led me to the local temple, and the Rabbi, an old friend, was very helpful. He remembered the name of Aaron Jepson immediately, but the Jepson he remembered had been dead for many years. Jepson was a Rabbi, or had been. He migrated to London about fifty years ago and made a home here, but even among his fellows he was shunned. Rabbi Jepson had spent years in the Arabian Desert, studying and fasting. He came away from that study—changed. He had scrolls and teachings that were unfamiliar to the others already settled here, scrolls dealing with legendary creatures and the Kabbalah. Scrolls dealing with the Golem. It is reported that he had a scrap of cloth that contained verses from Alhazred himself, inscribed in blood. Bits of a larger work."

"The Necronomicon?" I asked dubiously. "That work has long been passed off as legend. And what in the world is a Golem, Holmes, and what has it to do with Michael Adcott?"

"The Golem was an instrument of revenge," Holmes continued. "It was a creature formed of clay and brought to life by the will, faith and rage of a Rabbi. It would serve the purpose of that rage, and only the Rabbi himself could control it."

"And Adcott?" I asked, not certain I wanted the answer. "He was no man of clay."

"No," Holmes agreed. "He was a man brought to a sort of hellish, painful un-life by the science of Caresco Surhomme and the diabolical research of Aaron Jepson. It was the incantations, and the clay, Watson, clay from another place – another time. Clay inherited from Jepson's father, Aaron Jepson Senior—Rabbi Jepson. The substance in that sixth vial was the very clay of which I speak. When I found a bit of it on your doorstep, I was intrigued. When I saw the vial, I was certain.

"Through the power invested in the clay, Jepson was able to exercise enough control of Adcott's re-animated form to lead it about in public. You'll recall that Adcott never spoke, not at your first meeting, nor at any time thereafter."

"But he did," I said at last. "He spoke, right at the end. What do you suppose he said, and what enabled him to do what he did?"

"He spoke in Hebrew," Holmes answered at once. "The words were very clear, and I suspect, appropriate. I believe that Adcott's soul managed to make use of the same power that the elder Jepson would have used to animate clay. He used his will, and his faith, and he spoke the only words that could bring him peace.

"He said 'It is done.'"

I stared at Holmes for a long time, watching for doubt, or belief, anything in those wise eyes that would prove a clue to the mind beyond, but he had turned his gaze to the fire once again, and grown silent.

"I wonder," I said, rising and retrieving my coat, suddenly very tired and ready for my own home, and my bed, "who got the money."

Holmes didn't look up as I departed, but I sensed the smile in his answer.

"To the living go the spoils, Watson. Always to the living."

Shaking my head, I opened the door and made my way into the late evening fog.

AUTHOR'S NOTE: Stories are written for a wide variety of reasons. When I first started selling my work, I had some goals. One of those goals was to get into a magazine called **Deathrealm**. *I had tried, very literally, dozens of times to get past the editorial desk of Stephen Mark Rainey and the guinea pig who ate rejected stories. I was always close. One day, irritated beyond belief, I sat down to write a story intended for no other purpose than to break that market. It became one of my favorite works…one that has been reprinted several times, and that did—indeed—become my first (of several) appearances in Deathrealm. It is also, again, a very Lovecraftian tale. Maybe I DO write that sort of thing more than I believed…*

From My Reflection, Darkly

It has been hours since I last saw Eric, a lifetime of shattered reality, an age of dissolving foundations. An eternity. I know I should go to him, should try to help, but I know also that he would not answer if I called, would not come to the door, were I to knock. I must look horrible, hair unkempt, face scratched from my attempt this morning to shave. I could not use the mirror. Truth begins with proof, yet I will fight it until death forces its own truth upon me, if that is the choice. I cannot bear to know what he knows, to see what he has seen, and they may be watching, for they have seen me. I will not look into a mirror.

Eric Blount, student of the arcane, philosopher of dreams, academic genius, was my best friend. I grew up a quiet, shy boy, uncertain of what I would do with the great gift of life ahead of me. Eric knew from the beginning what he wanted. He wanted to go beyond the gift, to see whence it came and to follow it to the source. Life held no contentment for such a man. He inspired in me both awe, and an incredulous, half-hero worship that even the ridiculousness of the bulk of his conjectures failed to stifle. He was incorrigible.

It started harmlessly enough, or so it would have seemed. He spent hours alone, pouring over volumes of arcane "wisdom," searching page upon page of words left behind by such luminaries as Eliphas Levi, Aleister Crowley, and Madame Blavatsky. He spent a good three years among the adepts of the modern Rosicrucian Order. That was an amusing period, what with the candles and altars and assorted implements of their rituals. It proved not enough. Though he claimed certain successes with these unlikely arts, he was not happy with his progress.

"I would be dead twice over before I could discover anything truly valuable at this rate," he complained one day. "Rationality aside, for it is the greatest of hindrances in this type of affair, suppose, say, a poet, while writing, is in some sort of rapport with a higher state of existence? Or an artist? Certainly a writer can mold from mere words on paper images that warp reality as we know it, yet make it real for us at the same time."

"Are you saying, then," I asked with a grin, "that our reality can be made less real by these arts?"

"Not exactly," he answered. "I am trying to suggest, and I know that this will amuse you, but bear with me, that such creative acts have had a great part in the creation of our reality. I believe that man, given a choice, sees, touches, and believes in what is most convenient or beneficial to man. Were enough people to decide to perceive red as yellow, it would be yellow, and all those who still saw red would be issued corrective lenses and labeled as abnormal."

"Surely you can't believe this is true of everything?" I exclaimed, certain that I would get the better of this argument. "If that were the case, could we not disbelieve the chairs from beneath us and send ourselves crashing to the floor?"

Eric's eyes momentarily shared my amusement, but only momentarily. The light of the hunter on a trail was in them, and I resigned myself to another period of his eccentricity. We spoke then of other things until the bottles were both dry. Eric then rose, bidding me a good night's sleep, and departed to the shadows of the streets. As he left, he stopped by the large, full-length mirror I kept beside my door. Being particular of my appearance, I had purchased it some years before at an auction. He spoke no word as he gazed at his reflection, but his expression was odd, as though struck for the first time by some peculiarity of his appearance. At the time, I paid this no mind. Since then I have had occasion to dwell upon it in sharp detail. I wish to God I'd reached out and put my fist through that glittering surface and shattered it then and there, damning the risk to bone and skin.

It was several weeks later that I decided to return Eric's visit. After procuring two bottles of Campo Viejo, 1972, I began the mile or so trek to his flat I seldom made use, in those days, of public transportation, and the risks of operating a private vehicle on the roadways grew less enticing with each passing headline. Eric felt the same. Our visits invariably began with one of us making the journey across several residential blocks and through the paths of the Municipal Park. The trip was somewhat more uncomfortable on my part, with Eric living as he did among the more run-down tenements, and I hurried my steps upon reaching his side of the park.

The front door to his building hung open, dangling loosely from one hinge. I made my usual mental note to prevail upon him to move out. His reasons for remaining in such seedy surroundings had always remained obscure to me. His inheritance as last survivor of a well-to-do family left him amply provided for.

"It's the freedom, Percy," he'd once told me "No women peering from their window to yours, discussing things that are no business of theirs and drawing attention to where it is not desired. People there' respect your privacy, as long as you lock it away tightly enough."

He had indeed succeeded in this. I knocked on the metal-reinforced door loudly, nervously glancing every few seconds over my shoulder to the shadows that seemed to shift behind my back whenever I denied them my attention. After a few moments, I heard hurried footsteps within.

"Who is it?" Eric called, not opening at once.

"Percy," I answered, "only Percy, Eric, come to return your visit, and your wine. Open this door, you know how this place makes me nervous."

There was a clatter of chains, a rattling of bolts and locks, and the door swung wide. I did not enter immediately, my shock would not allow it.

The apparition before me hardly reminded me of my friend at all. He was gaunt, not in the manner of who is starved, but as though he'd not slept for days perhaps weeks. His eyes, bloodshot and dark with fatigue, darted about wildly, searching the shadows that had plagued me only moments before. I found my own fears magnified intensely. Pushing Eric aside, I darted into the room, slamming the door behind me.

"My God, man!" I cried. "What is happening here? You look half-dead, not to mention delirious. You've even gotten me nervous."

"Come," he replied, "to the den."

I followed, depositing the wine bottles on a table in passing and making a vain attempt to straighten my now disheveled appearance. I made to glance into the mirror in the hall, but to my consternation, it was curtained with a cloth of deepest jet. I moved to pull it aside, and Eric leapt, his shaking hands clutching like talons, and grasped my arm with surprising strength. My hand stopped inches from the dark cloth covering the' mirror.

"What?" I stuttered, backing away and pulling my arm free. "What in hell are you doing? I only wanted to comb my hair! Why in the blazes is the damnable thing covered, anyway?"

"Not yet," he hissed, tugging on my arm. "First come to the den, it is safe there."

By this time I was beginning to seriously fear for my friend's mental state. I had seen him act in peculiar fashion on many occasions, but never to the point of inducing discomfort upon himself. It made me not a little nervous to be alone with him in such condition. With a longing glance at the mirror, I allowed him to lead me through the beaded curtains that closed off his "sanctum sanctorum" from the more mundane parts of his home.

This room had never failed to invite my curiosity, even my awe, I suppose, in the intricately piled and jumbled displays of occult bric-a-brac it offered, the shelves piled with dusty, ancient volumes, and walls hidden behind brightly colored tapestries. It was truly impressive, or had been so on my last visit. Now it was filled with clutter along the walls. The furniture, even the rug, lay piled in corners, dragged as far as possible from the room's middle. A brazier stood, small wisps of incense smoke wafting ceilingward from its coals, marking the very center of the floor. Around it was drawn a circle in white, perhaps six feet in circumference. Concentrically, a larger circle, seemingly burnt into the wooden floor surrounded it. From the outer edge of the larger circle, the points of a pentagram shot outward toward the walls of the room. Strange symbols lined the space between the circles. With a final entreating glance to be certain I'd followed, Eric leapt over the symbols to land, breathing in ragged gulps within the center ring.

"Come on, man, for God's sake!" he cried. "I promise I'll tell you everything, but you've got to get within the circle!"

Seeing no alternative but blind flight, I succumbed to his wishes, walking slowly into the circle.

"No!" he cried, as my foot scraped accidentally across one of the symbols. Scrambling about on his hands and knees, he feverishly repaired the damage with a piece of charcoal from beneath the brazier. Sweating profusely, he turned to face me, sinking to the floor.

"I know how this must look," he finally gasped. Silently, I believed he did not, but I listened as he went on. "Believe me, if I could find a way to stop it, I would. There is no way out now, I have seen too much."

"What have you seen?" I asked, seating myself opposite him on the floor. "You look to be half-dead, man. When was the last time you slept?"

"Slept?" His eyes grew vague, as though considering it

himself for the first time. "What day is this?"

"You must be joking!" I exclaimed. "It is the 10th, of course, but surely you...."

"Nothing at all is certain any longer, Percy," he cut me off. His eyes seemed hollow, vacant and far-away. "I have found what I was searching for, you see, nothing can ever be the same."

"Humor me," I forced a grin, "and explain exactly what it is you've found. That seems a good place to begin to unravel this nonsense and return you to your senses."

He looked at me with eyes filled with such anguish that my mind whirled in confusion. "Nothing, Percy," he repeated, "nothing can be the same. I have rent the veil, torn it asunder, and I have peeked beyond it to that which was hidden. They are watching for me now, and I dare not leave the circle."

"They?" I queried, palms beginning to coat with cold sweat. "Who, and where are they? We are alone here, alone in a room full of old relics and scented smoke."

"No, that is only the outward appearance." He reached out, placing a pale, trembling hand on my arm for emphasis. "Do you remember our last conversation? We spoke of reality."

"I remember a silly notion you brought forth about reality being only a product of our own desires, surely you aren't referring to that nonsense? I am an imaginative man, but not that imaginative...."

"I am," he stated flatly. "I have come upon knowledge, forbidden knowledge, and now there is no way to turn back."

"Nonsense," I asserted, rising to my feet. "You are coming out of here with me now, before this gets completely out of hand, and we're going to see a doctor."

Eric made no move to follow, only dropping his head pathetically into his hands. "You don't believe me," he choked out. "Percy, for God's sake, I am not neurotic, I fear for my soul! They are in the mirror, waiting, waiting for me!"

It was worse than I'd thought. He was shaking uncontrollably, quivering in fear. Reluctantly, I resigned myself to humoring him for the moment. Returning to my seat on the floor, I said, "Eric, tell me, then. Convince me of what you fear, and, if you do not, then I will bear you out of here by the strength of my own two arms, and no nonsense!"

Staring intently into a shadow off beyond my shoulder, he began once more to speak. His voice had a distant, echoing quality, perhaps an illusion of the great empty chamber in which we sat, and the growing shadows that surrounded us.

"It started with the sky," he began. "I had determined that, if my theory were correct, there would be something else behind every sight that met my eyes, a deeper level of reality. The question, of course, was how to see it. The knowledge, or theory, that something lies hidden in an illusion, is not enough to dissolve the mental conditioning of a lifetime. I searched for hours, even trying hallucinogenic drugs, in an attempt to find a deeper truth in the sky. I found nothing.

"Then I had an idea. There are several occult practices in the realm of what is known as visualization. One is the manufacturing in your own mind an image of such clarity that you can smell, even taste it. I studied this at great length during my time among the Rosicrucian Order."

I stopped the smile from flooding my features, but only just. My memories of Eric during the period he'd just mentioned were both amusing and vivid. He'd thought himself quite the sorceror, for a while.

"I decided," he continued, "to take this concept one step further. Choosing the image of a great, curtained window, I put myself into a deep trance and began to visualize in the manner of my training. I have quite a talent for this particular discipline; it took very little time to create my window."

"Previously, this image, as well as that of a great, ornate door, had been used as links to certain realizations of self, doors to my subconscious, you might say. This time I determined to go yet another step. I opened my eyes slowly, forcing the image to remain clear by deepest concentration. What I now sought to achieve was the superimposing of my image onto the screen of the sky.

"At first, it wavered, all I could see was blue. Then this began to blur, my eyes crossing somewhat, as if looking not directly at the sky, but out of the corners of my sight. This began to create a void, one I was able to weave my own images upon."

"The window?"

"Yes," he sighed, "but that was just the beginning. After a few moments of the euphoria of success, I began to follow the visualization ritual to its conclusion. I began to open the curtains I had implanted on the sky, to seek what lay beyond the cool, pleasant blue we take for granted."

"And you saw something? A hallucination, perhaps?"

"No hallucination, Percy." His eyes snapped back from the shadows to claim mine with an almost audible snap of energy. I nearly jumped. "I saw a deepening, swirling void, Percy. There were no clouds, no dust, nothing at all but endless spirals. I felt drawn to their center—pulled—and I fancied that my back lifted from the solid surface beneath me, beginning to spin, turning with the vortex that spun faster, darker, and deeper every second within the squared expanse of the window I'd created.

"I ripped my gaze free with only the greatest of efforts, closing my eyes and struggling frantically to erase them the accursed image of that window. My arms and legs were numb, disconnected from my control, and the spinning sensation continued for what seemed an eternity. I was awash in nausea, unable to stabilize my churning stomach or my chaotic thoughts.

"Eventually, I awakened, as if from a dream. My head ached as if I'd single-handedly emptied a fifth of cheap Scotch. I rose and looked about myself. It had grown dark. I glanced upward at the starry blackness, or where it should have been, and was struck immediately by a wave of vertigo, dropping me back to my knees. The world seemed to shift beneath me, the air to whirl. I clamped my eyes closed again and staggered to my feet. I have never experienced such a terror, Percy. I feared to look upward, feared I would be sucked into the void and lost for eternities...

"When my mind had resumed control, I ran, my eyes rooted to the ground beneath my feet."

"Eric," I cut in, alarmed. "You mentioned a hallucinogenic drug. Were you...."

"No, Percy," he stated earnestly. "I swear to you that I was on nothing stronger than a single shot of scotch, and that several hours before. I saw what I saw, and it is still there. Percy, the sky is an illusion!"

Now certain that he was in dire need of help, I determined to get him out of the house. I placed my hand firmly upon his arm. "'Eric, you have to come with me, man. Look at yourself. This is insanity!"

"But there is more," he cried, shaking free and backing away slightly. "Mirrors, Percy, they are not what they seem, either. I have seen, and have been seen, and we are not alone."

"Surely you don't wish me to believe mirrors are conspiring to subjugate humanity," I tried to answer lightly. "I am an imaginative man, but not that imaginative."

"Do not jest, Percy," he cried, eyes flaring in anger. "I will show you, damn it all! You may laugh, then, but you will see! You will see more than you wish."

He leapt to his feet, then, running to the hallway, almost scurrying. I followed as quickly as I could, intending to make certain he did not escape me to return to that shadowed pit of a room.

He stood, when I found him, directly in front of the covered mirror. His countenance in the deepening shadow was spectral, ethereal. I shivered despite myself.

"Come," Eric demanded, "gaze into the mirror. You will see. Reflections are merely a defense, a screen erected by our minds against comprehension of truth we want no part of. Come on, if you dare, and prove me insane!"

My heart pounded, crashing so loudly within my ears that I could feel the warm pulse of blood through my veins, could hear the innermost workings of my body's organs. I could not, at first, do as he bid. Finally, I calmed somewhat, chiding myself for a fool.

"All right, Eric," I answered, moving and speaking slowly. I made every effort not to sound patronizing, no telling what his reactions might be. "I will look into your mirror, straighten my hair, which I am certain must be a sight, and then we will march out together, you and I, and gaze at the stairs. When this is all done, we will take the wine I have brought, retire to my own apartment, and I shall call you a doctor. Agreed?"

He merely nodded, a pleading in the depths of his eyes reaching out to me to pull him free, to prove he was wrong. My throat was strangely dry as I stepped forward, reaching up to grab the black covering and push it aside. Eric turned his head violently to the side as I did this, pressing his face into the wall. I paused for a moment, placing my hand reassuringly on his shoulder. He was shuddering his weakened frame wracked with convulsive sobs. My will hardened by the urgency of his need for help, I yanked aside the curtain and gazed, admittedly with great trepidation into the glassy surface of the mirror. Almost immediately I breathed a sigh of relief.

There, returning my stare was my own face, lines of such seriousness creasing it that I had to favor myself with a laugh. Wiping my face with one sleeve, I reached up, and straightened an unruly lock of hair before speaking.

"Now, Eric," I began, ""here I am staring back from your mirror, the only thing likely to abduct you—and that for your own good. Pry yourself from that wall and look, then we are leaving."

Very slowly, his movements stiff and disjointed, Eric pushed himself away from the wall. His head was lowered to the floor, and his voice faintly from beneath, low and subdued.

"You see what your mind projects," he said. "I know they are there, waiting. My mind has lost its ability to protect me. I've pushed aside the veil."

"For God's sake," I cried, grabbing him roughly by the hair in my exasperation "look at it, Eric, look! It's only your..."

I reeled backward, crashing painfully into the opposite wall and falling to the floor. Eric screamed, screamed in terror beyond my comprehension, screamed until the very pressure or the sound blocked thought from my brain. I could see him standing, eyes glued to the mirror, waving back and forth —entranced.

I could not rise to help. My mind would not even consider it. His reflection, when I had raised him to the mirror, had not been there. Instead, a swirling blackness had appeared, a hole in the reflective surface, a nothingness. As I'd fallen back, reaching to cover my eyes, a movement had grasped at my mind.

Eyes—I think they were eyes—coalesced in the maelstrom of nothingness, staring. They had seen me, just before I fell away, and now they had Eric!

I heard a scrabbling sound. Was something clawing free of that damnable hole? I looked up, fearing to the depths of my soul what I would see. I followed the scratching sounds to their source. Then I screamed. My mind blanked, bending with the sound, emptying of sanity. The scrabbling sound was Eric, his fingernails. They clutched vainly at the sides of a black void that had replaced the mirror in its frame. His head was gone, up to the shoulders, sucked into the whirling morass of darkness.

Scrambling to my hands and knees, I began to claw my way down the hallway, careening off walls, caroming from furniture. I broke a large vase and crawled through its shattered pieces, embedding them painfully in the flesh of my hands. The door loomed before me like the impenetrable wall of some vast fortress, every shadow, every object seemed to take on an ominous, other-worldly importance. Threats beckoned, thinly veiled, from pulsing shadows. My mind could not sort it out, fumbled open the door, rushed outside, and ran, never stopping, never looking up, through the park, across darkened streets, and finally into my home. I have covered the mirrors, and the windows. I have spoken to no one. Who could I tell? What if, in their ignorance, they tried to cure me as I did Eric? What if they put me before a mirror? Did I see what I believed I'd seen, or was it some strange, psychic projection from Eric's own madness? If he was right, were the walls around me solid, or illusion? The floor? Could I tumble to hell by looking deeper into the wooden slats beneath me?

There is no answer. Two choices have presented themselves to me. The first is this. I should go to the door, cast it open, and gaze into the cool, calming depths of the night-darkened sky. Then I should go to Eric and drag him from the insanity he'd enmeshed himself so deeply in that I'd been dragged behind, beyond the strength of reason and rational thought.

I have chosen the second. I have called the emergency room at the hospital, they are on their way now. If my theory is correct, my memories should hold the world together as long as no further disruptive data reaches them. The two pencils are sharp. I only pray that my eyes are the key. At least I shall never again look into a mirror. I will be safe.

AUTHOR'S NOTE: I have always been fascinated by ritual magic, the Tarot, I Ching, divination, talismans, anything bending one world in toward the boundaries of another. The Lost Wisdom of Instinct is another story I wrote specifically for Deathrealm – but I would have written it anyway. It involves doors, and rituals, the Tarot, and a healthy dose of erotic fantasy. This is the first story I ever read aloud at a convention with the result that a woman came up to me after the reading to tell me she had to go smoke a cigarette when I was done. I'll let you be the judge...

The Lost Wisdom
of Instinct

"Welcome," the woman said, bright luminous eyes glittering in the dim, yellowish light of the huge hallway. Behind him, Alex felt the heavy dampness of the storm. His hair was matted to his forehead, and he reached up self-consciously to brush stray drops of rainwater from his eyes.

He did not speak immediately. She was beautiful, despite being almost ten years his senior, and he was soaking wet; he'd hardly prepared himself for such an ignominious first meeting.

"I'm Alex Beauchard," he said at last, stepping inside and letting the huge door close behind him. "I've come to study the professor's papers."

"I've expected you, Mr. Beauchard," she said with a warm smile. "It's good to see that my late husband's work is still interesting to someone. My name is Madeline. Let me show you to your room at once so you can get dried out. Then, would you like to join me for tea?"

"That would be nice," he answered. Her eyes were intense, dark and compelling, and Alex realized he was staring. Thankfully, she did not seem offended, nor did she make an effort to avert her gaze. Turning away and breaking the contact with an almost audible snap of energy, Alex reached for his bags.

"This way," she said, motioning to the gloomy interior, an odd little smile forming on her lips. "For convenience's sake, I've put you in the room next to Robert's study."

Feeling a bit dazed, and still dripping from the deluge outside, Alex followed her up a lushly-carpeted stair to the building's upper floor. The walls were hung with tapestries and ancient portraits, only dimly illuminated by small, flickering bulbs mounted on ornate, mirrored sconces. For a long, strange moment, he felt like he was climbing into another world.

If the hallway below seemed large, the upper hall was immense. To the right, he looked out over an intricately-carved railing and down at the spacious dining room, while above, a giant, glittering chandelier hung from the peak of the sharply-angled ceiling. The aura of opulent, decadent wealth overpowered him. Paying more attention to his surroundings than to where he was going, Alex nearly tripped and fell over Madeline, who had stopped in front of one of the many heavy oak doors lining the hall and opened it.

Stepping inside, he was greeted by the strong aroma of sandalwood. A small desk lamp with a green-tinted globe provided the only light, which he quickly noted set the style for the entire room. Out-of-control spider plants cascaded down the sides of hanging baskets that flanked the windows. The drapes were deep, forest-green velvet over ruffled white linen. The bed was of mahogany, as was the roll-top desk that held the lamp and the one chair, which was padded in black leather. The carpet was also green.

"Robert called this his 'jungle room.'" Madeline smiled at him again. "There used to be many more plants here, and there were these horrid animal heads all over the walls. It's one of the few rooms I've changed since his death."

"But it's extraordinary," Alex said, genuinely impressed. He set his suitcase by the door of the closet and placed his briefcase on the bed. "I'll just change out of these wet things and join you—?"

"In the sitting room," she finished. "Downstairs. Just off the main hall to the left, before you reach the dining room."

She turned to leave, then glanced over her shoulder with another of those curious little smiles before disappearing into the hallway. Alex felt a prickle of—*something*—which he managed to dismiss as a product of his fatigued and disoriented state of mind. He turned his attention to getting out of his wet clothes. Grabbing his suitcase, he dropped it on the bed and flipped it open, grabbing the first set of clothes he found and headed for the small attached bathroom.

This room, he found, was equipped with a round, sunken tub, already filled with water! More of the encroaching plants hung in the corners and spilled over every ledge. In the ceiling above the tub, a shaft topped by a green skylight had been cut straight through the attic to the roof above. Occasional flashes of lightning sent shimmering beams of emerald light down this shaft, giving the gently rippling water a primeval, fathomless quality.

He stared, and stared.

Lush green foliage stretching out in every direction, blotting the sky above. Warm, loamy air—moist—tasting of forests and rivers. Smelling of vast, endless trees and ropy, hanging vines.

The cries of birds—deafening—padding footsteps crackling through the brush to the left and right. Sunlight filtering through leafy boughs that sway to the grasp of a cool breeze to trace intricate shadow designs on the ground at his feet.

A deafening crack of thunder split the night, startling Alex back to his senses. He found himself gazing dumbly down at the bathtub. Turning, he quickly flicked on the lights and bathed the room in bright, man-made light. He was shivering, and everything around him seemed somehow detached from reality. He went to the sink, splashed water on his face and stared at himself in the mirror.

Why in hell, he thought, *is that tub already full, anyway? And what's wrong with me?* His reflection didn't answer, and he managed to finally shrug it off. It had been such a long, tiring drive.

Stripping out of his wet clothes and hanging them across the rack beside the sink, he washed up quickly, slipped into clean slacks and a pullover shirt, and ran a comb quickly through his rain-matted hair.

He grinned at his still-disheveled countenance, and it grinned back. His good spirits were returning. He returned to his room and put on dry shoes, appreciating the comfort of the leather chair, and the strange daydream faded quickly. He had a lot of questions about the late Professor Robert Auburn Devonshire, the answers to which lay in the study just next door. Although he knew there was plenty of time to get to it later, he had to suppress a strong urge to open the door to that room and explore before meeting Madeline downstairs. He had gone through a lot to be here.

Robert Auburn Devonshire: parapsychologist, archaeologist, linguist, mystic, and Alex's mentor, had been one of the most controversial figures in several academic fields for decades. His death was as mysterious as had been his life, perhaps more so. One day he'd been teaching at the university, smoking his pipe and smiling that curious, all-knowing smile that Alex remembered only too well; the next day, he was gone. Dead. His heart had stopped, an occurrence that medical science had never been able to adequately explain. It just stopped. It had been seven days since Robert's death. Reluctantly, with the memories burning brilliantly in his mind, Alex turned away from the study door and descended to the lower floor of the huge house.

He found the sitting room with no trouble. Madeline sat in one of two antique Queen Anne chairs pulled close to a small table of the same design. Like all the other rooms, this one spoke eloquently of wealth and comfort. Glass-fronted cases lined the walls, filled with artifacts from the late professor's many archaeological journeys: grotesque, oddly asymmetrical pre-Colombian figurines from Mexico and South America, frightening tribal masks from ancient Africa, polished jade sculptures from the Far East, depicting inhuman, mythological creatures that somehow, in these surroundings, exuded an aura of disconcerting, eldritch awareness.

"Feeling better, Alex?" Madeline asked as he drew near.

"Almost human," he said as he sat beside her, again, barely able to keep from staring. This second meeting only affirmed his initial impression of her. She was beautiful. Her long, auburn hair hung loosely over her shoulders and halfway down her back. She was–his mind sought the proper word—willowy. She was tall for a woman, and so slender as to appear almost fake. As before, it was her eyes that held his attention. They seemed to reach out to him, speaking a language all their own in a sort of tandem, sensual echo to her words.

"Robert mentioned you many times when you were his student," she told him, handing him one of the delicate china cups of steaming tea. "You may not know it, but you were something of a favorite with him. That's why I agreed to let you come here. That, and the fact that the most important thing in Robert's life was his work. If it does some good, through you, and perhaps myself, his death will have more meaning. Did you know that before Robert and I were married, I was his student, too?"

"No," Alex answered. "He never mentioned it. As for giving his work meaning, I hope I can live up to that. Your husband was mostly responsible for my direction in life. I guess you could say I consider him something of a mentor. I was never much of a student before I met him."

"But you're close to your doctorate now?" She smiled again, and he almost blushed at the combined emotions the praise and her smile elicited.

"Just my dissertation to go. That's why I 'm here. But what I meant was, Dr. Devonshire gave me a new outlook on academics. I was struggling when I first walked into his class. I wanted to take on the world of archaeology single-handedly, and discover secret places and ancient magic. But I was much better at dreaming than handling reality—much better.

"Then I met your husband. He was like no professor I'd

ever met. He would really challenge the class. He'd pull out the most ordinary stone from some ancient battlefield or castle, and he would recreate more from that stone than I could from an entire building.

"I remember his words, 'Everything you learn on this planet, every morsel of knowledge you gain, no matter how mundane it may seem in the learning, has a purpose to serve. Never look at learning as work, but as something as natural as breathing. When you can take the stone knife of a man who lived a thousand years before your own conception, and you can draw him forth from the depths of your mind, clothe him and give him thought with your imagination and your knowledge, then you will understand. No lesson learned is ever wasted.'"

"And what lessons have you learned, Alex?" Madeline asked, still smiling. "Have you opened any windows of your own? I recognize my husband's words on your tongue. Have you learned enough, do you think, to bring him back in your words? To clothe him and return his thought? Are you ready?"

The questions caught him completely off guard. They were the sort of questions he'd been asking himself for a thousand-plus miles. Setting his cup down, he felt a kind of release inside—some subtle pressure removing itself from his mind. He found himself suddenly telling this strange woman things he'd told no other as though it were the most natural thing in the world.

"That is what I want to find out," he said. "I want the things he stood for to have meaning. Nobody else in the entire academic community wants to believe that he was close to the answers he sought. They are all afraid, and jealous. If I don't do him justice in this thesis – if I fail to prove his value and genius, then I have learned nothing, and they have won."

She drew a deep breath and her smile seemed to leak into the depths of her eyes. "Somehow I knew you would be the one, Alex. I wonder if you're aware that you were not the only applicant for this work? That others have tried to gain access to his papers before you?"

Alex started slightly. He'd been under the impression

that he was utterly alone in his interest. "Who?" he blurted, realizing his outburst might sound rude, flavored as it was with a sudden, inexplicable outrage.

"Other students, one of his old colleagues—even the university tried to obtain custody. They offered to buy his notes."

"But why? They never believed in him. All they ever did was question his work, even his sanity. Why would they want his notes?"

"Don't you see? They wanted to finish him off. He died trying to prove his theories with virtually no support. If they could get control of his papers, they could pass them off as whatever they wanted, seal them away in some vault in their library, and that would be the end to it. That was why I waited. I am very glad that you have come here, Alex. Very glad.

"But do not forget," she added, "that the dissertation is not the end in itself. The knowledge—the seeing—are what he would have had you seek. Robert had very little concern for the likes of his 'peers.' But his students, his true students—"

She leaned toward him, and her eyes grew larger, filling his vision. For just an instant he felt a tinge of vertigo, and he wondered—almost hopefully—if she meant to kiss him. She stopped just short, and said softly, "Robert would have been proud to know that you came."

She drew back, and the spell of the moment parted like the gossamer thread of a spider's web. For those few seconds, it was as though the professor had never died. His spirit seemed to inhabit every corner, every shadow and flicker of light, surrounding them with that aura of mystery and promise of power just beyond the ordinary senses that made every thought, every motion sensual and vibrant, alive with purpose and meaning. Alex knew that she must feel it too—that it was a shared emotion.

Sitting back slowly, he reached for his tea, which had begun to cool. Without a word, she warmed it with a splash from the teapot at her side. She refilled her own cup, never once dropping her eyes from his. Was she challenging him? His heart thundered, for she was such an amazing, exotic,

unbelievably attractive woman. He found himself suddenly—
perhaps wrongly, though he couldn't help it—looking forward
to more than the study to come.

Finally, rising, she said, "You must be exhausted, so I'll let
you go to bed. I'm afraid I'm a bit of a night owl, so I may not rise
as early as you. You'll find food and coffee in the kitchen. Make
yourself at home. You may want a bath—the tub in your bathroom
is actually a converted spa. The water cycles through once a day
from an automatic pump and drain system. The temperature
control is on the wall. Another of Robert's eccentricities. He did
like his creature comforts. I must admit, I've found that tub—
interesting—at times."

So that explained the full tub. Alex almost laughed. Still, he
thought, it would be easy to slip into that water first thing in
the morning, when the light of the new day's sun was cleansing
the shadows from the world. He wondered what she'd meant by
"interesting," but at the mention of bed, his body almost melted
with the sudden awareness of his fatigue.

"Until tomorrow, then," he said, also rising. "It has been a
pleasure to meet you, Madeline. Thank you for the opportunity
to proceed with my work."

She nodded, then turned and left the room. He watched
her go, and again, very unscholarly thoughts rushed through
his mind, synchronized with the subtle swaying of her hips. He
drained the last of his tea and returned to the stairs.

Upon reaching his room, he undressed quickly and slipped
between the sheets of the huge old bed, letting his head fall
softly onto the pile of down-filled pillows. He was unused to
such luxury. With green-fringed shadows all around and the
scent of newly laundered sheets filling his senses, he drifted off
to exhausted sleep. And he dreamed.

The air was heavy with the moisture of vast forests and roaring
rivers. Exotic flowers perfumed the air, along with the hint of lush green
foliage and the faint musk of unseen animals. Insects buzzed and flitted
about him, some larger than any he'd ever seen, and in wonder he moved
forward, parting branches and hanging vines with a brush of his arm.

Alex was on a path, though it appeared seldom used, walking
toward the sound of moving water. As he swiveled his eyes to the right

and left, he saw impossibly tall trees, the leaves of which he did not recognize, and splashes of colored flowers in hues so subtle he couldn't put a name to them. There were butterflies and large, bee-like insects humming among the blossoms. Like harmonic accompaniment to the sounds of water and insects, birds flushed from perches so far above him they were out of sight in the vast greenery, rustling and calling out to one another in warning at his approach.

The path ended in a clearing that revealed the bank of a river so wide he could just make out the tree line on the far side. The water was a green, algae-ridden color. Further out, he saw bubbles and foam moving rapidly downstream, but nearest the shore a small, nearly stagnant pool was trapped by a cut in the bank. The odor of rotting vegetation and the hum of insects was overpowering.

Turning again to the path, which now paralleled the river, he followed the line of trees whose branches overhung the water, draped with curtains of moss and clinging vines, until he reached a larger clearing.

In the center was a stone table—an altar? On the altar he could make out a prone form, and he moved closer, mesmerized by the sight. As he approached, he saw long tresses of auburn hair dangling from the end of the altar. It was a woman—Madeline, he realized with shock— and she was dressed in a gown of pure white linen. Her arms were folded upon her breast and her eyes were closed. He approached her, reaching out a tentative hand to touch her shoulder, but a mist rose suddenly, masking her from his sight. When he should have touched her skin, all he felt was rough stone, and he could not penetrate the hazy shroud that had appeared.

His senses slipped away from him then, with an odd twist, like vertigo, or a dream of falling from a great height, and darkness suddenly claimed him.

"Madeline!" he cried out, sitting up straight in the bed, sweat pouring from his brow. He couldn't immediately place his surroundings, and the shadow tendrils cast by the small forest of spider plants along the walls moved disorientingly about, as though a breeze blew through the room. It took a long time and several deep breaths to get his thoughts under control, and to realize it had been a dream.

"Damn," he muttered to himself. The sound of his voice rang comfortingly in the darkness, and the shadows receded. He almost laughed, but a slight chill remained in his heart. That hadn't been a run-of-the-mill nightmare. So vivid! He would almost swear the smell of decaying algae lingered in the air—and he could still feel the muggy dampness of that primal atmosphere.

Rising, he went to his briefcase and removed his journal. His eyes were already beginning to droop with weariness again, but before he returned and dropped off to a—thankfully—dreamless slumber, he recorded everything he could remember about the dream, adding a couple of comments about his strong attraction to Madeline Devonshire. The rest of the night passed without incident.

The next morning, he rose early and made his way to the kitchen, where he put on a pot of strong, black coffee. He found eggs and bacon, and made some toast, allowing his mind to ease slowly into full wakefulness. When he'd finished eating and cleaned his dishes, he poured the rest of the coffee into an insulated pitcher he found in a cupboard and headed back up the stairs.

He'd hoped that Madeline would, despite her warning, be up and around to give him an initial tour of the study, but she was nowhere to be seen. With any luck, though, the professor's notes would prove to be organized in his typical fashion, and it would be a simple matter to sort through them.

Approaching the study door, he found it to be much like the others on the upper floor, with a single notable exception: a brass plate was screwed into the wood at eye level. It read, "Enter with an open mind, depart with understanding."

He smiled as he slowly opened the door. He had seen those words, years before, the first time he'd entered Devonshire's classroom. He hadn't known at the time what a depth of truth was to be found in them. He had come to understand more in his two semesters in that classroom than he had in a lifetime of adolescent dreams and study.

The office proved to be an imposing sight, which was essentially what he'd expected, but he was undaunted. The desk itself was huge, covered with impeccably-stacked papers and writing materials. There were shelves, glass cases, tapestries hanging from the walls, all depicting various ancient lifestyles and religious beliefs—a wonderful hodge-podge of things that had made up the professor s life.

He moved around the desk, sat down in the comfortable leather chair, and focused his attention on the lower drawer, the large one designed to accommodate files. Pulling it open, he smiled broadly. There they were! The notebooks, literally hundreds of them, each labeled with that meticulous, mechanical script that he'd always admired. It would take countless hours to labor through these, but the rewards!

Breathing a great sigh of satisfaction, he closed the drawer reluctantly, and let his gaze wander over the surface of the desk, only to discover one more surprise. Pushing aside a stack of unanswered correspondence, he found a series of small rectangular lines engraved in the wood, arranged in the shape of a Celtic cross, with three more outlined boxes in each of the four corners. It took a moment for his mind to register, but it finally clicked. Tarot cards. The shapes were there for the arrangement of Tarot cards.

The windows....

He rose and went to study the cases along the walls. Here, he found tribal artifacts from some of the oldest civilizations ever discovered, pieces museums would kill for. The professor had always venerated the most ancient minds, deferring to what he termed, "the Lost Wisdom of Instinct."

Finally, after he'd browsed the books and the trinkets, the papers and notes left by an untimely departure from this world, he came to the window. It wasn't actually a window; it was merely the frame of one with the requisite curtains and blinds, but with no opening in the wall, no view of the outdoors or another room. It was symbolic—the center of everything that had brought him to this place, of everything the professor had believed in. It was the window in the solid wall, the veil that cloaked human understanding.

The barrier to be overcome.

There are other worlds, other levels, if we can only find the means to see them...if only we are ready.

More echoed wisdom from the past. He stood for a long time in front of the closed portal, staring at the grain of the wood that backed the frame, watching the way the light brought out the highlights in the paneled surface. He never heard a sound, and the hand that landed softly on his shoulder nearly stopped his heart.

"What do you see, Alex?" Madeline asked, her lips so close to his ear that he felt her breath tickling the hairs on his neck. "What do you hear?"

"I don't know," he admitted, forcing himself not to lean back against her, keeping himself rigid and erect and not thinking about the implications of that particular state. In the back of his mind, despite her subtle overtones of reciprocation, he couldn't rid himself of a certain guilt. She was, after all, the widow of the one man in the world that had truly made a difference in his life.

"The question, actually," he continued, "is what did he see? What did he hear? I've waited a decade to find out, and I always thought he'd be here to guide me when the time was right."

"Everything he learned is here," she said, gliding silently to the desk and running her hand smoothly over the wood, "in one form or another. Everything that was a part of him is here. I am here, for the first time since he died."

Turning from the blank window and its enigmatic challenge, Alex went to stand beside her. She was staring fixedly at the outlined Tarot boxes, lost in some world of thought all her own. After a time, she said, "Do you believe in the cards, Alex? Really believe?"

The question caught him completely off guard. He thought back to the first day Professor Devonshire had brought his cards to the classroom. Alex's attitude had been one of detached amusement, certain that it was all some sort of experiment, or a joke. There had been many moments since then for reflection on his own ignorance.

The cards—each student had been required to buy his own set, or, if he had the talent, to design and paint his own—had become an integral part of his life. Some of the students had never gotten it, had left with as little belief as when they'd entered the classroom, and, therefore, with as little understanding. Alex had painted his own cards carefully, checking and rechecking his notes to be certain that he had omitted no symbol, no pertinent reference. It had taken nearly two months to complete them, coating them at the last with clear lacquer to make them stiff and slick.

"Yes," he answered finally.

She raised her eyes to his, and crossed to one of the shelves that lined the wall to his left, passing so closely that the silky softness of her dress teased across his shoulders. She reached up to the top shelf and pulled down a small wooden box that he recognized instantly. The professor's cards. The first such cards Alex had ever seen and by far the most intriguing.

Turning back to the desk, she gestured to him to seat himself again in the leather chair. She perched on the edge of the desk, her leg so close to his arm that he felt himself tremble. What the hell was wrong with him? At a decisive moment such as this, all he could think of was what the widow of the one man he'd ever truly respected would look like without her dress!

Then she had the box open, and his eyes drifted thankfully down to the cards. They were bright, painted in the most vivid colors he could imagine. They seemed brand new, though he knew they were at least twenty years old. The back of each card, appropriately, he thought, bore the image of a window that framed only blackness. Tenderly, Madeline set the cards on the desk.

"He was the last person to touch them," she said softly, not letting her eyes drift from the cards. "He used to shuffle them each night, then read them the following morning before he began his day's work. He shuffled them his last day here—I watched him. They were never read."

The implications of what she was saying hit him like a sledge. Controversy had surrounded the professor's death, a long string of unanswered questions. Here, in front of him, he knew he could find those answers. Suddenly, he knew with complete certainty that he was not here merely to write a paper for a stuffy academic degree.

"Why didn't you read them?" he whispered. "Surely you know the cards. Why did you wait?"

"I know more than the cards," she answered enigmatically. "I had a dream, a dream that another would come. It was as if Robert were speaking to me as I slept. I was afraid if I touched the cards, if I disregarded my dream, that whatever message they contained would be warped, or lost. I didn't dare."

Alex could feel a tension growing in the air, linking her to him, and both of them to the cards, and sweat began to roll down the sides of his face. His mouth was dry and his hands trembled. So, this was it. This was the moment of discovery. There would be no weeks or months of study, no delving through notebook after notebook of meticulously recorded experiments and facts. It would come down to the moment, and the belief. The instinct.

Taking a deep breath, he reached for the cards, and closed his eyes. Normally this was the point where he would begin the slow shuffle that would place them in the proper order for reading. In this case, he merely held them, clearing his mind of all thought. It was not easy. He felt Madeline's hungry gaze, tasted her perfume in the air, sensed the beating of her heart.

Several moments passed before the familiar, warm peace began to settle over him, and he felt the beginning of the trance state calming his nerves. He didn't begin until he was absolutely certain he was ready. There would be no second chance.

The professor had taught him the pattern long ago. It was not the system used by most followers of the Tarot, nor were the cards exactly those one could buy in a store. Subtle changes had been made in the commercially available decks over the years; steps had been taken to obscure the strongest secrets locked in the ancient symbols and designs. A few questionable luminaries, such as Aleister Crowley and Eliphas Levi had hinted at these changes, even offering a second, and also erroneous, set of cards and numbers to further confuse things. The secrets were there, locked away in the collective unconscious of mankind. It took many years of study, however, to sort them out and make a usable system.

Alex turned over the first card, representing the person for whom the reading was done, in the center spot on the cross, face up. The Magus. *Of course,* he thought, flipping over the next card, crossing the first with it. The Queen of Cups. A water card. *Probably Madeline,* he thought, but he brushed the intruding images aside and continued. It was necessary to keep his mind clear, to not influence the reading in any way.

He flipped the next card and placed it directly above the first. The Knight of Wands. Fire. He was a Leo himself; could he be an influencing factor? At the bottom of the cross, he placed the foundation, the Ace of Pentacles. Primal energy. Earth. To the left, the Nine of Cups—Debauch—excess in pleasure, in indulgence; to the right, the Four of Swords. Four, a number of completeness—an air card.

He felt a slight ripple in the air around him, the familiar detached tingle that working with the cards always brought; but stronger than he remembered. He was aware, on a level just beyond his concentration, that Madeline had moved closer, that her thigh was pressing tightly against his shoulder, and her long auburn hair was draped down, forming a framework around the cards. Her perfume was like incense.

The next three cards he flipped in rapid succession: that which has gone before. The Fool, naive innocence and unshakable faith, walking into the unknown. The Ace of Cups, the fountain of malleable energies. The Four of Pentacles, stabilized power, completed work. An Earth card.

The next three cards, bottom left corner of the cross. The cards that expressed the central focus of the reading. The first, the Universe. Totality. Understanding. The second, the Two of Pentacles—the infinite inevitability of change. The Hanged Man, upside down, head to the stars, the earth and its control falling away below. Images began to fill Alex's mind, as if the meaning of the cards had begun manifesting itself, via pure sensation. Instinct.

Madeline's fingers touched his hand, and suddenly, his perceptions sharpened, heightening the sensation that he was observing the reading from a distance. The air felt heavier, moist and clinging. He made himself continue.

The third corner, the method—the answer. The Hierophant —a spiritual teacher. The Two of Cups—partnership, constant blending. Lust – originally labeled Strength– passionate energy, primal desire. Her fingers felt like fire on his skin, moving over his body in a sweet caress, but he could not be sure of its reality. His heart pounded so strongly, so fiercely, with the energy of the card and the heat of her touch that thought fled on its own this time.

Three more cards. One more corner of the cross. Powers that influence, but are beyond the control of the querant. His hand, somehow, reached out and flipped the cards and they fell into place as though unseen hands had guided his. The Ace of Wands – Fire, unleashed energy, unchecked passion. The High Priestess – the mother spirit – the source of all growth. And Death. Not the physical death, but the end of one thing and the beginning of another. These last three cards danced before his eyes as he felt himself falling back.

The chair was gone, but though he braced himself mentally for the shock, his head and back did not strike the floor. Madeline was pressed so closely against him now that they seemed one body, one being. Their clothing had melted away, and they drifted, afloat in some other-worldly bed of buoyant dream. There was a violent snap—a twist of vertigo that nearly drove him into unconsciousness. The walls of the room faded to green.

The trees stretched out in front of him, and he could hear the rushing of the river's water somewhere to his rear. His knees scraped on the stone of the altar, rubbing into the soft fungus that grew there, but he ignored the pain.

Madeline lay beneath him, her eyes closed and her head thrown back in ecstasy. Her long lithe body moved like the slow, powerful swells of an ocean, undulating with relentless, growing ferocity. Alex felt his naked flesh sliding over hers, thrusting roughly, pounding to a rhythm that rose from deep within him, pressing in from the trees and rushing over them in the sounds of the river and the buzzing flight of insects.

Madeline moaned, meeting every thrust with her hips, grinding back against him. Her cries blended in smooth harmony with the birds and the rushing of water. Dim thoughts invaded his passion, calling to him, calling him back but he cast them away with violent mental strokes, bending the energy to the motion of his body, and the heat of hers. The world around them, the impossible world of giant trees and primordial energy, ceased to exist. He bent his lips to her writhing form, slamming his tongue in to meet hers.

The moment rose toward ecstasy, toward a dizzying peak of blended sweat and blinding energy, pulling them both into a spiral beyond thought, where each motion, each bend of muscle or twist of limb was primitive – instinctual. The feeling was of such completeness, such fulfillment that he knew that he wept, and he could see the tears running freely from her eyes as well. He moved his tongue over her face, cleaning away the salty droplets and wondering at the sweetness of their taste.

They climaxed together, just as they had begun, one body blended of two psyches—trembling and quivering; his seed rushed into her in great spurts and his arms encircled her so tightly that he felt her tighten imperceptibly, then surrender to the moment, pressing himself into him as thought she might melt right through his flesh.

Then, overcome by almost maddening fear, he pulled away from her with sudden, desperate strength. She clung to him, called to him with her eyes, molded her limbs around him, but he was moving, shaking his head slowly back and forth. It was too much—and spinning now, losing clarity. He no longer felt the stone beneath him, or the silken sweaty touch of her skin. There was nothing but haze, whirling and receding to a face, a familiar face, fuzzy, yet discernible through the mist.

His head struck the desk with a sharp crack, and he slid to the side, dropping to the floor in a heap. The pain made it difficult to focus on his surroundings. He lay on beige carpet, huddled against the side of Professor Devonshire's desk. Although her perfume lingered tantalizingly in the air, there was no sign of Madeline. Shaking his head and regretting the action instantly, he rose to his knees, pulling himself back into the chair with great effort.

The cards were gone, all but one, and it lay in the center of the desk. It was The Universe, but it was not one of the professor's cards. Alex recognized it as coming from the Crowley deck, his own favorite prior to creating his own. His memory sought and found the text from Crowley's *Book of Thoth*, and a sad smile drifted across his features.

"We are come unto a place of which every stone is a separate jewel and is set with millions of moons.

"And this palace is nothing but the body of a woman, proud and delicate, and beyond imagination fair..."

Alex rose, walking around the desk to stand once more before the window. They were gone, on to the next challenge, the next level—or beyond. He now understood his role here, Madeline's need for his energy, which had been fired and consumed in the final Tarot reading.

But his own work was just beginning, for he now knew at least one of the answers he had sought; he was not ready. There were still things to draw him to this world, things that he could not take with him. He would follow, though.

Someday, in some way, he'd yet to discover, he would open that window again, himself, and he would step through.

Alex glanced over his shoulder at the desk, and the notes, and the work to come, but before he moved, turned once more to the window, gazing into its empty depths. Smiling, he raised a hand, and he waved.

*AUTHOR'S NOTE: This is another story written for a market. It was never published in that market—but I still love the story. I wrote this to try and get into the **Borderlands** series edited by Thomas Monteleone. The series died before it had a chance to be selected or not, but it was on a short list…which I consider a major coup. This story is about trying to reach deep inside and find what really matters…*

Rending the Veil

"So," Gretchen breathed in Toby's ear, "why *do* you write that stuff?"

"What do you mean," he returned, twisting his head to the side as her tongue slipped past his earlobe to the tender skin inside, "that stuff?"

"You know," she breathed, "killers, monsters, vampires. Why not write about what's real?"

"And what would that be?" he asked, pulling back and turning to gaze into her eyes. "What is real? What *should* I write about? Everyone is always telling me what *not* to write; suppose you do the honors?"

"I don't know," she said, turning her face away from him just slowly enough for him to catch the expression that told him she knew all-too-well. "Why don't you write about what turns you on?"

"You want me to write about you?" he grinned, reaching for her playfully. "You want me to write porn?"

"No," she said, her face a mask of seriousness, "I mean what *really* turns you on, you know? What's inside here." She tapped his forehead with a long, lacquered nail. "Write about what takes you away, what opens the doors. Write about what really matters to *you*."

"And what if it doesn't matter to anyone else?" he asked. "What if I empty it all out and nobody will read it, or worse yet, nobody even wants me around? Have you thought of that?"

"Have you?" she countered, her eyes narrowing a bit. "I'd read it."

"Would you still want me around, though?" he asked, suddenly as serious as she was. "What if I'm not who I seem to be? What if you hate me?"

"Oh, like you're the first to think of *that* one," she teased. "What did that old poet say, what's his name, ...uh, "all that we say or seem, is but a dream within a dream?"

"Poe. The poet's name was Poe. He wrote a lot of stuff that nobody read until after he died, and most everyone agrees he was mental. Maybe that's what happens when you write about what's important. Maybe it's not meant to be written."

"Maybe it's the *only* thing that is. Maybe he died because, once it was all out, his mission was complete. He was empty."

The conversation ended abruptly as Gretchen either lost interest or changed tactics, moving forward to plunge her tongue between his lips and press him back against the couch roughly. She never fooled around; even sex was serious – never trivial – never without some hidden, subliminal meaning.

As her fingers and tongue began to march across his skin, sending the world about him twisting away in waves of pleasure that insinuated themselves into his thoughts, then slammed through him like a battering ram, his mind detached itself, whirling off onto a tangent of its own. Or was it another of hers? He left his body, her body, all of it behind, left it in her eager, capable hands, and took off.

What turns you on?

The words took on shapes and substance all their own, pushing at him, nudging him, unwilling to release him without an answer. He didn't know the answer. He didn't know what it was that was important, and the sudden knowledge hurt worse than any physical blow, worse, even, than Gretchen's teeth, which he was vaguely aware of snapping at his nipples and tearing at his chest, more than her nails, which bit into his back and left little trails of plowed flesh and blood behind. Her mark. Her brand.

She had stimulated his mind, but she held him on a leash of the physical—gripped him by the endings of nerves that could distract thought and dissipate the very answers she'd sent him in search of. She was like a witch, or a siren, dragging him ashore with her body, by the beautiful, tinkling lilt of her laughter, which became the tearing, searing heat of her passion when he drew too close. He knew that once her hands were on him, once their limbs were intertwined, everything he did or thought was attributable, in some way, to her influence.

Were his thoughts hers as well? Did she want him to write about what turned him on, or about what turned *her* on? Did she know the answers, or was she seeking them through him? Maybe his answer lay in her eyes, or in her heart? Maybe she *was* that answer.

If so, could he write that down? Could he bring the essence of her to his fingertips, controlling her as she controlled him, and divert that essence into the firmament of words? If he did, would she be trapped, revealed to the world, or would he? What would come loose if he opened up the gates of his mind? What turned him on?

If he set it all free, would it even be he who was writing, or would she control that too? If he attempted to grab and hold her, blending her reality with his words, would he pour himself out instead? Would she take that as easily as she took his body, sucking it down and leaving him a dried out, empty husk? Would it matter?

He was brought back to his senses by the haunting music of her cries, back into a sweltering inferno of flesh and sweat, twisting hair and animal groans. He saw her eyes for just an instant as they flashed past his own, and he grasped at that vision. As they climaxed together, their hearts pounding as one and their flesh as nearly fused as the physical world would allow, he held that image.

He held her for long, sweet moments, letting his thoughts

settle, holding the image of her eyes. He felt her damp hair brush across his face, felt the scent and taste of her sweet, intoxicating breath insinuating itself into his own. He could not see, not with his eyes, but he had visions, clear visions. He drew them from the image he now cherished, the clear depths of her eyes.

He found answers there, too, or at least he believed that he did. Already his fingers itched, aching for the keyboard. The gates in his mind were bowed from the weight of words that must be released or drive him mad.

"What turns you on?" she whispered once more, pulling back slightly and slipping to his side. They lay there, skin pressed to skin, his eyes on the ceiling and his mind far away, her eyes studying his profile and her fingers dancing idly over his body. He ignored those fingers as best he could. He was after her mind.

He did not see her for days. Her class schedule and his own were so divergent that they seldom crossed paths. Too seldom, he thought, at times—at others far too often. He had not studied since she'd left him, had only been to one class – half a class, to be honest.

What turns you on?

His dreams were surreal, fevered landscapes that drew him in and sent him back to his own world writhing in frustrated fear and bathed in sweat. What was he afraid of? The answers he sought wove themselves into tapestries he could never bring to life before their threads unraveled. Secrets whispered from the darkness into his ears and slipped back out, leaving him clutching at their trailing edges – biting his lips in frustration.

He had not eaten. He was not fasting, nor was he suffering for art's sake. The concept of food was lost to him. Coffee cups littered the floor at his feet. His chin was a small forest of grimy stubble. His eyes stared with fevered intensity, burning from too much use – the smoke from too many half-burned cigarettes, hunger.

Trying too hard, he told himself. He was seated once more before the glowing green eye of his word processor, mesmerized and mocked by the blinking cursor, strobing like a solitary sentinel in neon garb.

The caffeine was replacing his blood. The CRT was leaking it's mucous green glow out to engulf his world. It was slipping away – everything was slipping away. He did not feel as though he were in the same place at all.

Trying way *too hard.*

When she entered the room, he hardly noticed. Her perfume wisped past his face, imbedded itself in the patterns of his thoughts, wound around and through him. Her arms twined across his shoulders, which were trembling with denied fatigue. Her hair dangled, tickling his skin and caressing him with an electric field of sensual intrusion. He fought it. He saw her presence in that moment for what it was—an interruption—a distraction.

Damn her, it was her fault. He was creating. He was writing what was important. He was doing nothing.

"Interesting plot," she observed, gazing at the screen over his shoulder and nipping playfully at his earlobe. "I foresee laurels; your fame will spread far and wide. You need a shower."

All true. He let her drag him to his feet, leaving the screen and the cursor to keep one another company as he dragged his sweat-drenched shirt and grubby jeans off in a daze. He staggered down the hallway in her wake, following the distant, jarring hiss of water steaming through pipes. She was waiting, naked in the steam, smiling at him with everything but her eyes.

He did not want this. His head was swimming with visions— the threads wove themselves together once more, taunting him. Once his keyboard was beyond his reach, he ached for it—yearned for it. Once the screen no longer faced off with him, holding him at a creative impasse – blocking the stream of his thoughts – he could picture it filling, letters dribbling from the top down to cover its green surface with words and phrases and syntax of literary perfection.

She dragged him into the tub, sliding the shower curtain closed behind him and drawing him close. Her skin was coated with a slick sheen of soap, and her lips were parted. She appeared hungry, needy—empty. He pulled away, tried to re-orient his whirling thoughts. Failed.

She opened her eyes to him then, just for a second, just long enough. He met them head on, forced his knees not to buckle and ignored the pull of her flesh on his own, on his soul. He caught a glimpse of something in that instant, something that ran and hid, scurrying to the back of her mind and twisting from the assault of his eyes—fear. He was sure of it. Fear, and something more. Then it was gone, scurrying deeper into her mind. She knelt down, diverting her gaze, and drew him down beside her.

The water washed over them. It streamed down his body, washing away his resolve, melting the tapestry. It was like rain across a sun-soaked beach, unable to quench the heat, misting to steam as it crossed their joined flesh. He fought it. He reached back—only seconds, seconds that stretched like years—reached for that glimpse into her eyes.

What turns you on?

Not this, he thought. "Not this," he murmured. She did not hear him. She did not listen. His thoughts swam, whirled. He grasped at them, struggled to free himself – failed. They broke free, sloughing off and slipping away, joining the soapy water as it swirled on downward and passed through the drain.

This time he clawed at her. This time it was *his* nails that bit, *his* teeth that found purchase in soft skin. It was her blood that flowed, her pain. He had no focus. He could not remember what he wanted—what was important. She sucked at him, drew him in, mocked him with the memory of her words – of her eyes.

It ended in a flash. He was there—joined with her—yet he was not. His mind floated, pleasure shimmering through and over him, and the heat that passed between them was incredible —blinding. He tried to speak her name, tried to call out to her to pull her closer—to push her away. He heard her voice—laughter? Tears? Then nothing. Nothing.

He woke with a start. She was there—beside him. He was still in the tub, but now it was filled with warm, bubbling water. Her hands splashed idly, running over his flesh with the soap, twisting in the hairs on his chest. She watched him as if from far away, watched him with deep, hollow eyes, eyes that begged to be filled, eyes that snatched hungrily at his innermost being.

He closed his own eyes, freeing them for a moment.

"What turns you on?" she asked. He did not answer, only laid back against the cool porcelain and the warm water, drooping, letting himself slip down until he was all but immersed. He did not open his eyes.

What turns you on?

Nights came and went, and finally he slept. It was not good sleep. He tossed and turned in the throes of dreams that would dance out of his grasp, fleeing the confines of his memory each time he shook himself to groggy wakefulness, only to return if he let his mind slip back into the darkness. At last he gave it up, returning to his vigil in front of the monitor screen.

What turns you on?

He began:

"There is pleasure, there is pain, and there is more. There are doorways within us that fade and reappear, windows that show glimpses of things that their panes, clearer and stronger than glass, prevent us from touching. There are veils, and there are barriers; none are permanent.

What is necessary is to divert your mind from its purpose —your protection. If you want to know what is beyond the veil, you have to rip it aside. Man's most powerful instinct is survival; your body will not allow you to pass the veil. You need a key.

Pain will work. Pleasure will work as well. In combination, they are more effective. There is another key, a truer key. That key is total release. Your mind protects you, your soul shies away from the truth. You must let it go, if you want to see—if you want to know."

Toby stared at the screen for a long time. He had no idea where the words had come from, nor where they were heading. He had no urge to write more, not yet. It would come. He feared that it would come in an avalanche, burying him so deeply that he'd never claw his way free. He did not erase any of what he'd written; he also did not save it. He watched, and he waited.

She came after six, small cartons of Chinese food she knew they'd never get to in a brown paper bag and an innocent smile with no depth painted across her lips. The scent of the food wafted across the room, itching at his starved body. He shut it out. He did not rise.

She came to him then, sensing the difference, feeling the subtle changes in the air—in the ether. Kneeling, she read over his shoulder as he continued to stare at the screen, ignoring her.

"What turns *you* on?" he asked. He didn't turn to her, nor did he move, just the words announcing his acknowledgement of her presence.

She didn't answer. She moved in closer, sliding her arms around him from behind and letting her hands roam across the emaciated skin of his chest. She did not speak, not to question, not to answer. Her answer was her silence.

He could feel his flesh responding—heat growing without fuel—burning out. He felt curiously detached. Something had clicked in his mind, drawing him sharply inward, distancing him from the moment.

She wanted him. Not his body, exactly—not *just* his body. Not his love, certainly. She wanted his pain—this he knew. She wanted his pleasure, as well. The words slipped back from the screen to haunt him, turning ghost tumblers in the locks of his mind. She wanted him to find his answer, and she wanted to be there when he did. At that moment, when the veil parted and he truly saw, he knew her goal. She wanted to feed.

He could feel her need, palpable, burning through her desire to singe his consciousness. "How do you know?" he asked her. "What makes you so certain that we will reach my threshold first, that it will be *my* vision? How do you know we won't find out what turns *you* on? I'd like to see that—would you?"

As he spoke, he turned and ran his fingers down her face gently—like a blind man searching for something hidden in Braille. He dug in suddenly with his fingers, rending soft skin and feeling it roll back beneath his nails. She flinched, but she did not cry out. She did not pull away. Instead, when his fingers slowed their descent, when the pain should have stopped, she twisted her head slowly, dragging them onward—offering up her skin to his assault.

He sought her eyes. They were the windows, the keys to her thoughts. She moved ahead of him, only enough to prevent contact, only enough to be certain that he would continue to follow. Their bodies blended, blood mingling with blood, tongues and fingers tracing hotter and darker passions across one another's skin. He fought the sensations, fought to control them—to bend them to his own will.

The veil would part if he could concentrate. His physical form, his conscious mind, both were linked to the sensations of the moment – to *her* sensations, her probing control. *He* needed to control that deeper place—that place where things not seen might coalesce. *He* needed to sidestep his self and cross the border. He needed to know she couldn't follow.

He galvanized the decrepit frame of his body, pressed it into service beyond it's limits. He grabbed her firmly, pressed her back and took control. She was using the physical as a union, a joining—he needed that to belong to him as well. He needed to control her.

She trembled beneath him, but she no longer struggled. Her eyes sought his, fought to grasp at him, to convey her need, to twist him from his focus. He ignored them, moving slowly toward his goal, roughly manipulating her flesh, dragging at her own control with the bite of his nails and the tearing of his teeth.

As easily as she had controlled his body, he held hers. Every motion she made he countered, every assault she made on his flesh he ignored with the growing force of his will. She moved to the pain, not away from it, sought a path beneath his control —an entrance to his mind. He barred her way, concentrating.

Moving quickly so she would not sense his intentions, he spun her over, straddling her and twisting the sleeves of her blouse around her like a straight jacket, pinning her arms to her sides and tying it off in a quick knot. Leaning very close and pulling her hair aside softly, he whispered his question into her ear, breathed it so that the breath would join with the rhythms of her own thoughts.

"What turns you on?"

He held her, and she struggled. Her power was in her flesh, and he had slipped the noose, removing her advantage. She squirmed, rubbing herself shamelessly against any bit of his skin she might reach, fighting to turn and meet his eyes, grasping at the control she'd lost.

He watched her, rode his growing arousal, but only on a distant level. It was no longer the focus, no longer the point of control. It would not bridge their minds. He was able to hold her easily. Every struggle, every bid for freedom or control he was able to easily counter with a caress, a bite, or a slap. He watched, entranced, as white images of his hand appeared, then disappeared into a fading redness on her skin.

He reveled in the moment—the discovery of control. He molded her movements, orchestrated the sounds that emanated from her throat. Her flesh was his tool. He would push her to the edge—the edge she'd been ready to cast him from such a short time before.

She stretched herself, grinding her face into the carpet as he pressed her from behind, slamming back into him, then away again as he rode the swells. He felt the climax that was building, about to burst from him in endless waves, but he did not release it. Not yet. He waited, forcing his tortured, weakened flesh to obey him, denying it completion.

She cried out at last, the sound primal and soul-rending, erotic on levels he'd never dreamed existed, within or outside his mind. Still he held on. He gripped her tightly, twisting her head so that he could find and meet her gaze, diving within them fearlessly and digging for what he sought, digging for her answers.

Gretchen shuddered against him, quivering with each spasm of release, gripping him with her body—arms and legs stretching up to confine him, to seek the control denied her, begging him to stop—and not to—all in one sound—one breath, begging for release. Still he held on.

He searched her eyes, deeper than he'd ever ventured, and he saw a flicker of light – of something beyond the hollow pits they had been – something alive and vibrant – fleeing as he pursued. He dove deeper. Dimly he was aware that his grip on her face— his hold on her hair had tightened, but he ignored it. The visions were coalescing, becoming clearer.

He felt her movements becoming more heated, liquid. She slid over his flesh, collapsing so completely against him that her entire being seemed to give itself over to his control, to release its own tenuous hold on reality.

He grasped again at the visions, pressing his advantage, diving deeper. Comprehension inflated within his consciousness like a balloon, nowhere to go—threatening to explode. Too late he felt the vacuum inside her, the horrible, gripping power. Too late he regretted his concentration on her flesh—on physical control.

She wanted his mind.

He came. His climax was beyond his ability to comprehend, beyond his failing body's ability to compensate. She drew him inward, her very supplication a trap, her pain a decoy. He felt himself releasing, a giant mind-fuck ejaculation, and he felt that release draining his essence, swirling down the twin drains of her eyes—stolen.

He fell away from her, small tufts of hair still gripped in weak fingers, but his mind could not pull free. It was beyond the eyes now—she had her claws imbedded in his soul. There was no sound, no breath or beating of his heart, only her mind, slamming into place around him like the walls of a prison, trapping him within her as completely as if all prior existence had ceased to be. Then it was over.

She rose. Toby rose. She pulled her arms free, draping her shirt haphazardly across her breasts and buttoning enough buttons to hold it in place. Then her pants. She moved slowly and deliberately, as if feeling the pain and the bruises for the first time, as if she had never, until that moment, been aware of the physical world that surrounded them, or the man she'd lain with.

She turned to him for the briefest of moments, mocking him with new eyes, eyes filled with a shining light and intelligence, with creativity and wonder. They danced with promises he would never see fulfilled. Familiar promises. Toby turned away.

As she took her things, retrieved her Chinese food, and left, he seated himself before the immobile cyclopic eye of his computer screen, staring into the void of his words. The hole she'd left was immense – a void beyond his capacity to fill. The words mocked him – the answer strobed with the cursor, and he ignored it.

He sat there for a very long time.

Charlene leaned back against Toby's chest with a purr. He was so – different. Every touch, every probing, sensuous movement of his tongue, drew desire from her like a vacuum. It was scary.

He wound his arms about her from behind, fondling her nipples and distracting her from his words. "Why do you paint *this* stuff?" he asked.

AUTHOR'S NOTE: This was written for, and published in an anthology titled New Tales of Zothique – it was an homage to Clark Ashton Smith. I really, REALLY enjoyed this. I researched, as I love to do, and found that some ancient cultures liked to take the graven images of their conquered enemies – a way of showing the superiority of their own deities. I wondered immediately, what if the deity was more powerful than the people who worshiped it? What if stealing that graven image…was a very bad idea.

The Temple
of Captured Gods

or

Let Sleeping Gods Lie

Xenocydes stood high on the growing ramparts of the temple, watching impatiently as slaves dragged yet another huge slab of stone up the ramps, pulleys and chains relieving only a part of their burden, fear hanging heavy in the air. More than one of the stones had broken free, sliding back down the ramp with sickening speed and adding the bones and blood of those who pressed up from behind to the mortar that bound the walls. In each case, Xenocydes had put all survivors to death. Slaves were incidental, the stone was not. None labored carelessly on the Temple of Thylosson, but many met their doom on his altar.

Xenocydes turned toward the inner court of the temple.

Below him Dendra's minions scuttled like vermin, bustling about the smaller walls of the containments. Their work was more critical, this day, as the first shipments would be arriving from far Xylac within the week. Xenocydes had questioned the wisdom of collecting so soon, but Dendra had been adamant, and the necromanceress was not one to be denied. Even Xenocydes shuddered at her approach, images and tales seeping from her history and his childhood to haunt his thoughts. Dendra assured him that each containment was a temple within itself, and that Thylosson watched over their efforts. Who was the king to deny this truth?

One truth Dendra had spoken undeniably. There was no way to choreograph the collecting of Gods. War was constant, and the conquered waited only to be carted off. The first three containments were nearly prepared. Each was a stone cylinder, sides smooth and carved with symbols Xenocydes could not begin to decipher, ring up on ring of cryptic incantations rendered in chiseled precision. Everywhere there were references to and images of Thylosson, The Captor, and on each there was a single space that remained un-blemished. The space whereon the name of that which would be contained would be carved. The names of the vanquished, the conquered. The captive Gods.

That knowledge drenched the slaves in deeper fear, lent yet another layer of caution to already trembling hands. The temple was a wonder of perfection. One did not capture gods lightly. The people talked behind his back, but none ventured near. Even empty the temple frightened them. Thylosson frightened them. Most of all, Dendra, ancient Dendra, older than their grandparents and beautiful as the spring, dark as the tombs of legendary Tasuun, and a voice like crushed velvet—soft with hidden folds that held things best unknown, frightened them. She frightened Xenocydes, as well, but ancient as she was she called to his soul in ways he was foolish to acknowledge, and powerless to resist.

Turning from the scene below, the king glanced a final time at the stone slab, inching its way to the top of the nearly completed wall, and turned away. Days, only, and the caravan would arrive.

Days that if dwelled upon too closely would become measured in hours, and then in minutes, counted in heartbeats. He could hear in his mind the cries of the vanquished, the crumbling walls and the shouting of warriors, the screams of captured women and children without fathers—the priests crying out to those who had forsaken them. The sounds faded to the creaking of wagon wheels, and he knew they were coming. The visions had been with him since the first stone was placed. Dendra saw the visitations as a sign, Xenocydes as a curse. No matter if it were sign or curse, no moment's sleep was free of the rolling, creaking wheels, or the images of shrouded, shadowy shapes covered in soft cheesecloth and waxed tarp. They were coming. The king only hoped that he, and Dendra, were truly prepared.

As He stepped down from the lowest of the stairs leading up to the walls of the temple, his foot striking soft earth, he whispered.

"May Thylosson bless us."

The caravan was making good time. Better time, in fact, than any such caravan Barsinious had ridden with. None wanted to tarry, or to camp early. None wanted to dally around the fires and drink toasts to women or adventure. The final wagon in the line trailed back several hundred feet from the rest. Not by the desire of the driver, a small, sallow fellow with rheumy eyes and a crazed aspect that did not speak of complete sanity, but by the wish of all others who traveled with them. The creaking of those wheels sounded to Barsinious like the whining dirge of an endless funeral procession.

The wagon's cargo was somewhat of a mystery, but there were enough rumors floating up and down the line of horses and wagons to fill in many of the blanks. Whether the blanks were filled in properly, or with truth, made no difference.

Idols. The wagon was said to be loaded with the most sacred idols of the temple of Sethran, blood hungry stealer of the strength of dark Klaa's enemies. Of course, Klaa had fallen, the temple lay in ruins. The idols were those of vanquished gods, and they were being transported to Xenocydes, and the temple of Thylosson, The Captor. None would bend their knee or prostrate themselves before the shadowed relics in that cart again. So it seemed. And yet....

Barsinious turned away, an icy stab of fear lancing through his heart, but receding as his gaze swept out and over the bleak landscape. Days only, between himself and the release of his burden. He had not slept since they had set out, halting the caravan only when begged by those who followed him, and up with the first hint of warmth, he'd gotten the wagons rolling before the sun had fully kissed the skyline. While riding he felt safer, felt the miles rolling away, and sensed that some end was in sight. It was the darkness, the time spent in front of his fire, staring into the dancing flames, that ate at his soul.

He would find his gaze sliding off down the line of wagons, drawn to that damnable cart. He would hear whispered voices, chanting. If he spun too quickly back to the fire, figures danced in the flames. No matter that he pulled his cloak more tightly about himself, or closed his eyes. Always the shrouded forms called to him. He feared to sleep. With his eyes wide, staring, he could be certain the dancing figures remained trapped in the flames, that the tarps did not slip free of their bundled captives, and that the voices did not become any clearer.

As the huge walls of the temple of Thylosson slipped into sight over the horizon, Barsinious nearly wept from relief and exhaustion. They were still many miles distant. So huge was the edifice that it appeared as a small mountain from afar, whittled to the sharp, severe edges of the temple by the passing miles. So many years in the building, Barsinious thought—so many lives ground to dust in the construction. And what gods had those men worshiped? What powers called out for their revenge? Were their gods captured as they fell to Thylosson's temple, or were their souls chinks in the armor of the great monument?

Barsinious found that even the coming dealings with Xenocydes and Dendra did not fill him with the same dread that had now latched onto his heels like a second shadow, leeching his strength. Gladly would he turn over the wagon, and its contents, and if they allowed it, he would remain until each of the idols had been contained. He would watch as Dendra and her minions swarmed around and over the pieces, securing them with stone and spell, incanting the cryptic prayers to Thylosson that would seal the nightmares from his mind. That would remove the dancers from the fire and the voices from his head. He would then leave an offering on Thylosson's altar, and depart. Forever. There were other trade routes, other cargoes. Thylosson would have to be content with a single offering, and a lifetime of fear. Calling out to the drivers, exhorting them to greater speed, he continued down the dreary road.

As soon as he heard the first cry of the watchman announcing that the caravan had been spotted on the horizon, Xenocydes summoned Dendra. The work was coming along more quickly, as if all involved, down to the lowest of the slaves, felt the imminence of danger. A single day. The wagons would roll into the city the following morning, and once the preliminary bargaining was completed, the one wagon that mattered would roll through the framework of the temple's huge gates.

Three. The king was almost certain that taking so many, so quickly, was a mistake. If he could have spread them out, found a way to concentrate on one at a time, he would have done so gladly. Dendra would not hear of it. Xenocydes had been on the verge of begging, had babbled a scheme for spreading the deliveries over three caravans, but that would have taken months, could have spread over the course of a year. War would not stand still, so Dendra explained patiently. Other temples would fall, and what would become of their treasures? Their gods?

And she had persuaded him, not with words alone, but with her eyes, ancient, lovely eyes glittering with energy, slender thighs and strong arms that drew him down to his own bed and fingers that stole sensations from his heart and mind, pressing them back through his skin with such intensity that he walked the thin line of madness. Her caress dangled him over the edge of endless chasms, dragged him back again, and each time he returned she was there, lips pressed tightly to his ear, whispering commands, and suggestions, incanting prayers to dark Thylosson, and winding the tendrils of her spells through his veins. He knew this, and yet could not turn her away. As his lips would move to deny her, his body drew hers closer. As his reason screamed that she was a hag, hundreds of years old and decayed as dust, his passion bound his ears and prevented understanding. Even when he awakened from their dark liaisons to find her, not at his side, but seated across the room, staring into the distance at the temple, he did not draw back. Did it matter if she had actually touched him?

Dendra entered the throne room in silence, as always, standing at Xenocydes' shoulder before he sensed that he was not alone, her breath chilly on his throat.

"My liege?"

The king could never figure out if her words were meant to mock him. Her voice was so husky, so melodic and charismatic, that it dimmed thought each time she spoke.

"They have spotted the caravan," Xenocydes said softly. "The wagons will arrive by morning." He turned to her slowly. "How long have you known?"

Her laughter rolled over him like rancid butter. "I have known since you told me, my liege. Your visions were the first indication, and I have charted the course by them each night as you related them to me. The idols of Klaa will indeed arrive tomorrow. I have been waiting for this moment a long time. Thylosson thirsts."

"Are the containments complete?" Xenocydes asked? "Will they hold?"

"Our efforts will only grow in speed once the idols are in our power, my lord. Thylosson will feed off of their energy, and I in turn will feed. The Temple will grow as if blown from glass by the mouth of our God Himself.".

"Sethran was a thirsty god," Xenocydes breathed softly. "Will he be so easily checked because a city of men has fallen?"

"You doubt Thylosson?" Dendra asked, eyes darkening.

"I doubt myself," the king answered slowly, "and though I have seen you work wonders, you are no goddess, Dendra. What if we are wrong?"

Her eyes were dark and unreadable, and she spoke softly the words he'd dreaded.

"Then our souls will fall to eternal anguish, and the Temple will crumble to dust."

Xenocydes turned away then, to the window overlooking the city below, and the nearly finished south wall of the temple, jutting like a small cliff from the sand and stone of the surrounding desert. His eyes could pierce little of the darkness, and the longer he stared, the dimmer his perception became. He was vaguely aware of Dendra's fingers tracing icy trails up and down his neck, slipping to his back—.patterns. The symbols were etched patiently into his flesh with each stroke of long nails, his soul drawn on like a parchment, or an oracle. His eyes clouded, the city and the temple replaced by other visions, darker images.

He looked out over another land, hills rolling off into the distance where moments before sand had stretched endlessly, and the crumbed remains of a city laid out before him in a panoramic nightmare image of destruction. The stench of death permeated the air, vultures circling and feeding, their cries and those of the jackals the only sounds of life.

He focused on the largest of the toppled buildings. One wall still stood, the others had fallen inward, stained by the deep black scorch-marks of sorcerous flame. He heard words, distant and too soft to be made out, but nearing. Dendra, the decadent melody that was her voice working its way into the tapestry of destruction.

"You see," she crooned. "Gone. All gone. Klaa lies in ruins, and Sethran? Mighty Sethran, who stole his strength from the vanquished has fed upon himself. His temple is fallen, his idols are stolen, captured—ours."

The vision shifted, and Xenocydes felt that Dendra's hands had slipped from his back, sliding around to pull him against her breasts, her nails tracing nearer to his heart, and down. His mouth was very dry, but he found that he could not even gather the strength or control of his own body to lick his lips. All of his blood seeped in slow trails down his body, following her stroking fingers downward. His face was damp, coated in a sheen of chilly sweat.

He saw the wagons again, saw them gathered, camped for

the night, not far from the temple, but too far to have been seen by daylight, too far to be seen so clearly. Dendra's fingers wrapped around his erection and despite his lethargy, he gasped. The fire in the center of the camp jumped into view. A single figure sat, staring into those dancing flames as if mesmerized. Xenocydes looked more deeply into those flames. He could just make out what appeared to be shadows, dancing in the fire, arms thrown wild to the sky. He heard Dendra's voice, still, but could not make out the words. Instead he heard a dark, rhythmic chanting that slipped into his soul, drawing him out toward the flames, toward the wagons. He did not understand the words, but his ignorance did nothing to lessen their power.

Suddenly he lurched, slapped from behind, and Dendra's words came to him with sudden clarity.

"Enough!"

Age crackled for that one second in her voice. A chink in her ancient armor. Glancing down in shock, shock that melted to icy terror, he felt the flaccid remnant of the erection that had threatened moments (hours?) before to stain his robes.

Seeing him move, Dendra fell silent. She did not touch him again, but watched in silence. He could detect no emotion in her eyes, but somehow he knew what had just happened had not been her doing, nor that of Thylosson. If she was frightened, there was no way to detect that fear.

"You must sleep my liege," Dendra whispered at last. "They will be here early."

Turning to gaze at her, before nodding in dismissal, Xenocydes whispered. "They are already here."

Word had been sent from the palace that the one wagon was to be brought to the temple at dusk. No sooner. Barsinious had cursed the messenger, but the instruction had come directly from Dendra herself. Now even the mournful creaking of the wagon wheels sounded cheerful as it wound its way through the streets of the city and on toward the palace, and the temple beyond. His mind buzzed, half from the chorna root he'd been chewing to stave off sleep, and half from the maddening visions, the voices that were never silent now. If he had not feared to be alone with the wagon in the darkness, he would not have lit the previous night's fire, would have sat in the pitch black of deepest night with his eyes shut tightly and not have let the dancer's steal his concentration. Now he wanted only to unload his cargo, see it sealed away, and be off to sleep the sleep of the dead in his wagon, miles from this thrice-cursed city.

Fires burned deep within the temple, their light dancing beyond the stone walls, sending shadows groping out toward the road. Barsinious shivered. He did not want to be near those flames. He heard voices. Not the voices in his head, but somehow similar. As the wagon rolled slowly forward, entering and passing through the gates, the voices grew clearer. Barsinious could make out none of the words, but the sinuous rhythm of the chant pounded through his head with a subtle familiarity. He shook it off and hurried the wagon's pace, coming to a halt near the first of the containments and sitting, waiting to be noticed by those crawling over and around the stone cylinders.

He glanced to the fire and regretted it instantly. Dendra stood there, her ancient eyes locked on the wagon and its draped cargo with a hunger that rose from deep within. For just an instant Barsinious didn't see the beautiful sorceress. He saw age—more age than he could measure—dry, shriveled skin, clinging to the skull beneath and draped over with ratty, decaying hair. Barsinious drew back with a gasp, but as her gaze shifted to meet his, she was herself again, the vision had passed.

Dendra stepped forward, crying out in odd, shrill tones to her followers. Four of them broke off from the work on the containments and followed her, drawing a smaller cart behind them. Barsinious watched them approach dully, wanting to leap and run. His heart thudded wildly in his chest. Atop the furthest containment, Xenocydes stood watching. He was silent, still as the stone beneath his feet. If he was aware of the chanting, of the rhythm, it showed in no way visible to Barsinious' weary eyes.

Dendra and her followers moved past him without a word or glance, to the back of the wagon. Barsinious closed his eyes, breathing heavily. He heard their soft voices, chanting, working subtly into the back beat of the dark rhythm that permeated the temple with dark, insidious sound. The words made no sense, and yet formed images in the merchant's mind, familiar images. There was a deep thud as the gate on the back of the wagon dropped open. He felt the vehicle shake and sway, creaking heavily as the idols were moved toward the back, slowly, and lowered to the cart. The rhythm of the chant thrummed through the earth, rising through the wagon seat and synchronizing with the pounding of the merchant's heart. He wanted to watch, to know the three abominable things were gone from his cart, but he could not. His gaze was locked on the dancing flames.

Dendra's minions pranced around it, mincing steps and odd gestures mating with the licking tongues of fire, but Barsinious looked beyond and through them. The fire was alive, figures pulsing, bobbing and weaving among the shadows of the living dancers that ringed it. Dendra's voice blended with those of her followers, her high-pitched keening counterpoint to their low rumbling chant. Barsinious concentrated on that sound, skin suddenly clammy with sweat, though the night was cool and a soft breeze ruffled his hair. The words sifted through him and away, as if caught on the breeze, and other sounds, other voices replaced them. He shook his head, trying to cry out, though he did not know of what, or to whom. The voices were deeper, war-like and dark.

Shivering, the merchant forced his gaze from the flames with a soft cry, turning in time to see the first two idols roll past him on the cart, being hauled to their tombs. Dendra skipped along beside the them, her head thrown back, face turned to the night sky, voice rising and falling in an impossibly intricate cadence. She seemed not to hear the voices. None of those who circled the huge fire acknowledged the dancers within. The cart rolled slowly toward the first cylinder and Barsinious cringed back into his seat, shivering in dread.

Nothing. The stone idol was rolled carefully from the cart, worked slowly along the soft earth into the small opening that had been left to accommodate it. Dendra danced, her acolytes chanted, and the stone casing was slammed into place with a deep, decisive boom of finality. The cracks were sealed carefully, mortar and incense, darker things, pressed into the cracks and smoothed over, prayed over and bound in ways Barsinious would not dare imagine. The flames were stilled, for a moment, and all sound faded to Dendra's voice, and her accompaniment. All the while the dancers were in motion, a moving puzzle, fitting piece to piece, matching step for step.

And then the cart was rolling again, the second idol perched precariously near the back, carefully drawn to the next containment by strong hands, draped in the deepening shadows of the temple and bathed in the warm glow of the fire. The air was alive now with the sound, the incense smoke so thick it hung like a blanket of cloud, rising to the height of the statues center and wafting about the feet of those who danced.

Beyond them, Xenocydes had begun to sway slowly back and forth, caught in the rhythm. Barsinious was too far away to hear, but the king's lips moved in time with the voices of Dendra and her followers, his body moving to the controlled rhythm of their spell. His eyes glowed brightly, and his arms rose slowly up until they reached toward the darkened sky, his head thrown back in dark ecstasy.

The cart stopped and the idol was rolled free, walked to its casing and bound within, no break in the sound or the dance, and the incense thickening again so that all that was visible was Dendra's long hair, dancing about her as she flung herself left and right, somehow winding her way through the deep mist without a misstep, leading the cart back to Barsinious, and the last idol.

The wagon creaked as they levered themselves up once more, and Barsinious felt the heavy shift of the idol, heard Dendra's voice so close it seemed to whisper in his ear, then away, blown on the wind, and his heart began to calm. It would end. He closed his eyes, felt his heart shiver back to a steady thumping beat. The idol shifted again, and he jumped, but then the soft scraping of stone on wood told him that it was sliding off the wagon, onto the cart below, and seconds later some intangible sense told him it was moving away.

Barsinious opened his eyes once more, but at first he could

make out nothing. The mist had risen to a deep grey fog, billowing about him, heady with the scent of sandalwood. He blinked, listening for the soft creak of the carts wheels, hearing nothing but the chanting. Something had changed and he strained to hear, but it would not come clear in his mind. He glanced toward the fire and realized that his sight was clearing somewhat. He could make out the glow of the firelight through the haze, and the shifting, flashing shadows of those who danced.

But they were wrong. The shadows danced as before, but their steps did not match the rhythm of the chanting any longer. They leaped to the high, keening drone of Dendra's voice, but Barsinious realized with a sick, clammy clutch of fear at his heart that he could barely make that voice out. No longer did her words rise above the others, but whispered through the background, weakening steadily.

The chant had shifted subtly, lowering in pitch. The voices were rougher, but more powerful, the beat thrumming through the mist, each word, each note shimmering through the air and gripped at his heart. Barsinious drew in a long, shuddering breath, and waited.

The first cry was hideous, a long, ear-splitting wail of pain and terror. It split through the mist, dispersing the chant for that split second and bringing a moment of clarity. Barsinious reached for the reigns, drawing back hard, gasping as the mist split over the third containment and whirled up and away with a sickening wrench of air and light.

Barsinious stood suddenly, the horses shying, backing into their harness and the wagon, threatening to dump him and trap him beneath the dusty wood frame. He clutched the reins and stared.

The final stone cylinder stood stark against a background of mist and shadow. Beside it the cart lay broken, canted to one side, one corner embedded in the soft earth, and the front wheels shattered. The idol was nowhere to be seen, and the niche in the stone cylinder lay empty, a deep red glow seeping from its depths, rising and melting into the mist. Where Xenocydes had stood, a dark stain marked the stone, clearly visible in that momentary flash of clarity, seeping downward, and Barsinious recalled the scream.

Unnerved, the horses spun, managing not to upend the cart in their terror, and took off in a sudden bolt across the temple floor. The mist settled over the containment once more and Barsinious rocked back into his seat, clutching the wood and adding his own scream to those now rising all around him. The chanting continued, but it was the voices of his nightmares, and he heard as well the pounding of war drums, and the resonating crash of hundreds of booted feet, slamming to the dirt in unison, the clatter of weapons filled the air.

The fire. With a scream Barsinious dragged on the reins, fighting with all his remaining strength to turn the horses. They were pounding straight at the point where the fire had blazed such a short time before. He could make out the glow, growing brighter and he screamed to the animals, his terror dragging the sound, finally, from his heaving chest. He felt the wagon lurch to the left, felt it career wildly, rocking up onto two wheels, balancing precariously and then slamming back to the earth.

Barsinious was tossed roughly back, the reins yanked from his hands and his shoulder cracking painfully back into the seat. He teetered for a moment, nearly falling from the edge of the wagon, the clutched the seat and righted himself.

Rising, groping for the reins, he gazed into the mist, gasping for breath and felt it sucked from his lungs by the image that flared as the right wheel of the wagon glanced off the edge of the fire, shooting an arc of sparks high above him.

Dendra writhed in the flames, hair caught fast in fiery talons, back arched like a bow and her mouth open wide in a silent scream. Behind her a darker image glowed, not moving, but hovering in the center of the fire on invisible supports. Barsinious screamed again, giving voice to the terror mirrored in Dendra's eyes as she was dragged back and down, withered hands clutching her own hair, trying to tear free but held helplessly.

The wagon lurched again, smacking the merchant's head solidly into the wood of the wagon beneath him, and his vision blurred. He could make out the dancers, shifting through the flame, as he had seen them night after night, could hear the pounding rhythm of their chanting. The idol glared down at him. He knew it was the idol, though he'd never laid eyes on it during the long journey. He fought the shadows that clutched at him, fought to keep his eyes from closing. Failed. As the war cries of the shadow-men faded to the dull roar of blood, rushing through his veins, the glow faded to shimmering darkness.

Driverless, the wagon careened against the right side of the temple gate with a sickening crunch, and off into the streets of the city, weaving wildly form side to side. The flames fed in the temple of Thylosson, beyond walls that would never rise to completion. In mist and ash, the tomb was sealed.

Old Barsinious, hair as white as mountain snow, though he'd known but forty years, sat atop the old rug, eyes downcast at the memory, speaking in hushed tones as the story drew to its close. He fell silent then, lost in memories, and the children shifted about restlessly, wanting more.

"It is late," the storyteller said at last, "and there will be plenty of tales for other nights. It is time for you to go to rest."

"No!" one boy cried. "Let us feed the fire and hear the rest. Tell us of the idol."

Barsinious' eyes widened at mention of the flames, and he held up a gnarled hand. "There will be no flames in my camp," he said softly, and there is no more to tell. "I went back to that temple one time, with the nobles of the city, seeking their king. Nothing remained of Xenocydes but a scorched bit of stone and the ring of his office, molten to that cylinder. The idol was gone. There was dust and ash where the fire had burned, nothing more."

"Where did it go?" the boy demanded. "The sorceress and the king were dead..."

"Yes," Barsinious agreed. "Yes they were. His hollow, deep-set eyes shifted their gaze to the shadows beyond the camp. "It is dark, young ones, and it is best that you leave me now."

There was a murmur of protest, but Barsinious had already turned away. In his head, the soft drumbeats had risen, and the chanting begun. Beyond his camp, fires burned brightly and he tried not to stare into their depths. One day he would falter, step too near the fire too late in the night. They were waiting, hungry, patient, vengeful, dancing in the tattered shadows of his mind.

AUTHOR'S NOTE: Okay, you've got me. Every time an anthology came along with a Lovecraftian theme, I jumped on it. This story was for a Chthulu in Space anthology, and was accepted. I don't believe that anthology was ever published, and this story is presented for the first time here. Ancient gods…high-tech computers…a sort of Philip K. Dick influenced story.

Anomaly

Roberts stared at the screen above his workstation. Sweat crawled down his spine and dampened his armpits. His hand rested on the base of a compact electron microscope. The screen depicted the contents of the slide currently under the lens. The sudden realization that he was touching that instrument, and the instrument was touching the—thing—on the screen cut through his lethargy like a white-hot blade.

With a small cry he withdrew his hand and jerked back from the workstation. What writhed in the pink, jellied solution he had used to prep the slide could not exist. He worked in a clean lab. The samples he worked with were genetically pure —proteins and enzymes. The entire workstation was cleansed three times daily, as was Roberts himself. All of this flashed through his mind and speared his brain with a single word. No.

He should already have hit the large, red, mushroom-shaped button that rose beside his keyboard. The button would set off alarms, flashing lights, and galvanize a dozen men in pristine white lab suits into action. He should have sealed his workspace until the cleansing unit arrived. He did none of these things.

Instead, Roberts sat down, forced his reluctant fingers to the controls, and increased magnification on the microscope. In the back of his mind, he knew that the alarms should be sounding, with or without action on his part. The spike in his own nervous system was detectable. In the white, clean world of EXOTECH, it was an infestation. As much as he hated the word for all its science fiction connotations, it was an anomaly.

The thing moved. Tentacles shot out from either side, seeking sustenance. Roberts blinked, glanced at a small graph display on his desk, and swallowed. The thing was twice the size it had been when he first spotted it, and appeared to be growing exponentially. Roberts calculated from what he'd observed, whistled, and backed away again. Too fast. It was growing too fast, and if it continued, more than just his workspace might be compromised. Still he hesitated. There was something in the slow, sinuous motion, something with a barely concealed pattern. He tried to place the sensation but failed.

He reached out his hand to smack down on the contamination alarm, and froze. He stared at the perfect image on his screen and bit back a scream. The thing—the anomaly—was gone. The slide contained only the standard "control" base he used every day. In his mind he still felt the tug of spiraling tentacles. He tasted the bitter bile in the back of his throat brought on by the thought of the cleansing to come, the quarantine, and the silence. He blinked his eyes but the screen remained clear.

Trembling, he sank back into his seat. Soft leather formed about him, separated from his clothing and his skin by slick plastic. Roberts reached for his control panel, stopped as his hands were gripped by an intense trembling. He closed his eyes and breathed deeply until his nerves calmed.

When he glanced up, he saw that the roving security patrol had stopped outside his "pod" and was staring in at him. Roberts raised a hand to signal all was well. The guard didn't move. He pressed his shielded face close to the window and stood, watching.

Roberts reached out for his controls. This time his hands were steady. He lowered the magnification back to its standard level and began his process. The guard watched for a few moments longer, then moved on down the corridor. If it hadn't been for the built-in gauges and fail safes, Roberts was sure the guard would have questioned him.

Roberts focused on his work and tried to press the disturbing hallucination from his mind. There was no room for error. The proteins and genetic material he worked with was brought in from Earth in small quantities. Supplies were limited, and it was months between deliveries. A single small error could cost millions.

His work, combined with that of a team of more than two hundred other scientists, each working in a similar environment, formed the backbone of EXOTECH'S prime technology, a process Roberts' colleagues termed genetic cleansing, and that was marketed to governments and the masses as "Exotechnology". The term had no serious meaning. EXOTECH'S earliest work was in the field of exoskeletal human enhancement. When they slipped over into the realm of genetic manipulation, they used the company name as a smokescreen. The scientific community, as a whole, did not endorse what they were doing, which was another reason for the off-world facility.

Roberts never gave it much thought. He was a technician, and the pay for this project would allow him the freedom to complete his education on his return to Earth, or to retire. Twenty-four months of isolation in an absolutely clean environment. The compound, a space station locked into orbit around Mars, was a hive of separate quarters, workspaces, and routines. Each and every person assigned had volunteered for the work and only been accepted after strict background investigations were complete. They were joined at the brain via the main computer bank when off duty, able to converse, share ideas, and retain their sanity, but in the workspace even this weak umbilical was cut.

The isolation had begun even before they left earth. Biological, emotional, and mental examination, testing, and monitoring cleared their minds and their bodies to interact with the super-clean environment of EXOTECH'S lab. The training was simple enough; memorization of sequences and codes, and a thorough grounding in procedure was the core. The experiment itself, and the results gleaned from the research, had been outlined and was monitored every step of the way by technicians on Earth. Roberts had only to provide his data in a constant flow and to maintain vigilance against contamination.

The rest of the day's work proceeded without incident, and Roberts closed his workstation with a heavy sigh of release. There were no more incidents with contaminants that didn't exist, and the guard passed him by without notice on all rounds subsequent to what Roberts now termed "The Anomaly." He sealed his results, began the decontamination sequence. He stepped into the bio-suit he wore between his workspace and his quarters, and stood motionless inside the door of his pod until scanners had checked every inch of his protective clothing for the slightest hint of anything outside the strict parameters allowed on the station.

Roberts would be back in the pod in sixteen hours. He would eat, read for a while, spend a little time on the computer system trying to find something to talk about with the other technicians, and then he'd sleep. His vital signs would be checked and monitored as he slept, and when he woke, any deficiencies that might affect the quality or efficiency of his work would be addressed by supplements added to his breakfast, which would be delivered to his quarters through a thirty-minute decontamination process and a tri-level lift system that would not proceed from one step to the next until the preceding level was sealed.

A claustrophobic person would have gone insane in an hour, but Roberts was very self-contained, and after four months barely missed the distractions of the world he'd left behind. He did miss sex, but there would be plenty of time for that when he got back. He told himself over and over that he'd managed to make it the first seventeen years of his life without it, and a few more months wasn't going to kill him.

In fact, nothing but very random chance could kill him until his assignment ran its course. His health was monitored and pampered constantly. There was no illness on the compound. There was little or no discomfort. There were no germs. He felt like he worked in a dream state. Only the short periods of conversation with the others broke the illusion. They had little to talk about after the first couple of months. Each of their jobs was very similar to the next. They monitored the effects of certain chemical and sonic reactions on gene structure. Each change was infinitesimal, the results carefully recorded and transmitted, but none of them knew the exact purpose of their own part in the greater puzzle that was EXOTECH. There was speculation, but it fizzled under the weight of apathy. It was more stimulating to talk about what they would do when they returned to Earth, and that is what filled most of their on-line hours.

Roberts logged off early that night and sat staring at the white, blemish-free wall of his quarters. His mind painted the writhing tentacles across the smooth surface. He still felt the itch of something just beyond the reach of his memory, or his perception. There was something he should know, but he couldn't bring it to the forefront of his mind.

The walls dimmed from luminous white to blue. Roberts rose, went through the familiar rituals of cleaning his teeth and washing his face. None of it was necessary, and all water that contacted his skin was immediately purged from the station to be recycled, cleansed, and purified off-station before returning to the system.

As the walls faded through shades of blue toward deep purple, he lay on his cot and drew his thin blanket up to his chin. He didn't need it. The environment was programmed to respond to minute reactions in his nervous system. If he got cold, the small bedchamber would simply become warmer. The blanket was another old habit that had refused to leave him. Too many such rituals could disqualify a person from service with EXOTECH, but some ritual was encouraged. It made transition back into life on Earth simpler.

Roberts closed his eyes and wiped the last of the writhing image from his mind. The air was slowly infused with a mild sedative. The deep purple glow of the walls soothed him. The world dropped away to darkness, and he slept.

EXOTECH INTERNAL MEMO 1009-53-0

Step one of the key accessed. Source genes human, as prophesied. Trigger is acoustic. Subject Roberts activated. Standard sensor array disabled, decoding sequence initiated. Subject is stable.

The first sensation was helplessness. Roberts could move neither arms, nor legs. His head was gripped on either side by padded braces. His eyelids would not close, and when he tried to blink, the pain was excruciating. His fingers were individually banded to a cold, hard surface. Someone moved, and the motion sent a soft breeze rippling across his skin. He was naked.

He scanned the periphery of his limited vision. The walls were bright, luminous white, like those of his bedchamber. A painfully bright light glared down at him from above. He heard the sound of voices; at least they seemed to be voices. He could make out none of the words. He tried to speak, but his lower jaw was clamped in place. His tongue was so bone dry it crackled when he moved it and a wave of thirst so excruciating it knifed into the base of his brain and caused his entire body to go rigid stung his throat.

Someone moved close by, out of sight. He tried so hard to see them that his eyes actually cramped from the effort of trying to twist them sideways. Something hummed. A large, polished metal bar slid into view above his toes. It stretched across from one side of the table to the other. The whirr repeated, followed by a loud THUNK! And the bar swiveled. A whine rose, like a turbine firing up, the sound louder and louder until it became painfully piercing, beating at his eardrums with insistent, malevolent pressure.

He heard more mechanical movement to either side of his head, but he saw nothing. Moments later he felt soft pricks of pain just forward of either ear. The pressure increased slowly; something long, thin and very sharp slid through his skin. He wanted to scream and could not. The effort brought the thirst again, and he nearly blacked out.

Then the bar glowed bright blue at the end of the table, shifted to

*white, and a solid beam burst from the base of the thing, bathing his feet
in its glow. The pain was incredible. He trembled, fought to scream,
and fought the urge to scream because it brought the thirst. The bar
moved so slowly down the length of his body that he only knew it was
moving at all by the burning, searing pain of its passing.*

*Ice cold pricks of sensation formed where the long, thin probes had
pierced his flesh, behind his ears. He started to shake, and then grew
still. The pain ceased. He still followed the progress of the scanner
up his calves toward his thighs, but the burning, searing pain was
gone. He floated, detached from all sensation. In the back of his mind,
something itched. He wanted to watch the scanner move over his form.
He wanted to think about how he would remove the icy probes from
the sides of his head. He wanted to scream, but he had no more control
over his lungs and vocal chords than he did over his arms and legs.*

*In the air above him, particles joined, separated, and joined again.
They swirled. He watched, fascinated, as they formed an image similar
to the thing he'd seen on his slide. It pulsed. Tentacles stretched out
to either side, probing. It whirled slowly, and he followed each motion,
picking out the pattern as it moved. He wanted to speak, though
only to seek a certain word. The thing was like a letter in an arcane
alphabet—something he'd known and forgotten. It meant something
important and was communicating that thing to Roberts, but he could
not understand. Tears formed in the corners of his eyes and rolled
down, sliding around the probing lengths of metal piercing his skull.*

*The scanner passed over his torso and reached his neck. There was
an unpleasant ripple about an inch beneath his skin. His jaw ached,
and as the scan rippled over his face and up to his cranium whatever
the icy pain relief that had flooded him had been, it was overmatched.
All thought ceased and the blinding white of the light wiped away the
room and the machinery, leaving him silently motionlessly screaming
into a luminous void.*

The walls pulsed from deep purple shades up into shades of
blue. A light mist of stimulant, laced with the scent of fresh
coffee misted the air. Roberts sat up slowly. Wide awake in

seconds, as always, he slid his legs off the side of his cot, leaned his head into his hands, and fought the urge to vomit. His skin tingled. The dull throb of the memory of machinery echoed in his head and his ears were filled with a buzzing, ringing sensation.

If he didn't move, sensors would alert the central control. Roberts stood shakily and began his morning routine. For once, the absolute monotony of his existence worked in his favor. Synthetic coffee and breakfast slid up through the multiple airlocks; he ate and drank quickly, and the tray disappeared. Next, Roberts stepped into a clear tube. It closed around him. He shivered, as always, as the chemical and sonic cleansing removed any and all impurity from his skin. He stepped clear of the tube and straight into the bio-suit that now hung in front of the tube.

At the door he stopped again, moving through the airlock sequence and the careful scan of the exterior of his suit. His heart pounded. What had become a simple routine terrified him. What if they saw it? What if there was something left on his skin, in his blood? What if he hadn't been dreaming? Had they done that to him – EXOTECH? Was it possible? If he asked, his time here would be over, along with his dreams of retirement. If they were behind it, they'd silence him. If not – well, then he was going crazy, and they'd ship him out on the next freighter home with a partial pension.

He stepped into the hall and headed for his pod. Once he was inside, he could drift into the mechanics of the job and try to forget this. The quicker he wiped it all out of his mind, the more likely he was to relax. He passed none of the guards, and made it into his workspace without incident. Once he'd passed through the safeguards and left the bio-suit behind, he set to work quickly.

He worked methodically. He would get no extra pay for extra output, and EXOTECH frowned on hurried results. If his standard time parameter for a particular task varied too much, they would light a warning on his control panel and withhold samples. Too many variations and he could be called out for examination. They allowed this to happen one time during the tenure of employ. Any variation beyond this was considered an unacceptable expense, and that technician was replaced.

Everything went smoothly, and within half an hour he had several slides prepped and had set his "control" data carefully. All that remained was to submit the slides to a set of sonic pulses. In his time on The Compound, he'd been through several batteries of tests. Each time the control was exactly identical to the last. Only the slight variation in sonic pulses changed, and each time the test ended, the results were whisked off by the sensors and monitors to the central memory banks to make way for the next batch of data. Clockwork.

Roberts liked to think of the pulses as notes. Each vibrated differently, and over time he'd fancied he could detect the minute differences himself. It was ridiculous; they were far too subtle for anything but very sensitive electronic equipment to monitor, but he couldn't help toying with the notion. Maybe the pulses were affecting his mind, as well. Maybe they caused the hallucination that had invaded his screen the previous day. It could be that familiarity with the sonic patterns was what he'd been unable to put his finger on when he saw the waving tentacles. A similarity in patterns.

He shook his head. He swapped the first of the slides out and replaced it with another. He studied the chart beside him on the bench, and performed very minor adjustments to the sonic equipment. He pressed the toggle that began the sequence of pulses and watched as the invisible lines of force interacted with his slide.

The back of his hand itched, and he glanced down. In the valley formed behind the knuckles of his index and middle finger he saw a tiny black dot. Roberts stared. The itch continued, and he knew he wouldn't be able to stand it long. What in hell could it be? Not an insect. Not here. No dirt. Had he slipped up somehow in prepping the slides?

Very carefully, he reached down with his free hand and flicked at the dot with the back of his fingernail. He felt nothing. Whatever it was, it was flush with his skin. He leaned closer, but still couldn't make out what the offending spot could be. The itch grew more intense with each passing moment. Roberts shifted his gaze back to his screen, grunted, and reached for the slide. He could barely grip the edges as he slid it out, deposited it in the disposal slot, and clicked on the button that transferred his data. Gritting his teeth, he ignored the itch on his hand and grabbed the next slide. He managed to get it into place without mishap, changed the setting on the sonic pulse, and flipped the toggle for the next sequence.

Just for a second, the itch on his hand abated, and he leaned back. Then it hit harder and faster, a sudden stab of pain. He stared, horrified, at his hand. Tiny tentacles branched out from the perimeter of the spot, groping across his skin. Each touch burned like fire. Tears in his eyes, frantic, Roberts glanced up at the screen. Everything looked normal, except…

The settings. He'd changed them. He ran back over the past few moments in his mind. There was no way to doubt himself, despite the distraction of the pain in his hand. He'd moved the pulse settings to the next combination in line, but now they'd changed back. He hadn't touched the dials, and yet there it was. The previous settings had been restored, and the test was running a second time. On the screen the mirror image of the spot on his hand stared back at him. Under the lens of the electron microscope it was so large it threatened to writhe off the edge of the slide.

Roberts cried out and flipped the toggle, ending the test early. He backed away from the workstation. The image on the screen faded. His hand stopped burning. He glanced at the slide, and at the disposal slot. He knew that somewhere in the complex, alarms were sounding. Lights flashed on security desks and in medical to warn them of an "anomaly." Still, he stared at the slide. He could return the settings on the switch to the position they were supposed to be in and finish the test. He might get on to the next setting before anyone arrived, and he could always claim that the glitch was in the machinery, and not himself. No one needed to know of the spot on his hand, stretching out and groping across his skin, or the way it had burned. No one needed to know that the slide had been contaminated, because all sensors indicated it was as clean as any before it.

Roberts decided quickly. He'd get away with it, or he wouldn't. He had nothing to lose by trying. He flipped the controls to the next setting again, double-checking, and held them there. With his thumb he flipped the toggle. There was a small jerk in the controls, as if they wanted to twist back again, but he held them firmly, and after a moment, the pressure subsided. He was just sliding the finished test slide into the deposit slot when the guard's faceplate pressed against the outer window of his pod.

Roberts ignored the man. He grabbed a third slide and slipped it into place. He fought to keep his hand steady, and it only trembled a little. He made the adjustments to his controls, and flipped the toggle. The settings remained intact. There was no flip back to an earlier position, and there was no spot on his hand. He felt the weight of the security patrolman's gaze on his shoulders, but he didn't turn. If they wanted him out, they were going to have to reach him. He wouldn't give them the satisfaction of admitting he'd screwed up. If they didn't catch it, what harm could one slightly irregular slide in half a million make?

Finally, unable to endure the strain, he slowly turned his gaze to the window. The patrolman was gone.

The day finished in a blur. He worked through his slides, secured his equipment, began the cleansing sequences right on time and sweated bullets through each, expecting bells and whistles and flashing lights, and getting nothing more than the hiss of the inner pod door sliding open, followed by the clinging security of his bio-suit, and, finally, his room.

He knew it was a risk, but after eating, he didn't log on to the main system. He didn't want to risk the temptation of asking questions. Had anyone else noticed the anomaly? Did they know about it? Were they readying themselves to remove him, even now, or worse yet, to study him? The calm, glowing walls took on a sinister aspect, and the strictly structured life and world surrounding him felt like some strange kind of prison.

The wait was interminable, but eventually it was time for him to sleep. He lay back on the cot, pulled the blanket up to his chin as always. His heart raced. His skin was clammy. He knew the sensors would pick it up. Was it fever? Had he managed the impossible, becoming ill, or infected, in a place devoid of illness or infection? No alarms sounded. The lights shifted through their color spectrum and the misting sedative tugged his eyelids closed, despite his best effort to keep them open. Roberts slept.

EXOTECH INTERNAL MEMO 1009-53-1

Subject appears to be near the key. Mental stability questionable, but motor skills normal. Sensor readings indicate partial solution. Initial scan incomplete. Risk of damage to subject in second scan acceptable. Sonic pulses, even at reduced control rates, caused reactions in multiple workstation pods, despite shielding. Subjects cleansed. Recommend commencement of pulse ray construction. Next scheduled flight to Earth in less than 60 hours.

The pain was immediate and excruciating. Roberts felt the cold metal table against his naked flesh. His limbs were secured as before, eyes clipped open, and the two long, slender needles were already in place just forward of his ears. He felt the numbing, icy touch of whatever they dispensed, but it wasn't enough. The pain shot through him and despite the danger, and the additional pain, he fought to force a scream through immobile lips.

The walls glowed white. He heard whispered voices, but, again, could make out no words. The ringing in his ears, accompanied by a sizzling, chemical hiss each time he strained to move, gave the voices a rhythmic, hypnotic quality. Like a chant in some foreign tongue. He wanted to call out to them. He wanted to beg them for mercy.

The metal bar slid into place just beyond his toes and the balls of his feet. Roberts' eyes rolled up into his head in panic as the turbine sound returned and the scanner kicked to life. It wasn't a steady beam this time, but a pulse. It flashed so brilliantly he felt as if his eyes would boil from the heat of it. The flashes recurred at a steady rate, like a hideous strobe light. The bar began its excruciatingly slow ascent of Roberts' body and he shied away. He couldn't move, but his skin drew back, and up, and every muscle in his body was clenched. Though he fought against it, perversely, his penis stiffened, stretching up obscenely as the scan made its way slowly upward.

Something was different. He grasped this thought and clung to it. Maybe it was important, maybe not, but it was something. If he sat and watched and waited for that pain to leave his toes and ankles and work its way up to...

What was it? The pulse? He tried to blank his mind. He couldn't close his eyes. He couldn't look away from the inexorable ascent of the bar, and each time the light pulsed his nerves screamed with pain, blanking thought. Between those pulses, he fought to think. There was something he should be seeing, something just out of reach. The pulse came again, radiating his upper thighs and teasing at the edges of his groin with fiery tendrils of agony.

He held that thought. Hairs, sticking out at angles, brought the image of the anomaly to his mind. The pain flashed again, and thought vanished. When it returned, colored dots swam before his eyes. He knew he was nearing unconsciousness, but as he slid away, the dots formed patterns, like motes swimming in his eyes. They whirled into small circles, each with strands of something – tentacles? – trailing from their perimeter. His skin crawled, though the next pulse had yet to fall. Something deep inside detached moved slowly from a point directly above his navel.

FLASH and the scan reached that same point. His thoughts extinguished like the quick flash of a camera, and all was darkness.

EXOTECH INTERNAL MEMO 1009-53-1.b

Subject stabilized, scan complete. Sonic pulse settings verified as key. Construction of pulse ray reported in stage four with expected completion in thirty-two hours. Freighter conversion complete and ready for installation of Pulse Generator. Test subjects transformation terminated at various points, not to exceed safety parameters. Final solution imminent.

The walls shifted color, and the stimulant misted the air. Roberts blinked. He stared and blinked again to convince himself he had control of his eyelids. His body was on fire with a burning ache that permeated muscle and nerve endings. He moved his toes slowly, and then bent one leg. It hurt, but the pain was bearable. He slid his legs off the couch and stood.

Everything was as it had been every single day of his time at The Compound. Roberts forced his aching body through the motions of his daily routine. Something was horribly wrong, but the central control team didn't appear to be aware of it, and lacking any other form of defense against his world crumbling, he decided to delay their awareness as long as possible. If he were sick, they would have come for him. If his synapses fired erratically, they would note this too, eventually. Everything was monitored. Everything was clean.

He managed to make it into his bio-suit and into the hall without incident. Normally he didn't pay much attention to the other pods he passed. When he'd first arrived, he'd been fascinated, staring into each and trying to imagine what kind of person the other technician was, where they'd come from and where they were going when all of this was just a memory. Then the novelty faded, and he paid them no more attention than he did the walls, or the floor. Now he glanced from side to side surreptitiously. Everything looked much as it had the last time he'd bothered to check until he got within two pods of his own. He knew they had technicians assigned. He also knew both should be at their stations. The work was scheduled on a cycle so that none of them hit the passage at the same time, and the two pods directly before he reached his were on an earlier start schedule. They were empty. No lights flashed. There was no indication that anything was amiss, except for the missing technicians.

Sweat slicked his skin. The bio-suit was suddenly very tight, warm, and restrictive. Roberts forced his steps to remain steady, and when he reached his pod, though the desire to be free of the suit was overwhelming, he fought it back. He stood quietly through the layers of decontamination and moments later stepped free into the workspace.

Inside, he stared. The electron microscope seemed alien to him, the chair something from a bad dream. The row upon row of blank slides awaiting his attention gleamed, and he thought of their sharp edges. He wondered how his blood would look under the microscope, and how long it would take the system to sedate and remove him if he tried to find out.

He wondered where the missing technicians had gone.

Mechanically, Roberts grabbed a slide and began to prep it. The work took little of his concentration, but there was nothing else to focus it on, so he stared blankly at his hands as he worked and ran through the past few days in his mind. The screen flashed on and he cringed, nearly dropping the slide in his hand. The flash of light had triggered memories of the scan. His skin itched and his bones ached. He managed to get the slide into place and focused.

He glanced at the chart beside his workspace. He stared. Each day when he came in the chart had changed. He wasn't allowed control over keeping track of his tests because this allowed for error. The system itself made the shifts, always slight, in the control settings.

Except the settings were the same. He forced himself to visualize each knob position, as he'd set them the day before. It was hard to concentrate. His fingers, while not broken, were stiff and did not want to bend to his will. The date on the chart was new. All of the information was as it should be except the first setting. It was identical to the previous day's setting. Exactly the same.

Roberts' hand shook, but he didn't hesitate. If this was a test to see if he would deviate, or become a problem, he was up to the test. If they were using him in some way for a separate study, he had no doubt he'd be compensated for it. He flipped the knobs into position and hit the toggle. The pulse bombarded the slide with its subtle pressures and "tones."

The shift was more immediate than before. He saw the thing tug itself to the surface of the slide. It was larger, still, than before. If it got any larger, it would not be contained on the slide, and all he'd see was a black splotch. Roberts felt a stabbing pain in his hand. He glanced down and screamed. The black mark he'd noticed the day before had grown. It was a splotch, pressing outward from inside the skin of his hand. He could clearly make out the outlines of tentacles, reaching down the length of his fingers and groping toward his wrist. It throbbed, and each throb ground the thing into his bone.

It was too much. Roberts lurched forward and smacked his hand down hard on the alert button. If they were going to cleanse him and deport him, fine. He hoped they would hurry. He reached out with his free hand to flip the toggle down and stop the pulse. At that moment the thing burst through his skin. He whirled and stared in horror as it oozed out of his vein and gripped his arm, tugging itself along, and growing. In its trail his hand shriveled and sank in upon itself.

The screen had gone dark. Whatever pulled itself free of the slide had completely blocked the lens.

Gas hissed through nozzles set deep in the walls. Roberts clawed his way upright and used his one good hand to drag himself toward whatever it was they'd piped in. He hoped it was a sedative, or a pain killer – some sort of antidote. He never reached the nozzle. Whatever sprayed from its tip solidified, like a bubble. Within that pale surface he saw a familiar swirl, and he screamed again. His arm no longer existed below the elbow.

Grinding his teeth against the pain, he turned to the window. Nothing, there was no one there. He turned to the table along the far wall, and the row upon row of blank slides. The thing passed his elbow and gripped his bicep.

With a hoarse, maddened scream he gripped one of the slides, dragged it free of the rack, and drove it into his shoulder. He sliced, drawing a long, bright red burst of blood. The sensation was warm and almost comforting in the face of the agony in his lower arm. He ignored the screen, and the microscope. With desperate, slashing strokes he worked the slide through skin and muscle, tears streaming down his face as he fought to reach the bone.

There was a searing flash of light, and everything in the room went still. The light filled the pod, glaring from the windows.

Smoke rose from the screen and the equipment. Where Roberts had stood, there was nothing. On the floor the clean, broken shards of a glass slide gleamed like forgotten crystals.

EXOTECH INTERNAL MEMO 1009-53-1.c

Subject terminated. Test exceeds parameters. The key is functional and programmed. Installation is complete. Launch for Earth is one hour. Remaining subjects terminated. Destruct sequence engaged. Pulse ray primed and programmed for release upon achieving Earth atmosphere. The key functions exponentially, as expected. Projected annihilation of host cells twenty-four hours. Rebirth achieved. Ia Cthulu.

AUTHOR'S NOTE: This is one of my favorite stories ever. It is a tribute to William Hope Hodgson, and at the same time, to my own childhood. My step father was a barber in southern Illinois. Much of what is written here about the barber shop is from my childhood. The bedroom – the old house – cobbled together from things I've lived, seen, known, and loved. This story was reprinted in The Year's Best Horror Stories 2005. It was first published in my Bram Stoker Award nominated collection Defining Moments and has been one of the most critically praised works of my career. Welcome to the story that named the collection…welcome to Cedar Falls.

The Call of Distant Shores

The barber shop in Cedar Falls was more than just a gathering spot for tired old men with nothing better to do than to trim the few remaining wisps of gray from their temples and pass on the latest fish stories. Brown's small shop sported two chairs, three barbers, off and on, the memorabilia of dozens of lives. Terry Brown was the sixth generation of Browns to run the small shop. His father had come back from the war, honored and decorated, just in time to take the reins from Jeremiah Brown, who'd cut hair in Cedar Falls for nearly forty years. There were sighs of relief when that torch was passed. More than a few heads of hair had borne the mark of a slight palsy and unattended cataracts, but it hadn't been enough to keep them away.

Jeremy stood on the steps, taking in the changes time and weather had etched across the face of the old building. He hadn't stepped foot in Cedar Falls in nearly ten years, but he remembered the last time he'd mounted the steps to Brown's Barber shop with a clarity that ran like cold rain down his spine. Small details surfaced, details with more clarity than those he could have brought to mind from the breakfast barely cool in his stomach. The aroma of his father's cigarette-scented flannel shirt, the rustle of leaves, rolling and scurrying down the sidewalks as he'd stepped up onto the curb. Cars had been larger in those days, and Jeremy smaller. The scents of gas and oil had carried on the wind, blending with wood-smoke and the acrid scent of burning leaves.

There had been chairs outside the shop in those days, metal chairs that bounced if you hit them just right, and leaned back nearly to the sidewalk behind if you had the proper size and age. They were usually full, pulled close in beside the sand-filled ashtray and flanked by a Thermos cooler.

Now anti-smoking laws and open-container fines had ended all that, and what remained of the chairs themselves were deep scrapes in the wooden planks of the Main Street boardwalk. Jeremy hesitated outside the door. The exterior changes had done nothing to still the *presence* of the place. He closed his eyes, and years melted away in an instant.

There were animals of all sorts lining the walls, some heads, fish so large they seemed surreal and improbable to a young boy whose fishing experience extended to Bluegill and catfish. There were the heads of deer, a bear, a wild pig, and in the corner, Jeremy's favorite, a stuffed mongoose poised in eternal battle with a coiled, moth-eaten snake. There were tools of unknown use and origin, black and white photos so yellowed and dusty you had to stand with your nose pressed to the glass of their frames to make out the images. Squat figures in black pants, black shoes and white shirts, standing in front of buildings that only peripherally resembled the city streets Jeremy had walked as a child.

And the wooden figurehead. Jeremy stood, leaning against the frame of the doorway, and shook as the memory of that worm-eaten chunk of wood invaded and took over. Dark wood, so dark it seemed soaked with sea-water, damp and rotting, the thing had glittered with coat after coat of varnish. Jeremy's father had told him it was to fight off the rot, but Jeremy had never believed it. The varnish – so thick it clogged the lines of the original sculpture – had seemed more a prison, holding that rot *in* so it couldn't escape and infect those standing too near.

It was a woman, or had been, at some point in history. Carved from a single log, long angular features, huge, mournful eyes that stretched down and down to high cheekbones and a slender, pointed nose – almost Roman, he'd heard others say. You could tell the woman the piece had been modeled after had been beautiful. Even the ravages of the ocean, the weather, and the years hadn't been able to mask it. There was an eerie sense of something hovering just beneath the surface of the wood, staring back at you if you studied it too closely and watching you move about the room if you pretended not to notice. Always.

In his pocket, sharp page folds pressing through the worn denim of his jeans to scrape his thigh, was the letter that had dragged him home. The type had smeared from sweat, too many folds, and too many readings. The return address was one he'd never seen before, and would likely never see again. Probst and Palmer, Attorneys at Law. The address wasn't local to Cedar Falls. Jeremy's father had left him with two standard rules. Never do business with friends, and even if you break rule number one, never do business in your own back yard. The less people knew about what lay behind your smile, or your frown, the less likely they were to be able to find a chink in your armor and take you down.

Jeremy had never understood who in Cedar Falls would want to take him down, or his father, for that matter, but he understood the rules. Probst and Palmer's offices were in Kingston, 100 miles to the north, and Jeremy had stopped through on his way to pick up paperwork, and keys. His father had left things in good order. The house was paid for, the taxes good for the year and the insurance caught up both on the property, and the ancient Chevrolet sedan he'd left behind.

All of it was ordered and neat, empty and far too bizarre to be handled all at once. Jeremy had driven to the house, parked out front and stared at the door and the windows for about fifteen minutes, then driven away. He knew he should have gone in, checked the place over and unpacked. There were more papers to sign, and the utility companies would have to be notified that services should be restored. Jeremy knew, but he just couldn't face it.

So here he was, head against the wooden frame of Brown's Barber Shop, sweat trickling under the flannel collar of his shirt as he fought for balance against suddenly weak knees and a whirling panorama of memory and pain. He didn't need a haircut, but he very suddenly needed to sit down, so Jeremy twisted away from the wall and slipped inside with a deep breath.

There were two bright overhead lamps, one swinging over each chair on a single stainless steel chain and funneled toward the floor by aluminum shades. The edges of each were yellowed and dusty, and Jeremy wondered, just for a moment, if some of that stain wasn't tobacco from his father's cigars.

Some things hadn't changed at all, except in perspective. The once-giant sailfish, while still huge, seemed possible through adult eyes, the mongoose and snake seedy and dusty rather than mysterious and dark.

The room was empty, and though the lights were on, there was a sensation of – emptiness. Deep, dark emptiness that matched the hollow ache in the pit of Jeremy's gut. He stepped in and let the door swing closed behind him with a squeak.

For a moment, he just stood there, taking in the room, the scent of old leather chairs and hair tonic, the slightly acrid scent of oil burned in the gears of Chrome and Bakelite clippers that should have been retired in the sixties. Whispered voices from his past spoke of presidents and congressmen long dead, bake sales and sea stories. Dust motes danced beneath the hanging lamps, and Jeremy turned to the wall at the back, taking a step deeper into the gloom.

She was there, just as he remembered. There were a few more photographs lining the wall to either side, some in color, which didn't fit his memory at all, but Jeremy's gaze was focused. The wood seemed to grow from the wall, curving and taking shape slowly as it built up to the deep-set holes that were her eyes. Long, flowing hair, deeply etched into the wood, each line darker in the center and lightening as it neared the surface of the wood. The longer Jeremy stared the more real she became, the room fading around her until all he could see was a woman, gazing back at him in quiet desperation. He stepped closer, one foot hesitantly sliding through the dust, then the other. Just as he reached out his hand to trace her cheek with one finger a voice cut through the shadows.

"Can I help you?"

Jeremy spun, eyes wide and his mouth dropping open. The man who'd spoken leaned against the second barber chair on one elbow, watching Jeremy with interest. The cheeks had grown heavier, and wrinkles lined the skin beneath his eyes, but Jeremy recognized Terry Brown instantly. It had to be Terry. He was the spitting image of his Father, and in that instant the echo of Jeremy's father's voice, and the scent of smoke and leather nearly overwhelmed him.

"I ..." his words caught in his throat for a second, then he turned, stepped forward and offered his hand shakily. "I'm Jeremy Lyons," he said. "I used to come here with my father."

In that moment, the other man's face shifted through a series of emotions, surprise, a deep, impressive smile – a quick flash of insight, and ended in a sympathetic frown. "Jack Lyons' boy?"

Jeremy nodded. "The last time you cut my hair," he said softly, "was for my high school graduation."

"Flat top," Terry nodded, "high and tight, just like always."

Jeremy turned back to the wooden woman mounted on the wall for just a second, then stepped away and walked toward the barber's chair, extending his hand.

"I'm guessing you aren't here for a trim?"

Jeremy grinned wryly. "I don't know why I'm here, exactly. I went by the house, just wasn't quite ready for it. When I came back into town, it just seemed natural. I don't know how many afternoons and evenings I spent in here, reading – drawing – listening. Guess I thought it would be a little more like home than that empty house."

"Not a lot of action these days," Terry smiled. "I get busy about one or so, but by three or four it thins out. Only a few old-timers remember the way things were, and mostly they come around on the weekends. Not a one of them has needed a real haircut in years, but they come, and they pay, regular as clockwork."

Jeremy smiled. "Just like always."

The two laughed comfortably, and Terry moved away from the chair toward the front door.

"Let me lock up," he said. "I've got a few bottles of beer in back. No one waiting up for either of us."

Jeremy almost bowed out. He had no right imposing his depression on someone else. The more he thought about it, the less sense it made that he'd come to the old barber shop at all. It was a place to get your hair cut, and all the magic, if there'd truly been any, had long departed. He turned to the wall a final time. Almost all.

Jeremy had never been in the back room of Brown's Barber Shop. He'd seen his father disappear through those doors countless times, but he'd never been allowed past the entrance. Even now, as Terry slipped in ahead of him and flicked on the dim light, he hesitated. It was like violating his father's will beyond the grave.

"We had to move most of the social activities back here as the years passed," Terry said conversationally, pulling open an aged refrigerator and grabbing two long-necks from the frosty interior. "Health inspectors were cracking down, mothers dragging their children in where father's had always done so before, complaining about the cigarette smoke and threatening to close us down.

"Hell," Terry chuckled, plopping into one of the old leather chairs lining the wall of the back room and twisting the top off his beer, "we even had animal rights activists protesting the animals on the walls."

"I don't know how you survived it all," Jeremy said, shaking his head and taking a seat a few feet away. "I don't know how you stayed here at all."

"Well, the staying is in my blood," Terry smiled. "Been a Brown in this shop almost as long as there's been a Cedar Falls. Wouldn't want to be the one to break a streak like that. The rest was easier than it seemed. They opened a new shop in the mall out Whitewall way. It's got a big clown chair for the kids and a play room with Nintendo. That left us to the regulars and the few too lazy to drive that far. It's enough for a living, and that's all a man can rightly ask of life, I think."

Jeremy thought about that for a moment, taking a long pull from the beer bottle.

"I wish I could have thought that way," he said at last. "I wish I'd been happy to come here every week, get a trim and hear the old stories. I wish I could have been more like my father – at least a little. I feel like it's all been lost, and all I have to show for the years is an empty house and dreams I have no one to share with."

"Never married, huh?" Terry turned away for a moment, then took another long drink, draining his bottle and rising for a second, glancing at Jeremy, who shook his head. "I never settled either. Never could find anyone I felt comfortable with, not after Dad passed on. There's been a couple of times I thought I might be on the right track, but ..." He shrugged and opened his second beer. "Some men are meant to be alone."

Jeremy nodded.

"I miss those days, sometimes," he said softly. "I miss the stories. I miss hearing old Mulligan talk about catching that Marlin out there. I knew, even then, that he never set foot on the deck of a fishing boat in his life, but the words were magic. It wasn't the truth, but the story, you know?"

Terry nodded. "I do. Don't get much of that any more. Mulligan passed on about seven years ago, Billy Jensen shortly after that. Mostly they come and talk about those who've died, now, and wait for their own turn."

"There's one story I never heard," Jeremy said suddenly. "I know there's a story, because my father used to let bits and pieces slip. That figurehead on the wall out there, the woman. He said your father brought her back from the war ..."

Terry grew suddenly stiff, and for a moment Jeremy thought the man would chase him out of the shop and lock the doors behind him forever. Tension rippled through the air and tingled along the hairs on Jeremy's arm. His hand shook, and he forced it to steady.

"Some stories are best left to the dead and their memory," Terry muttered, downing his second beer and rising quickly.

"Did I say something wrong?" Jeremy asked quickly, taken aback by the sudden reaction his words had brought.

"Not at all," Brown said brusquely, "but it's getting late. I know you need to get settled in. Maybe you could stop in during regular hours for a trim."

Jeremy sat, stunned, staring at the bigger man and trying to figure out whether he was kidding. There was no humor in the barber's slate-gray eyes, so Jeremy rose slowly, downing the beer and handing over the empty bottle.

"Nice to see you again, then," he said, turning. "Nice to be back."

Terry's features trembled, as if he were fighting some inner battle. Maybe he wanted to say something, take something back, but in the end, he held to his silence, only nodding as Jeremy slipped out of that forbidden room and into the shadowed barber shop once again. Jeremy glanced at the wall, and in the darkness, shadow cloaking the carved wood, it seemed a woman stood, watching him. He could have sworn her eyes glittered brightly and that a slender arm reached out – fingers beckoning.

Then Brown was at his side, ushering him toward the door with a firm hand on his back, mumbling something about the good old days. The air was cool, and the streets were deserted. Jeremy stood on the walk outside in confusion, then shrugged and turned to the road, and his car. Might as well get to some memories of his own.

The old home was full of stale air and dim memory. Jeremy had had vague ideas of cleaning up, arranging things and putting them back in order, but he should have known that his father would leave no such satisfaction. Everything was in its place. A very light sheen of dust coated everything, but beneath it the floors gleamed. The glass glittered – even the silver had only the faintest tinge of tarnish. The power was alive and waiting. There was a yellow note, hanging from the knob of the front door, to let him know they'd stopped and cut it on. "Just as his father had asked."

Jeremy's room was much as he'd left it last visit home. He'd been in his senior year of college, and the remnants of that time littered the desk and the walls. His bed was turned down, as if expecting him. Too much. Jeremy closed the door on that particular set of nightmares and moved down the hall. He pushed and the door to his parent's room swung open easily, hinges oiled. No sound. There had never been a sound. Jeremy had listened and listened, but he'd never been able to tell when they came and went. The room beckoned, dark and – inviting. It was a strange, exhilarating invitation, but an invitation nonetheless. For the first time since driving into the tiny, dirt-water town, Jeremy felt as if he were home.

The switch beside the door didn't operate a ceiling fixture as he'd expected. A single, dim light pooled yellow illumination over the floor from the dresser to his right. Rather than cutting the deeper shadows, the lamp's glow accentuated them. The bed was an expansive darkness, flanked by low-slung nightstands of still-darker wood. The windows were hung with heavy drapes of indeterminate color, pulled tight across closed blinds.

Odd shapes hung from the walls, and a huge old mirror glittered across the back of the dresser. Jeremy stared at that mirror. He couldn't make out anything in the silvered surface, but he stood, still and quiet, and watched the reflected glow of the lamp.

His mother had sat there, right in front of that mirror, brushing her long hair for hours. Jeremy had never actually set foot in his parent's room, but he'd watched her from the doorway, when she didn't know he was looking. He wondered if a part of her might be captured there. If he stared long enough, would her face appear? Would he feel the soft stroke of the brush through his hair? And where had his father been when...

Shaking his head, Jeremy turned from the mirror quickly. Again, too much.

Moving to the bed, he laid his suitcase out and unsnapped it quickly. He needed to get his mind out of the past. There were a lot of things to accomplish, clearing out the house, gathering his parents papers and belongings, the lawyers. All of it loomed over him like the specter of his father, leering and poking, tugging him first one direction, then another, and the last thing he needed in the midst of it all was more illusion and memory. Illusions and memories had haunted him for too many years.

Before he could think of his father's accusing gaze, he opened the drawers of the old dresser and shoved his clothes hurriedly inside. It was nearly comical, the way the finality of the gesture washed through him in a wave of sudden relief. He was in. The dresser was his, not his father's, not a thing he would be punished for violating. The room – the house – everything in it – was his.

With a sigh he pushed the drawer shut and turned, seating himself on the edge of the bed. The woman stared down at him, smoother than he remembered, and darker, her hair seeming to drip from the polished wood surface.

Jeremy grew very still. His heart pulsed, slowing with his breath painfully until it felt as if it might stop altogether. The moment was identical to a hundred acid-tripping moments in his youth, pulsing with the neon-beat of bar-lights and the sultry back-beat of strip clubs, pounding with the rhythms of a thousand songs. Still and silent.

Beside the window, sliding out from the edge of the heavy curtains, was the wooden figurehead from the barber shop. He knew it couldn't be the same one. He had just seen it – had reached out his hand and touched it – but the sensation it was there – that it was real and identical and WATCHING him was undeniable.

Mesmerized, Jeremy rose, stepping forward. He heard the soft echo of Terry's words in his ear. "Some stories are best left to the dead, and their memory," but the words flitted through his mind and away, as if whispered across a great distance.

Jeremy reached out one hand, letting his fingers come to rest on the smooth, polished wood, and his stomach lurched. The scent of hair tonic and musty leather assaulted his senses violently. His vision blurred, then focused. The wall had changed. Lengthened. For just an instant, the floor pitched beneath his feet, and he clutched the wooden carving tightly for support.

"No," he whispered.

Everything had shifted, and the pungent scent of tobacco smoke hung in the air. To his left, dim, yellow light flickered, and he could hear the scrape of feet, the groan and squeal of old springs as heavy bodies settled into aged chairs. The shadow-forms of dead, mounted animals surrounded him, glass-eye stares too-high. As if he were shorter. As if he were younger.

As if time had rewound its tape.

A heavy cough, then laughter, deep and guttural. Jeremy's heart lurched. He knew that cough, and that laugh. He pressed into the wall, nearly collapsing, and closed his eyes so tightly that they squeezed shut on the heavy smoke, burning and tingling. He thought about the bed behind him. He thought about the door, still ajar, less than three feet away, and the hallway beyond. He thought about his father's liquor cabinet, and with a sudden shove he pushed away from the wall and spun.

His knee banged into something hard, and he cried out. His eyes opened to shadows, flickering, and a huge, dark shape silhouetted against yellowed light.

"Who is it?"

The words hung in the smoky air, mocking Jeremy's sanity.

Jeremy held his breath, pressing back to the wall.

"That you boy?"

Jeremy tried to remain silent, but it was too much. That voice, a voice he'd been conditioned from birth to obey, was irresistible.

"Dad?"

The world shifted again. Jeremy felt his mind whirl, saw the lights shift and heard heavy footsteps approaching like the beating of primal drums, timed with his heartbeat. He knew he was falling, but somehow he couldn't react to it. Strong arms clasped him under his arms, hands too large, covering his shoulders, fingers gripping and lifting.

Then – mercifully – it was dark.

Jeremy woke next to the scent and cool caress of leather. He was curled in a chair. How was that possible? A single chair, club-style with brown leather and metal rivets. Voices droned, the sound shifting and growing clearer with each beat of his heart. He smelled smoke, thick in the air above him, and he saw that a single dim bulb hung from a bare wire in the center of the room.

Jeremy curled tighter. He wanted to know what was being said, to put it into perspective before he sat up. It was all a mistake, obviously. He shouldn't be there. Not like this, not small and vulnerable, shivering in a chair shrouded in shadow, but alone and brooding in his father's room. It would all fade if he sat up. He would be passed out across that bed, nothing on the wall behind him at all. Nothing but a mirror to stare into that would stare back and mock his meaningless life – that would show him the younger face of the father he'd lost.

"She's hung there nearly ten years," a deep, guttural voice cut through Jeremy's thoughts. "Hung her there myself. The nail is a square one; drew it by hand from the very wood of that ship."

There were murmurs, but no words, in reply, and the voice continued until an image twisted into shape in Jeremy's mind. It was Terry, but not exactly Terry. It was an aged, too-squat Terry with a beard gone half-grey down the center and gnarled, liver-spotted hands. It was a Terry two generations back, when the barber shop had been so much more than a barber shop, and the back room had been sacred.

"She'd ridden the waves so long it took a good hour's work just to wipe away the salt scum that held her to the prow. She was bolted down, of course, but those bolts had long since surrendered to salt and wind. They crumbled like dust when I tried to pry them loose. For all that, it was no easy task. That ship clung to her like a lover, green mossy slime stretching like some god-forsaken glue. Two more days and she'd have dined with Davey Jones himself. The plan was to scuttle her over the far side of the reef, where her bones could blend with the coral and not be a hazard."

"Seems a shame," a softer voice replied, floating out from the far corner of the room. "I mean, that ship was a beauty.

Shame to see her go down."

The silence that followed grew heavy, and despite the ludicrous notion of cowering in a chair much too big to be real, Jeremy felt himself shiver as the weight of it settled over the room. Someone coughed, and a glass hit the table with a heavy clunk.

"Maybe you should have let her go, too." The words echoed. Jeremy recognized his father's voice. For some reason this was more comforting than disturbing in that moment.

There was a quick, grating sound as a chair pushed away from the table. Heavy footsteps followed, and then Terry Brown's grandfather's rough voice continued, as though no other words had been spoken.

"I couldn't bear to see her go. Not that way. Not after all I knew. She didn't belong to the sea, not then, not ever, though the barnacles and the weather had done their best to disguise her as one of their own." He paused again, then added more softly. "I couldn't send her back to him. Not that."

"Tell us," the soft voice Jeremy didn't recognize cut in. "Tell us again."

Jeremy dared to uncoil his small frame slightly, peeking just over the arm of the old leather chair. He saw a tall, broad-shouldered man with his back to the table, one hand gently caressing the cheek of the figurehead on the wall. The woman's eyes returned that gaze with more emotion than was possible, and Jeremy ducked back into the tentative safety of the chair.

"They said she was beautiful," the elder Brown's voice rose, a practiced storyteller practicing his art, "so beautiful that men would travel miles just for the chance to see her face, or hear her voice. They say she had the beauty that starts wars, or ends a dynasty. They say ... she was loved ..."

Jeremy felt the world shift again and he started from the leather seat. His balance failed, and he teetered to the side, clutching at the arm of the chair. It wasn't there. He grabbed an armful of air and toppled, crying out softly and striking the floor hard. His senses reeled, and he felt the soft brush of something on his cheek. The acrid scent of mothballs filled his nostrils and he coughed violently, rolling to his back.

The silence of his parent's room surrounded him. The ceiling, lowered tiles he remembered his father laying in place, one at a time on the rickety, dangling framework that held them suspended over the room, shimmered.

"Makes the room look longer and wider."

Jeremy heard the voice clearly. His father's voice. Staring at the tiles, the room in the back of the barber shop fading from his mind slowly, he could still hear the words as clearly as the day they'd first been spoken. He remembered the skeptical frown in his mother's eyes, and the silent nod. He remembered thinking that the tiles did nothing but make the room short, and squat. He remembered saying nothing.

Rising slowly, he reached to the bed for support and levered himself to his feet. The wall was bare. Nothing. Not even a photograph, or a gilt-framed mirror to fill the space. The mirror he might have understood, because then the face he'd touched could have been his own.

On the nightstand beside the bed, a framed photograph of his parents watched him.

"Not this time, old man," Jeremy whispered.

He grabbed the pillows from the head of the bed and yanked free the down comforter, heading for the hall. Moments later, without a backward glance, he slipped through the doorway into his old room. He didn't flip on the light. He sprawled out over the bed and wrapped himself in the comforter, sliding his head between two down pillows and closing his eyes, drifting off to sleep before the dreams could descend and trap him in that netherworld between rest and reality.

Autumn in Cedar Falls was a quiet time. Things were ending, and beginning, school in session and the football season in full swing. Churches were gearing up for the final bake sale before Thanksgiving, and the road crews were oiling and winterizing their equipment for the annual war with the weather. Despite the comfortable familiarity of it all, Jeremy couldn't shake the cold knot of ice free from his chest.

He could still hear his father's voice, and every time he closed his eyes, the scents of leather and tobacco permeated his world. He drove straight through the center of town, skipping the market and passing the "General Store," still in operation despite the competition of the new Super Wal-Mart down by the highway. There was only one place he was likely to get his answers.

He parked right out front of the barber shop, waiting until the dust had settled before he stepped out and closed the door behind himself. There was no light inside, but he knew Terry was open. The barber shop had always been open – Jeremy couldn't remember a time when it had not been. Of course, most of those memories were of visits with his father, and there was no clarity of time, or space. Jeremy had been more of an accessory than a companion, brought along because it was what father's in Cedar Falls did.

Now there was no father, and the town was slowly dying around the edges. So little remained of what had seemed so huge and imposing those many years in the past that the town hung against the sky like a tattered and torn postcard. Not many people were up and about on a Saturday morning, at least not in town. There were a couple of kids playing in the park out front of the Post Office, and just before Jeremy reached the barber shop door, a police cruiser rolled slowly past behind him, moving on to other pockets of inactivity en-route to the diner by Route 12.

Jeremy wondered fleetingly why he hadn't noticed the general decline the day before. Everything had seemed so – quaint. So rural and down-home comfortable. Now it looked like a too-old prop in a bad horror movie. The buildings leaned, ready to fall over backward at the slightest provocation, nothing more than propped up plywood silhouettes.

The barber shop was dark. Even more so than before, and though the door was open, there was no sign that Terry was open for business. There was no sign of any activity at all, in fact. Dust covered the chairs and the walls were dingy. Jeremy released the door and it swung to with a squeal of old metal in need of oil. The only illumination came through the slats of the blinds to his rear, and from beneath the crack of the door to the back. From there a soft, yellowish light trickled, slipping to puddle just beyond the base of the door, which was closed.

"Terry?" Jeremy didn't call out too loudly. Something held him back. There was no answer.

He called out again, a bit more insistently, and stepped closer to the door in back. "Terry? Are you there?"

Nothing again, and moments later he stood, ear to the wooden frame of the door, trying to press his eye to the crack that was releasing the light. The sound of feet shuffling reached him, and the soft murmur of voices.

Hesitantly, Jeremy reached out and rapped on the door. At first he thought no one had heard him, and he was hovering between the desire to knock louder, pounding until they let him in and told him what the hell was going on when the door swung wide. The floor beneath him lurched sickeningly, tumbling him forward, and Jeremy reached out with a cry drowned quickly in the roar of ...

Waves. Crashing, rolling high above and tumbling toward him, foam-tipped and peppering face and eyes with hard, stinging salt-slaps of spray. His stumble brought him up abruptly against a wooden rail, and he clutched the slimy surface tightly as his chest slammed into the solid wood and his knees threatened to buckle from the impact.

The water hit then, and everything else disappeared. Jeremy pressed himself tightly to the wood, clutching with his hands and gripping with his knees, fighting the crushing weight of the cold, relentless pull of the seawater as it pounded, then receded with a sickening, sucking sound over the side and the world tilted backward as quickly as it had leaned forward. Closing his eyes, Jeremy clung more tightly still to the rail, fingers slipping and groping along the wet-slick wood for purchase and feet threatening to slip off behind him and down.

For an eternity of deafening sound and flashing lightning, he hung nearly perpendicular to the sea, then he rushed back the other way, compressed tightly to the wooden rail and his breath left him. Voices cried out, nearly lost in the gale, and Jeremy's mind swam with the words, trying to order them so they made sense, trying to find the courage to release the rail, turn, and step back through the door and into the barber shop – the world.

The same world that chose that moment to lurch again, not so violently this time, and Jeremy felt the ship turning beneath him – felt the prow coming about, just in time, slicing the next of the monstrous waves that had threatened moments before to wash him from the deck into a sea of insanity. The voices grew clearer, and Jeremy risked releasing the rail with one hand to brush the soaked hair from his eyes.

It was dark, too dark to make out anything much more than the length of his arm from his face, but the lightning flashes gave a strobed pseudo-light just visible through the stinging salt. Jeremy could make out the prow of the ship, dropping down with a stomach-stealing lurch to shimmy at the base of a huge swelling wave, then rising, so high that only the sky and the angry face of the storm, creased in deep green, blue-black and silver by the searing crackles of lightning, filled his vision. There was a shape, solid and unmoving, like a body leading the ship through the storm. A woman. Droplets of water washed back and off, giving the illusion of silver hair in each lightning burst.

From behind, strong fingers gripped suddenly beneath Jeremy's arms, and he was jerked from the rail and hauled up and back. The ship was no more steady than before, but the danger of slipping side to side had passed, and moments later Jeremy crashed to the wall of what must have been the ship's cabin.

"Get inside!" The words screamed through his eardrums, blocking out the storm, just for an instant, and Jeremy turned, wild-eyed. Terry stood there – not Terry – taller with similar features. The man's hair waved wildly about his head and his eyes smoldered with barely-controlled anger – and strength.

"Get below, damn you!" The man repeated, cuffing Jeremy on the side of the head. "I've not enough men to make it without you."

Other hands groped from the shadowed doorway of the cabin and Jeremy was jerked inside, just as another wave crashed across the deck and threatened to drag him back to the railing, or further. As he tumbled backward into the shadows, Jeremy caught a last lightning flash. The woman's figure stared out over the waves stoically.

His foot caught on the top stair, and he tumbled, ignoring the loud cursing of whoever it was that had dragged him to safety. He felt the contact as the two of them slammed into the wall, then continued back and down, banging one knee painfully and twisting mid-air to try and get his hands beneath him. There was nothing. Nothing but shadow, and as he passed to darkness, he felt damp wood as his hands struck first, chin following in a jarring tangle of tar-soaked hemp and salt-soaked planks. The darkness that followed was sudden, and complete.

Jeremy returned to consciousness amid the scents of leather and tobacco. His head pounded painfully, and his eyes refused to focus. The room was adrift in smoke – tobacco smoke, pungent and overpowering. He coughed, hand rising to cover his mouth and body convulsing until he bent nearly double from the effort to draw clean air into his lungs. His eyes stung, and he could barely focus through the pain, so he closed them tightly.

"Quite a tumble."

The words hung in the air, making no sense coming from the direction and voice that they did. Jeremy brushed his fingers gingerly over the growing knot on his head and forced his eyes open once more.

He was in the back room of the barber shop. The old refrigerator hummed too-loudly against the wall. Terry sat across the table from him, an open beer resting between cupped palms.

"I was wrong," Terry went on. "Been here by myself so long, I'd started to think things would come full-circle and end. Seemed right. Now I see she's been callin' you back all along."

"She?" Jeremy coughed the word out, making it a question.

Terry just watched him, raising his beer and taking a long drink.

"You know who I mean," he said at last. "Now I have a story – *the* story. You just sit there and try to concentrate."

Terry rose slowly, moving to the refrigerator and drawing forth a second cold beer, which he carried across the room and placed in front of Jeremy on the table. The barber untwisted the cap with a quick jerk of his wrist and left the bottle to stand, tiny wisps of steam rising from the neck to remind Jeremy of the ship – the waves. The throbbing in his head subsided to a dull ache, and he rose, moving the leather chair he was leaning back in closer to the table and grabbing the beer tightly. He raised the cold glass to press against his temple for a moment, then took a drink and met Terry's gaze.

"Tell me."

"It started in Scotland," Terry began slowly. His eyes, and his voice, took on a distance and a depth they'd not seemed to possess previously. "None of our fathers were even gleams in their own father's eyes at the time, but one thing was the same. The ocean. Even then, when women waited by the fires and wars were fought hand to hand, enemies staring one another in the eye and defying death, she called to us. There was one who answered.

"Angus was his name, and he took to the sea so young they say he was sailing from near the day he was born. The son of a son of a sea captain, bred to the ocean – the far shore. Born with the burning need to see what lay beyond the next wave. Angus Griswold belonged to the sea.

"Until he met her," Terry stopped, nodding toward the door, and the barber shop beyond – the woman hanging on the wall – the world that seemed so distant Jeremy could scarcely grant it credence.

"She was the daughter of a merchant he met in his travels. Angus wasn't one to settle in one place, but the day he met her, he found that an anchor had been cast that would not dislodge. She was beautiful. Beyond anything he'd seen, rivaling even the blue of the deepest lagoons and the scent of the islands after a storm, she drew him. At night, on the deck of his ship, he would think of her, writing letters long into the night, only to crumple them and toss them aside in anger, drowning his imagination in rum and dark thoughts, until even his men began to talk.

"He returned to Scotland, soon after, and erected a keep overlooking the waves, tall and strong of stone dragged from the very edge of the sea. All that time, he kept her face in his heart. He wrote more letters, and eventually, a few of them weren't crumpled. He sent the first, then the second, and when she replied to his third, he wrote again, until at last he found himself before her father, a tall, thin man with piercing eyes. You've seen those eyes, mirrored in the countenance of his daughter.

"They were wed, soon after, and settled into that keep. That prison."

"Prison?" Jeremy asked, finally finding the courage and strength to take the beer in a shaky hand and draw deep. "You said it was a keep."

"It was that," Terry said softly. "It kept him from his other love – his oldest love. It kept him from the sea while holding it out before him like a carrot dangled before an ass. She loved him, Jeremy. She loved him with all her heart, mind – soul. She loved him, and in the end, it wasn't enough.

"Ten years to the day after he brought her home, Angus bought a boat. He told her it would be for short trips - jaunts up the coast and back, but she knew. In his eyes, the waves danced, and the sun set over shores with unknown lines.

"He sailed within the year."

"Sailors have always sailed away," Jeremy said, lifting his eyes to meet the barber's. "They come home."

"Not Angus," Terry shook his head and sipped his beer. "Not that time.

"He was gone a year before she began to really worry, sending letters home to her father, who was less than sympathetic. He'd received her dowry, and she was aging – still beautiful, but not of marrying age, and still married, in any case, to Angus. The year stretched into another, and another – ten years, Jeremy. She lived alone in that keep for ten years, spending the money Angus had amassed in a life of sailing and trade, and pining for the one thing that had drawn her to the ocean's side. The one thing she couldn't have.

"Every night she watched at the balcony outside her room until the sun set and the moon rose high above the waves. Every night she prayed. Some say, near the end, when the loneliness had started to make her crazy, that she prayed to others than the God we know. There were books found in her towers, books none could place, or translate – some written by hand, others printed in far-away lands. Angus must have brought them home, but it was obvious that his lover was the one to find their use.

"Then one day, the ship returned."

"You said he never came back."

"And he did not. The ship came back. Most of his men came back. Angus died of a fever, wasted him away to nothing in the cabin of that ship. They buried him at sea, but before he died, he set them to bring his boat home. To bring her the treasures and secrets of the world he'd found. To tell her he loved her.

"None of it mattered. They pulled in and she flew to that shore a woman possessed, to find no man, but only wealth. Only salt-soaked board and men too-long away from home. Only more loneliness washed ashore.

"They brought it all to her, and she held a feast such as had not been seen in those parts since Angus himself was alive. They drowned themselves in the food they'd missed and the local girls, washed it all down with barrels of wine. She watched, smiling all the while as if she was sharing their good humor.

"When they woke, every man-jack was locked in that ballroom. She'd had men come in during the night and bar the doors with stout planks. They were left to rot with what remained of the food, and the wine, even the women who'd joined them. They carried on and wailed at her, even tried to set the place on fire. None of it worked. They were trapped, and she was going to go and let them stay, leave and never come back."

Jeremy shuddered, casting a glance at the door – toward what lay beyond. "What happened?" he asked softly.

"That night, she stood on her balcony as always," Terry replied. "As she stood, staring into the waves, he came to her. Moss was matted and woven into the long hairs of his beard, and his eyes were half-eaten by fish, but he came, staggering from the waves. She just watched him come, no effort to help him, or to hinder. She watched as he staggered to the walls of the keep and beat his rotting hands against the stone walls.

"Let them go," he cried. "Let them go, my love. I've come back."

"No one knows for certain if she listened," Terry said at last. "She released the men the next day, giving them back enough of what they'd brought her to build a new ship. She made certain that everything was perfect – every board, every sail – hand-picked. And she sent for an artist. A young man, some say a Eunuch. He brought the wood with him from Egypt, a solid block of it, taking up half his cart. As the ship was built, the man worked."

"She sailed with that ship?" Jeremy asked, breaking the silence.

"No. She died. She died, alone in her tower, leaning on the wall that overlooked the waves below, but the work was finished, and when they saw what she'd commissioned, the work the eunuch had left, the men would not leave her behind."

Both men stared at the doorway now. Beyond it, they could feel the draw of the wood, dark and curving tightly to the wall behind, eyes sockets of something darker than shadow. In their heads, a voice, calling out softly.

"Your great grandfather found that ship," Jeremy breathed. "He brought her here."

Terry rose, turning toward the refrigerator again without a word, and the lights flickered, suddenly, threatened to die, then steadied. They were dimmer, their radiance more yellow, and Jeremy staggered half to his feet, bracing himself on the arms of the chair as the floor lurched sickeningly.

"Damn," Terry cursed. He turned back, a brown-necked bottle in his hand. Tipping it up, he took a long swig and strode across the deck to where Jeremy now stood, wild-eyed and staring at the doorway, now a stairway once more. Beyond the walls, the waves crashed, and Terry – not Terry – handed over the bottle with a wild-eyed stare.

"We can't let her go down," the man whispered softly, almost plaintively. "We must keep her afloat. She ... she loves me."

Jeremy took the bottle, turned to the stairs, and staggered through – into the clear night air beneath the stars. The moon was bright and full. He downed the beer in a single gulp and fell heavily over the hood of his car. In the shadows behind him, he felt the weight of eyes, and the call of farther shores.

It was good to be home.

ABOUT THE AUTHOR

DAVID NIALL WILSON has been writing and publishing horror, dark fantasy, and science fiction since the mid-eighties. An ordained minister, once President of the Horror Writers Association and multiple recipient of the Bram Stoker Award, his novels include *Maelstrom, The Mote in Andrea's Eye, Deep Blue, the Grails Covenant Trilogy, Star Trek Voyager: Chrysalis, Except You Go Through Shadow, This is My Blood, Ancient Eyes, On the Third Day, The Orffyreus Wheel,* The DeChance Chronicles, including *Heart of a Dragon, Vintage Soul, My Soul to Keep, Kali's Tale,* and *Nevermore – A Novel of Love, Loss & Edgar Allan Poe.* He is the author of the Cletus J. Diggs supernatural mystery series, including *The Not Quite Right Reverend Cletus J. Diggs & The Currently Accepted Habits of Nature,* and *The Crazy Case of Foreman James.* His newest novels include *Crockatiel – A Novel of the O.C.L.T., Gideon's Curse, Reember Bowling Green – The Adventures of Frederick Douglass—Time Traveler* (With Patricia Lee Macomber) and *A Midnight Dreary,* Book V of The DeChance Chronicles. David can be found at www.davidniallwilson.com and can be reached by e-mail at david@davidniallwilson.com.

David is CEO and founder of Crossroad Press, a cutting edge digital publishing company specializing in electronic novels, collections, and non-fiction, as well as unabridged audiobooks and print titles. Visit Crossroad Press at http://store.crossroadpress.com

Curious about other Crossroad Press books?
Stop by our site:
http://store.crossroadpress.com
We offer quality writing
in digital, audio, and print formats.

Enter the code FIRSTBOOK
to get 20% off your first order from our store!
Stop by today!